"Well, if it ain't Rafferty, the pretty drugstore cowboy," the foreman drawled.

"Back in the big city, they probably all think you're a real wrangler, don't they? I'll bet a handsome fellow like you has a string of women a mile long. But, hell, you probably kiss like a greenhorn."

LaRue had to stifle a smile at her foreman's barbs. She shot a quick glance at Rafferty, trying not to laugh.

Before she knew what was happening, Rafferty whirled to face her. Seizing her shoulders with both hands, he thrust her backward against the trunk of a cottonwood tree, his long legs straddling her so that he could press up against every inch of her body.

LaRue struggled briefly, but rational thought spiraled away like campfire smoke in the wind the moment his lips ground into hers. When he ended the kiss and stepped away, she was convinced she'd feel the imprint of his body for the rest of her natural life.

Rafferty cocked a glance at LaRue's astonished foreman and said, "I may kiss like a greenhorn, but your women certainly seem to enjoy it."

Dear Reader,

The name Silhouette **Special Edition** represents a commitment—a commitment to bring you six sensitive, substantial novels every month, each offering a stimulating blend of deep emotions and high romance.

This month, be sure to savor Curtiss Ann Matlock's long-awaited *Love Finds Yancey Cordell* (#601). And don't miss Patricia Coughlin's unforgettable *The Spirit Is Willing* (#602), a deliciously different novel destined to become a classic. Four more stellar authors—Tracy Sinclair, Debbie Macomber, Ada Steward and Jessica St. James—complete the month's offerings with all the excitement, depth, vividness and warmth you've come to expect from Silhouette **Special Edition**.

Deeply emotional, richly romantic, infinitely rewarding—that's the Silhouette **Special Edition** experience. Come share it with us—six times a month!

From all the authors and editors of Silhouette **Special Edition**,

Best wishes,

Leslie Kazanjian
Senior Editor

JESSICA ST. JAMES
Showdown at Sin Creek

Silhouette Special Edition

Published by Silhouette Books New York

America's Publisher of Contemporary Romance

This book is dedicated, with love,
to my son, Don—
someone who bears a great deal of
resemblance to Rafferty.
Oh all right . . . to all my heroes!

–L.V.

For my sons, James and Chris.

–C.N.

SILHOUETTE BOOKS
300 East 42nd St., New York, N.Y. 10017

ISBN: 0-373-09603-8

First Silhouette Books printing June 1990

Printed in the U.S.A.

Books by Jessica St. James

Silhouette Special Edition

The Perfect Lover #561
Showdown at Sin Creek #603

JESSICA ST. JAMES

is the pen name for a Kansas-based writing team. Friends since high school, the two women began writing together about four years ago. They have published two historical romances, set primarily in Scotland and England, where they enjoyed doing hands-on research. In their contemporary novels, they have welcomed the opportunity to show readers that Kansas can be as romantically inspiring as Europe. In addition to writing and travel, the authors share a love of books and cats.

* * *

Authors' Note

This book is a fictionalized account of a very real controversy that has raged in the Flint Hills of Kansas for more than a decade. Combining elements from the several attempts that have been made to create a Tallgrass Prairie Park, we have altered the facts to fit our story.

Only time will tell how this dilemma will be resolved; meanwhile, this book is our salute to the indomitable spirit of the keepers of the land—the people of the Flint Hills.

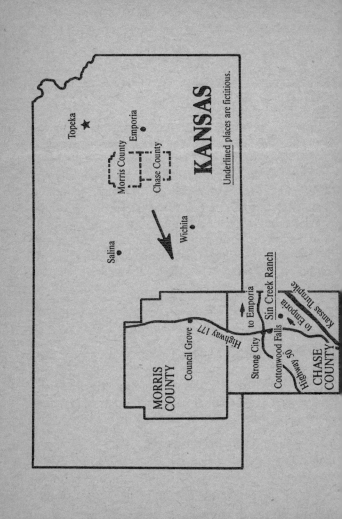

KANSAS

Underlined places are fictitious.

Topeka

Morris County

Emporia

Chase County

Salina

Wichita

MORRIS COUNTY

Council Grove

Highway 177

Strong City

to Emporia

Sin Creek Ranch

Cottonwood Falls

to Emporia

Kansas Turnpike

Highway 50

CHASE COUNTY

Chapter One

"It don't matter none who draws first—it only matters who's left standin' when the smoke has cleared away."

—Ned Culpepper, bank robber,
Matfield Green, Kansas, 1872

J. B. Rafferty stepped into the bright light of midday and stood, hands on lean hips, surveying the dusty one-horse town spread out before him.

Wearily, he realized it looked pretty much the same as a dozen others he had drifted in and out of in the last few months.

Then as his eyes adjusted to the glare, he saw a figure settle into a belligerent stance in the middle of the street, not more than fifty yards away. Clearly, the young cowboy had been waiting for him.

With insolent grace, the lad began pacing off the distance between himself and Rafferty, one gloved hand nervously slapping the butt of the Smith & Wesson revolver strapped to his leg. The spurs he wore danced, making a silvery sound that was somehow menacing in the stillness.

Rafferty's sigh of disgust whistled through his teeth. Damn! No matter where he went, it was always the same—some fired-up young hotshot anxious to take him on. Oddly enough, there was a time when he would have relished the challenge. Lately he was just too everlasting tired to even care.

The youngster came to an abrupt halt, studying Rafferty in a way that clearly was meant to be insulting. The kid didn't look like much of an opponent, Rafferty decided. He was downright scrawny, dressed in a faded denim shirt, jeans covered by scarred leather chaps, and boots that had seen better days. The felt hat pulled low over his eyes looked as if it had been trampled in a cattle stampede.

Oh, hell, thought Rafferty. *How can I confront a kid, for God's sake? The least they could do is send a grown man....*

"You the government agent?" The boy spoke suddenly, the timbre of his voice surprising Rafferty. He'd expected it to be higher, with the painful crack peculiar to adolescence. Maybe the boy was older than he appeared.

"Yeah, that's me," Rafferty drawled. "What about it?"

"I just thought you might want to know you're not welcome here."

"Somehow that doesn't come as any surprise. How'd you get elected as the welcoming committee?"

"I guess I volunteered."

"You planning on running me out of town?" One corner of Rafferty's mouth quirked up in sardonic amusement.

Though the cowboy's face was shaded by the hat he wore, his scowl was apparent in his tone. "Could be. But if you had any sense, you'd leave of your own accord."

Something about the way the cowhand spoke didn't add up. The voice was low, slightly husky, as if roughened by long hours of breathing the same dust that shadowed his clothing, but there was almost no trace of the usual flat midwestern twang. For the first time, Rafferty felt curiosity about his challenger, though experience had long ago taught him the danger of that particular emotion. It wasn't smart to become distracted when facing down a cold-eyed stranger on a lonely back street.

"I've got a job to do, sonny," Rafferty informed the cowboy. "So it doesn't matter a whole hell of a lot whether you want me here or not."

"I'm not the only one. Nobody in this town has any use for you . . . or your darn-fool ideas."

"We'll see about that, won't we?"

"I reckon we will." The boy's hands dropped to his sides, his fingers flexing involuntarily. "I think you'd better know, mister, that I intend to do whatever it takes to stop you."

The taller man tensed. "What's your beef, sonny?"

Rafferty was unprepared for the boy's lightning-quick move. The gloved fingers curled around the brim of his disreputable hat, pulling it off his head to slap it savagely against one narrow thigh.

"Quit calling me sonny," the cowboy ground out through clenched teeth. "And my *beef* is that I live on Sin Creek Ranch—right square in the middle of the land you're trying to steal."

Rafferty managed to close his mouth long enough to mutter, "Well, I'll be damned!" Then it fell open again.

The kid was a woman. A dirty, brawling, bull-headed snip of a female, to be sure—but the streaked brown hair spilling over her shoulders in two loosely tied ponytails proclaimed her a woman all the same.

Rafferty took another, closer look at her denim-clad body. Either he was getting old or his job was becoming too much for him. How could he ever have mistaken her for a boy? he wondered.

Well, hell, he rationalized, she'd come whirling down the dusty street like a small Kansas tornado—he couldn't blame himself for a failure to recognize the presence of feminine attributes.

"Surely you've heard of Sin Creek?" the girl prompted.

"I believe it's Levi Tate's place. But who are you?"

"I'm LaRue Tate, his granddaughter. And part-owner of the land the government is trying to cheat us out of."

"The government's not trying to cheat anyone, Miss Tate."

"That's not the way we see it."

Rafferty heaved an impatient sigh. He'd been through this before, too many times. "I'm sure that if you'd give me a chance to explain . . ."

"I suppose that's why you're holding a public meeting at city hall tonight—to explain?"

"That was my intention."

"I'll just bet. I've seen you government men before, and you're all full of shi . . . fty explanations. And fancy promises. None of which mean a blasted thing."

"Look, lady . . ." Rafferty didn't believe it—he was actually beginning to enjoy himself! He raised a hand to hide the smile that lurked behind his stern expression.

Lord, her fury was raging like a prairie grassfire, so hot he could imagine its heat singeing the hair on the back of his raised hand. He could almost feel the flames lapping at his feet.

"You look," she snapped, jabbing a finger in his direction. "My granddad and I plan to be there tonight to keep you in line. We're not about to let you get by with your lying propaganda."

Rafferty couldn't help it—his lips twitched.

"Is that a threat?" he asked, knowing what she would reply even before she opened her mouth.

"No. It's a promise." She whirled and stalked away, pausing after only a few steps to hurl one last parting shot. "And you'd better, by God, not be laughing at me."

"What if I am?" he asked softly, unable to resist. "You going to shoot me?"

She stood still. The palm of her hand longingly stroked the gun she wore. After a moment she spoke. "No, I guess not. But only because you're one rattlesnake it wouldn't be worth wasting a bullet on."

She clapped the bedraggled hat back onto her head and strode away.

Rafferty, barely aware that a crowd had gathered, leaned against the side of the green sedan with the government insignia on the door and watched her departure.

LaRue slammed the door of the rickety red pickup and rested her forehead against the steering wheel, groaning aloud. How could she have let herself get riled up enough to create such a scene? Half the population of the small town must have been watching.

Straightening, she twisted the key in the ignition and put the truck into gear, peeling away from the curb, leaving strips of rubber the old tires could scarcely spare.

A quick glance in the rearview mirror told her that the government conservationist was leaning against his car observing her, arms folded across his chest. A tide of fury swept over her again.

Damned arrogant city-bred upstart, she fumed silently. *Thinks he's so all-fired important because those silly sons of bureaucrats in Washington sent him out here. I'll bet he just can't wait to start showing his authority.*

LaRue cursed the bad luck that had sent her into town in the first place. Riding and repairing fence all morning, she had run out of metal staples and made a quick trip to the hardware store at Cottonwood Falls.

But when she'd finished her errand, what perversity of fate had prompted her to circle the block instead of simply making a U-turn and heading out of town? As she had driven down the back street behind the courthouse, she'd seen the government car and knew immediately who the man getting out of it had to be. After all, a notice of tonight's meeting had been posted for some time, and the whole county had expected him. Before she knew what she was doing, she had parked the truck and jumped out, hell-bent on raising a fuss.

LaRue didn't know why she had acted that way. She'd made up her mind long ago that when the Department of Parks representatives arrived in Chase County, she was going to be cool and organized in her battle against them. Well, she'd certainly blown that plan all to Hades and back....

She made a turn off the blacktop, rattling over a cattleguard and up the steep ascent of graveled road. The pickup coughed and wheezed like an old horse; at the summit she pulled over to let it rest. Through the years, stopping in this place had become a ritual with her. The view never failed to soothe her troubled spirits.

Before her lay the prairie, thrown like a warm coverlet over the aged bones of the earth, its haze of spring green seemingly stretching to eternity on every side. Wildflowers and half-grown bluestem grasses swayed gracefully in the restless south wind.

LaRue let her eyes slide over the long ridge off to her right, knowing that Sin Creek Ranch lay just beyond. Sin Creek—her home in actuality for the past nine years; in her heart, the only home she had ever known. How could she survive losing it?

But, she admitted bitterly, losing her home was becoming more of a possibility all the time. The government had decided a portion of the only remaining virgin prairie in America should be preserved as a national park. Unfortunately the proposed site most highly favored by the Tallgrass Park Committee included the vast acreage of Sin Creek.

LaRue tried to shrug off a feeling of hopelessness. Until the federal representative arrived in town, the threat of government seizure of the land had been only that—a threat, an unlikely possibility being mulled over by a group of unknown men in a distant city. Now, suddenly, the threat had become all too real, taking on form and substance in the person of the agent she had just confronted.

Unexpectedly, the memory of that confrontation sent a thrill of excitement zinging through her. It had felt good to stand up to him and speak her mind, she realized. And knowing who and what she had to contend with helped to vanquish some of the dark, nameless fears that had haunted her. Despite the danger he posed to her way of life, she was actually looking forward to the evening meeting. He was about to find out what a determined adversary she intended to be.

"Better gird your loins, mister," she muttered, grinning wickedly at the thought. "There's going to be one hell of a showdown before this is settled!"

She shifted into low, the gears protesting all the way. "Come on now, Bessie. We need to get home."

She spoke soothingly as she might to a contrary horse and eventually the vehicle snorted, backfired and then rumbled on down the road toward Sin Creek.

Chapter Two

"Just cuz that horse was in my barn ain't no sign I stole it. A man oughtn't to be called guilty and hung without gettin' to speak his piece."
—Will Hildebrandt, hanged as a horse thief,
El Dorado, Kansas, 1883

LaRue confessed to her grandfather on the way to town that night. It irked her to have to admit she had done something so stupid, but she knew he was going to hear about it one way or another, so she figured he might as well have her version.

He took it pretty well, just chuckling when she got to the part where the government man had asked if she intended to shoot him.

"I'd like to have shot him," she mumbled grumpily. "Right in his Department of the Interior."

"Reckon he didn't know for sure what to make of you," the old man said with a grin. "But I guess it's best the fellow found out what he was up against."

LaRue fell silent. They were passing through one of her favorite parts of the ranch. Levi Tate had taken the long way around to the highway in order to check on some cows and calves on the north range, and they were approaching the creek, which was running low because the usual spring rains were late.

More than a hundred years earlier an event had taken place there that had resulted in the name Sin Creek. A wagonload of prostitutes—"soiled doves," historic chronicles called them—had arrived in Cottonwood Falls one summer day, prepared to ply their trade. Too many righteous citizens had voiced strong disapproval, inviting the madam and her girls to move on. Levi Tate's great-grandfather, Rutherford, gave his permission for the women to camp on the banks of the creek that meandered through his property. Since there was no record to attest to the form of payment he may have received, it was generally assumed he allowed the prostitutes to set up shop, so to speak, out of the goodness of his heart. At any rate, for a time the road to the ranch was well-traveled—until irate wives forced the local marshal and a Baptist preacher to put an end to it. Even then, one of the girls, a pretty young thing named Faith, stayed behind to marry Rutherford and produce the next generation of Tates.

LaRue had loved the story long before she really understood it. It gave her a sense of the colorful history of the Old West, and more especially of the men and women who had settled this land and lovingly passed it on to their descendants.

A sudden surge of frustrated anger twisted through her. "I can't believe those big shots in Washington think they have the right to come in here and take all this away from us!" she said. "What kind of a government does this country have?"

"Now, calm down, sister," cautioned her grandfather. "Least we can do is wait and see what this here fellow has to say."

"He'll say the same things the last one did. Damn it, he's simply one more braying jackass...."

"Watch yer mouth, girl." Levi shifted gears and turned onto the highway.

* * *

J. B. Rafferty sat at the back of the darkened room and observed as his assistant, Hollister Ames, began the presentation by showing and explaining slides illustrating the destruction of the American tallgrass prairie by man and industry. As Hollister talked, Rafferty let his gaze roam over the backs of the heads silhouetted in the projector's glow.

She wasn't there.

His first reaction—disappointment—surprised him. He should be relieved that she hadn't shown up to cause more trouble. The general mood of the townspeople wasn't all that great to start with.

Still, as mad as she had been, he couldn't quite imagine her *not* being there to carry out her threats. He'd bet his new laptop computer she'd had every intention of being right in the middle of tonight's meeting.

The lights went up and Hollister started handing out printed sheets containing facts and figures garnered by several government polls. When he finished, he briefly introduced Rafferty and took a seat in the corner.

Time to go to work, Rafferty thought, hauling his lanky frame out of the chair and moving to the front of the room amid polite, restrained applause.

He nodded to the crowd, then turned to the chalkboard behind him. He printed Tallgrass Park—Pros and Cons on the green surface and in the Pros column, began listing reasons why the government felt creation of a national prairie park was necessary. When he straightened and faced the audience again, his eyes were drawn to the back of the room.

LaRue Tate and a man who must be her grandfather stood just inside the door. The old man whipped off his Stetson and muttered, "Sorry we're late. Busted the fan belt on my pickup."

Rafferty smiled to himself. If the pickup in question was the pile of junk the girl had been driving earlier, it was a wonder they had arrived at all.

"No problem," he replied. "We're just getting started—have a seat."

"Obliged," returned Levi Tate.

The man was a caricature of the old-time Western cowboy, Rafferty decided, taking in the faded denim shirt and starched, ironed jeans whose knifelike creases only served to emphasize the bow of the man's skinny legs. His face was tanned and weatherbeaten, the lines bespeaking a stern, just character, with underlying humor. The eyes were obviously keen, though almost hidden by bushy white eyebrows, and his beak of a nose soared proudly above a bristling white moustache. The hair on his head was so thin his shiny scalp showed through, adding a note of vulnerability to an otherwise trail-toughened appearance.

LaRue followed her grandfather to the last empty seats, refusing to meet Rafferty's eyes. She looked a lot cleaner than she had that afternoon, but only a little more feminine. Her shirt, a cotton plaid with rolled-up sleeves, was tucked into a pair of new jeans that made her look slim and long-legged. Her hair was neater, but still gathered into a ponytail, tied with what looked like buckskin thongs.

So, Miss LaRue Tate scorns such fripperies as ribbons, mused Rafferty, absently fingering the piece of chalk he held. *It's a wonder she doesn't have a crewcut.*

Right in the middle of wondering what color her eyes were, Rafferty remembered where he was and cast a quick, guilty look at Hollister, who was staring at him with a puzzled expression. Giving a slightly testy shrug, Rafferty launched into his speech.

"Two hundred years ago, the entire midland of this great country of ours was prairie—an unspoiled land of lush grasses teeming with birds and wildlife. Today, this same prairie is being destroyed by man, decimated by industry and its pollution...."

As the government man warmed to his subject, LaRue stole a few surreptitious glances. He was as big and arrogant as she had thought this afternoon, she decided, though she had to admit she was somewhat surprised by his general appearance. He looked more like a mild-mannered college professor than the dangerous man she remembered. Had she simply been too mad to see straight?

She let her gaze run over him again. He looked casual, yet scholarly in khaki pants, a white shirt and a deep green cardigan sweater. His face was all lean, square, hard angles, with softness only in the dark eyes behind horn-rimmed glasses—and his hair, which under the fluorescent light was black with brownish highlights, looked clean and soft, a temptation for wayward hands—LaRue nearly choked as she realized the direction her errant thoughts were taking. This man was her enemy in every sense of the word. A logical woman wouldn't be daydreaming about running her fingers through an enemy's hair.

Unless, she mused with wicked glee, *she was about to take his scalp!*

That idea consoled her, allowing her to stoke up stony anger once again.

"And now I want to give you the chance to speak your minds," Rafferty was saying, removing his glasses to gaze earnestly at the audience. "I've gone over the reasons our government thinks we need this park, but I'd like to hear your side of it, too. I'm aware there has been a great deal of opposition to the idea and I want to know why. Why shouldn't there be a tallgrass park?"

A thin, stoop-shouldered man in the front row rubbed his jaw thoughtfully. "'Cause we jist don't want it," he said.

There was a smattering of tense laughter, and even Rafferty had to smile. In true midwestern fashion, the man had laid it all on the line.

"But why not?" Rafferty questioned.

"Why should we want it?" asked another man.

"For the reasons I've written on the board," Rafferty patiently explained. "And for the extra income it could bring into your county. That makes sense, doesn't it?"

"Nope. Don't see no advantage to it."

There was a buzz of agitated voices. Rafferty felt as if he was trapped in a room full of angry bees. He stuck the glasses in his pocket and automatically reached up to loosen his tie before remembering he wasn't wearing one.

A woman at the back of the room stood up. "There are thousands of acres of prairie in America. Why has the government declared this its first choice?"

"Because this is the largest expanse of virgin prairie left in the U.S.," Rafferty replied. "*Virgin* meaning that it has never been touched by a plow."

There was a chuckle or two at that statement, and he could feel his cheeks turning a dull red. For the first time he was at a disadvantage in front of a crowd. It probably had something to do with Miss LaRue Tate sitting out there, staring steadily at him as though she thought he should be bagged and sold for fertilizer. It was impossible to be at ease under the circumstances.

"Look at it this way," he said in frustration. "Tourist dollars could bring in a lot of revenue to improve your schools, your roads—"

"Man, have you ever looked at the prairie?" asked a young cowboy. "It's grass . . . miles and miles of grass. Now can you tell me who in the hell is going to go out of his way to see acres of grass?"

"Yeah," chimed in a man holding a small child on his lap. "Are you trying to tell us tourists from New York or Alabama—or anywhere else, for that matter—are gonna drive clear out here to look at *grass*?"

"The country is becoming more ecology minded all the time. There will be thousands of people interested in the preservation of nature. Thousands who will want their children to see buffalo and antelope roaming the plains just as they did in the past."

"Yer full of it, mister," the man on the front row drawled, succinct as ever.

Rafferty began to sweat. He knew these people had been opposed to the park since it was first suggested, but he hadn't realized just how dead set against it they were. He had assumed it was merely a matter of explaining the facts, but that didn't seem to have much impact. They were too stubborn to listen to reason, that was for sure. Perhaps LaRue Tate was simply a product of her environment.

"We'd be lucky to get five hundred tourists a year, and you know it," protested a man in an expensive suit with a pocket full of cigars. "My name is Claude Hirsh and I'm an attorney.

I've been retained by the citizens of Chase County to fight this governmental interference in their lives.''

"We're not trying to interfere in anyone's life," Rafferty stated, realizing the townsfolk had dragged out one of their big cannons. Experience had taught him that men like Hirsh could be a real pain. "And surveys show that a significant number of tourists would pass through here each season."

"The thing is, the citizens I represent don't give a damn about your park," said Hirsh. "Don't their opinions carry any weight?"

"Of course they do—" Rafferty began, but out of the corner of his eye he caught a flash of blue plaid and knew LaRue had stood, apparently ready to join in the fun. Briefly, he wondered if a government agent had ever been hanged in this county.

"Mister, you've said a lot about the preservation of the bluestem prairie," she said clearly, "and about the money we can all make by having a park in our backyards. But why don't you get to the bottom line?"

"Bottom line?" he echoed, his nerves set pleasantly on edge by the huskiness of her voice.

"Yeah. Why don't you just level with these people and admit that it doesn't matter one bit what they want or don't want? If the government decides to make a park, there's nothing we can do about it. And all because of a little technicality called *eminent domain*."

"Yeah, I've heard of that," someone behind her said.

"I hain't. What is it?" The old man adjusted the control on his hearing aid in anticipation of Rafferty's answer.

Damn, thought Rafferty. He really wasn't ready to get into this just yet. He should have known she'd force his hand.

"Well, you see, if the government should decide they are going ahead with the project, they will need to obtain the acreage on which to build the park. Now, experts will determine the most suitable location and then—"

"The government will take it over," LaRue finished. "Whether you want to sell or not."

"Is it true there isn't anything we can do to stop something like that?" Levi Tate spoke for the first time, fixing Rafferty with his hawklike gaze, as if daring him to lie.

"Well, yes . . . it's true, I suppose. But, you see, the federal government will give you more than adequate recompense for your land."

"Ha!" snorted LaRue. "I'd like to know how they figure this adequate recompense. How do they put a price on the hours a man has worked to build a ranch or a herd of cattle? How can they possibly evaluate the pride he feels in knowing he's got something important to pass on to his sons and daughters?"

"Of course, no one wants to lose his home, Miss Tate, but with the money an owner receives, it would surely be possible to purchase other land in the immediate area. And, sometimes, the individual citizen is called upon to make a sacrifice for the sake of the country. It's part of the way America was set up."

"Do you really believe that?" she snapped. "Because, if you do, you're worse off than I thought."

"I have a job to do here," Rafferty returned, forcing himself to remain calm. "It isn't a personal thing. I wish you could all see that."

"And I wish you could see our point of view," she countered. "I wish you could understand exactly what this land means to us—why we want to go on taking care of it, not turn it over to a bunch of strangers. They can't know as much about it as those of us who've lived here for generations. I wish I could show you—"

LaRue broke off, filled with a turmoil of emotions she couldn't find words to express.

Rafferty saw her hands, which had been so active as she spoke, drop listlessly to her sides. But just as he thought she was going to admit defeat and sink back into her chair, she bent to whisper something into her grandfather's ear. The old man considered, nodded and smiled, and with new determination, LaRue raised her chin and issued her challenge.

"Mr. . . . ?"

"Rafferty. J. B. Rafferty."

"Mr. Rafferty, I have a proposition for you."

Why didn't anyone snicker at her choice of words, Rafferty wondered with asperity. Why were they hanging on every syllable with a suppressed glee that made him distinctly uneasy?

"All right," he said quietly.

"My grandfather and I own a few covered wagons and sometimes, when there's enough public interest, we do overland wagon trips through the Flint Hills. In a couple of days we're taking the representatives of several ecological groups out on a fact-finding mission. Would you consent to joining our wagon train for a week or so?"

"What?"

"It'd give us the chance to acquaint you with this country—show you firsthand what the farmers and ranchers are already doing in the way of conservation. You could observe the prairie up close, see the condition of the grasses and plants. Check out the quality of the animals the ranchers are raising."

"Well, it all sounds very educational, but I really don't see any purpose in my—"

"I didn't think he would be interested, sister," Levi Tate said, his moustache twitching. "Mr. Rafferty's from the big city. He probably can't ride a horse or—"

"I can ride a horse," Rafferty said evenly. "And I'm not afraid of coyotes or rattlesnakes. I just don't see the point of all this."

"Afraid to give us a chance?" LaRue taunted. "Afraid we might show you something that you don't want to see?"

"Such as?"

"That the so-called need for this park is a trumped up excuse for the government to grab more land it really doesn't have any right to."

Rafferty sighed. So this was the form her retribution was going to take. He hated to admit it, but he had to admire the sneakiness of her plan. If he refused, he was going to come off looking like a bad sport, a city slicker too arrogant or wimpy to risk tackling the prairie. And worse, if he resisted her conniving little scheme, he'd appear disinterested in what the people of Chase County could show him. It would be as good as saying she was right, the government had already made up its mind despite the wishes of those most closely involved.

But on the other hand, if he went along on her stupid overland trip...

Suddenly he realized that, in all honesty, there was no reason not to go. The worst that could happen would be that he would have to spend a week in the company of a smart-mouthed tomboy with a major chip on her shoulder. Maybe he would figure out why she intrigued him so. Maybe—of course, it was a long shot—he could discover for himself whether the woman had one single spark of femininity in her body.

The prospect of a few days on the open prairie had a certain appeal, he decided. God knew he could stand a change of pace, something different from town meetings, strange motel rooms and endless driving. He began to think of meals cooked over an open fire, sleeping under the stars—the chance to rid himself of shirts and ties and wear comfortable Western clothes.

"Okay, I'll do it," he said quickly, before he could talk himself out of the crazy notion.

Both LaRue and her grandfather looked surprised.

"You will?"

So, she had just been hoping to make him look bad. "Sure, but only under two conditions."

"What are they?"

"One, I want to take Holly along."

"Holly?" she repeated, faintly. "Is Holly your wife?"

He laughed. "No, my assistant." He nodded toward the astonished man in the corner. "Hollister Ames."

"Oh. Well, of course Mr. Ames is welcome to come with us. What's the other condition?"

"I want to be free to talk to the ranchers we meet without input from yo—from anyone. I don't particularly like being made to look like a villain, Miss Tate. I'm not here to cheat people, and I resent being made to feel like lowdown scum."

"Are you implying that I make you feel that way?" she asked, a glint in her eye.

He grinned. All at once he was beginning to enjoy himself again.

"I am, and you do."

"Well, I beg your pardon. From now on, I promise I'll do my best to make you feel like a higher class of scum."

Smart mouth? he thought. *Much too tame a description for the little hellion.* He only hoped the overland trip offered him an opportunity to pay her back in spades. Something told him it would. His grin stretched wider.

"I'll appreciate that," he murmured. "When should I show up at your ranch?"

"Day after tomorrow," she shot back. "The others are meeting at eight o'clock in the morning."

"Good. I'm looking forward to it."

Not half as much as I am, LaRue thought. *Not a tenth as much!*

"Well, ladies and gentlemen," Rafferty said, "this looks like a good place to end our meeting, but you're all welcome to stay for coffee and doughnuts. When I come back from the Tates' wagon trip, I'd like to schedule another meeting."

If you come back, LaRue thought nastily.

"I'll discuss what I've learned and how it will affect the recommendation I'll take back to the government committee. Shall we make the meeting a week from next Wednesday?"

There was general agreement and then Hollister Ames started steering people toward the cloth-covered card table in the corner where a coffee urn gurgled and steamed.

"Want a cup, sister?" asked Levi.

"No, thanks, Grandpa," LaRue said, sneaking a glance at the big man at the front of the room. She was glad to see an elderly couple had him cornered. "I'm ready to go home."

Levi chuckled. "Reckon you've got a few plans to make, all right."

As graciously as he could, Rafferty eased the man and his wife toward the refreshment table, then went in search of the Tates. He was disappointed to learn they had already left.

Oh, well, he reminded himself, *I'll have my chance to get to know her—them. Day after tomorrow it'll be just me, Miss LaRue and the wide-open prairie.*

Wide-open? he reconsidered. It was only several thousand acres. Knowing the way she felt about him, it could turn out to be pretty close quarters.

Chapter Three

"On the prairie, there are two things a man needs: a good horse and a good woman. If he can only get one of them, he'd better settle for the horse."
—Wes Faulkner, blacksmith,
Bazaar, Kansas, 1875

LaRue swung the saddle into place on the horse's broad back.

"What're you grinning at, Quincy?" she asked testily, reaching under the animal's belly for the cinch strap.

The tall, thin cowboy nodded at the horse. "That government man must be a real pansy if you're saddlin' Slow Dancer for him. Only thing tamer would be a kid's rocking horse."

"So?"

"Ain't he ever been on a horse before?"

"He said he could ride," LaRue answered, grimacing as she tightened the cinch. "But I'm pretty sure he's a tenderfoot, and there's no sense taking any chances. After all, I invited him on this trip to show him what's being done in the Flint Hills, not to maim him. Much as I dislike the thought, I've got to take care of him."

Quincy's eyebrows went up. "You really think this is going to do any good?"

"I don't know, Quince, but I've got to try. I can't figure out any other way to prove to them that we don't need their consarned park."

"Well, I hope it works. Sure would be a shame to see the ranch bulldozed under to make parking lots for the tourists." Quincy Needham, although a young man, had been the foreman at Sin Creek for nearly a decade, and his loyalty to LaRue and her grandfather was unshakable. "Let me know if there's something I can do."

"Thanks. I may need to take you up on that offer—these college men can be pretty tough to convince of anything."

At that moment a horn sounded outside the barn, and LaRue made a face.

"That must be him. Wouldn't you know he'd be the sort to sit in his car and honk? Arrogant jerk."

"I'll finish up here," Quincy said. "You go on and see what he wants."

"If he's like most big-city men, he probably needs to know where to stash his Gucci luggage," she sniffed. "Or maybe he just wants to inquire about the vintage of the wine we'll be serving with our meals."

Quincy chuckled. "It really galls you to have to be nice to him, doesn't it?"

"He's trying to take my home away from me," she pointed out. "What do you think?"

"I think that if I was him, I'd be checkin' that wine for more than vintage."

LaRue sighed and started down the hay-strewn aisle between the stalls. "No, I don't plan to poison him. I have to be as nice as possible," she said over her shoulder. "Damn it all."

To LaRue's surprise, the man driving the government car was not Rafferty, but his aide, Hollister Ames. Rafferty was sitting on the passenger side and the two seemed deep in conversation. Because she approached from the back, neither man saw her and as she stepped close to Ames's open window, she clearly heard Rafferty's words.

"Of course, it's not going to change my mind, Holly. I'm only going along with this idea because I'm tired—I could use a change of pace. You know how many meetings we've held in the past four months...how many nights we've spent in strange towns. I'd just like a little time off."

"This might not be exactly a vacation, you know," Holly pointed out.

"I realize you're not overjoyed about chuckwagon meals or sleeping on the ground," Rafferty said with a laugh. "But, look at it this way, the experience could really put us in touch with the prairie. Maybe it'll even give us some ideas we can use in structuring the park."

Sudden hot, immobilizing anger poured through LaRue.

Rafferty had no intention of changing his mind about the need for the tallgrass park! He was merely going along with the wagon trip because he needed a vacation! He'd eat their food and accept their hospitality, and then recommend the government take their ranch as planned.

A hazy mist swirled before her eyes and she wondered if she was having some sort of apoplectic spell. God knew, she was mad enough....

"Oh, Miss Tate," exclaimed Hollister. "I didn't see you there. Uh...where are the others?"

LaRue was proud of her swift recovery. Reaching deep inside, she drew from reserves she hadn't even known existed. Taking a slow breath, she smiled broadly.

"Good morning, gentlemen. You're the last to arrive. Everyone else is down at the cottonwood grove by the creek. That's where the wagons are pulled up, ready to go. I thought we could ride down. Your horses are being saddled now."

"Horses?" queried Hollister. "Surely we don't have to ride? I mean, I'd really prefer to travel in one of the wagons."

"Fine. What about you, Mr. Rafferty?" she asked sweetly. "Do you want to ride in a wagon, also?"

He opened the door and got out, observing her over the top of the car. "I'll ride a horse," he said.

"Good. I'll...."

Her words trailed away as Rafferty walked around behind the car and stood facing her.

Damn, with a capital D! LaRue thought. *Why in thunderation does the man have to look so all-fired good?*

J. B. Rafferty was the antithesis of a pansy if she'd ever seen one. Wearing boots, faded Wranglers and a denim shirt, he had the dangerous aura of an outlaw. Gone was the college man, glasses and all, and in his place was a rangy cowboy so big and mean looking it wasn't hard to imagine him going grizzly hunting with a switch.

She found herself staring at his long-muscled legs, wondering how he managed to stay in such great shape with a desk job. She had just begun a detailed survey of the hard planes of his abdomen when she became aware that Hollister had come around behind the car to unlock and open the trunk. She wrenched her gaze away from Rafferty and concentrated on the luggage. There were two large duffel bags and a briefcase, not a piece of Gucci in the lot. LaRue wished she could have been as mistaken about Rafferty's lack of honor as she was about his taste in luggage. She forced herself to speak calmly. "Now, Mr. Ames, if you'll take your things and get into that old pickup over there, I'll drive you down to the wagons." She turned back toward the barn. "You can wait here, Mr. Rafferty, and I'll bring out your horse."

Quincy looked up as LaRue stalked past the stalls toward him. "What's wrong?" he asked.

"That lowdown, weasel-lipped polecat," she fumed. "He thinks this is going to be a pleasure trip. He never had any intention of changing his mind about the park."

"What are you gonna do?"

"Put Slow Dancer away, will you? I'm going to saddle up old Mert for him."

"Mert?" Quincy pushed back his cowboy hat and scratched his head. Slowly he grinned. "Well, now," he muttered, "I reckon things are gonna start gettin' real interesting."

Rafferty exhaled gradually. So far, so good. At least he'd made it across the barnyard without incident.

He'd been relieved that the horse LaRue Tate had brought out of the barn for him hadn't been a raging, rampant stallion. The lazy-eyed, slightly spraddle-legged mare looked just fine to him. After all, he hadn't been on a horse since he was ten years old, visiting his uncle's dude ranch. There was no telling how much he had forgotten about riding. He'd never learned *that* much in the first place.

Fortunately he'd remembered which side to mount from, and it had only taken a light tap with the toe of his boot to start Mert, the horse, ambling off.

He took it as a good sign that there had been no discernible amusement on LaRue's face as she'd watched him climb aboard the dun-colored animal. "Be sure you follow this path," she'd said. "Just over the hill it skirts the pond and leads down to the cottonwood grove. You'll see the wagons."

Rafferty had merely touched the brim of his cowboy hat in thanks, trying to look nonchalant.

Keep your back straight, he silently reminded himself. *Try to look relaxed.*

After a few bouncing steps, the mare settled into her own particular rhythm and Rafferty felt better.

"Piece of cake," he chortled under his breath. *Good thing I had the class in method acting that time. All I have to do is be-lieve I'm John Wayne, and I'll be John Wayne.*

But he hadn't really breathed easy until he had cleared the hill and was finally out of sight of the barnyard.

God, he thought, mopping his brow with a red handkerchief, *I'd have hated making a fool of myself in front of that woman. It'd give her the upper hand for sure . . . and with a female like LaRue Tate, that's something you don't ever want to happen.*

Rafferty began to look around him with pleasure. Up ahead, the pond glimmered in the bright May sunshine and the pasture was dotted with purple cowslips. Spring was one of the prettiest seasons of the prairie year, he knew, but it had been a long time since he had really looked at it without his usual clinical detachment.

A capricious little breeze sprang up, teasing Rafferty's nose with the elusive scent of wildflowers. He had just pursed his lips to commence whistling a cheerful tune when, without warning, Mert's head snapped up and she sniffed the air with unmistakable relish. She whinnied sharply, her rubbery lips slapping noisily against her teeth, and shook her head with wild abandon. Then, nearly unseating Rafferty in her unseemly haste, she began running.

"What the hell?" he gasped, clutching the reins and gripping the horse's heaving sides with his knees. "Whoa, Mert—whoa, old girl!"

Mert was having none of it. If anything, she lowered her head and galloped faster. She was listening to a siren's call stronger than Rafferty's commands and threats.

The pond! Some deeply-buried instinct for self-preservation stirred to life, warning Rafferty that the damned horse was headed straight for the water and nothing was going to deter her. In a split-second he had weighed all the consequences and made his decision.

Pulling his feet free of the stirrups, he threw one leg over the mare's neck and with a short, fervent prayer, allowed himself to slip out of the saddle. He hit the ground with a dull thud, like a sack of potatoes. No sooner had he determined that he hadn't broken anything vital, than he heard a mammoth splash. Forgetting caution, he sat upright and stared at the scene in front of him, mouth ajar.

Mert hadn't slowed her pace for an instant; she belly-flopped into the pond with all the enthusiasm, if not the grace, of an Olympic diver. The tidal wave she created inched toward Rafferty's feet as he watched in amazement. He'd never seen anything like it.

The horse splashed and rolled, frolicking like a dog. She turned and twisted, even swam a few strokes, her front hoofs churning the water. Occasionally, she lowered her nostrils below the surface, snorting and blowing bubbles.

Rafferty shook his head, aware that he'd been set up.

Painfully aware, he mused, getting to his feet and rubbing both palms over his newly tenderized rear end. That little witch knew precisely what she was doing when she put him on Mert and told him to head for the pond.

He allowed himself a few satisfying thoughts of revenge before reluctantly conceding his gratitude for having had the sense to bail out when he had the chance. Something told him that LaRue would be anxiously awaiting his appearance at the cottonwood grove. No doubt she'd expect him to show up soaking wet and madder than a hornet.

"Well, my girl," he intoned through clenched teeth, "now it's my turn to surprise you."

Eventually, Mert seemed to have had her fill of cavorting in the pond and lumbered out, streaming water like some hairy all-terrain vehicle. Her coat glistened with moisture. The leather saddle was wet clear through, which might be difficult to explain, but Rafferty had no intention of admitting he'd had any problem on the short ride from the ranch house. His mind busy with rationalizations, he used his handkerchief to wipe as much excess water as possible from Mert's neck and sides while she stood grazing placidly. When he had done all he could, he mounted up again, and they headed toward the distant line of cottonwood trees.

LaRue and her granddad had just stowed the last of the groceries into the chuckwagon when Rafferty rode up. LaRue was aware that Quincy, who had been assigning wagons to the various guests, had laid his clipboard aside and started her way. He probably didn't want to miss the fun.

With satisfaction, LaRue noticed that old Mert was wet—very wet, indeed—but, what had happened to Rafferty? Her smile faded. For some reason he looked as dry as the Sahara. She exchanged a puzzled glance with Quincy.

Rafferty swung down off his horse, greeting them with a mild half smile. "Sorry if I kept you waiting. It's been a while since I was on a horse..."

"Something happen?" asked LaRue innocently.

"Well, it was my fault, really."

"What was your fault?"

"I gave Mert her head and we crisscrossed that pasture hell-bent for leather."

"You...what?"

"I'm afraid I let her run...seems she got pretty lathered up." He patted one of the mare's steaming flanks. "Sorry about that. I'll give her a good rubdown." As he walked off, leading Mert, he added, "Guess it was just too hot to trot."

Hands on her hips, LaRue flashed a look at Quincy. She knew Rafferty was lying. And she was pretty sure he knew that she knew. What kind of game was he playing?

She wanted to make some snide remark about his wet seat, but somehow the slight twist of the tautly-muscled rump encased in faded denim held her spellbound until he had disappeared from sight.

"Kind of a nasty trick to play on the man, givin' him old Mert to ride." Levi Tate made the observation in a reproving tone, following it with a stream of tobacco juice aimed at a flat rock.

"You wouldn't think so if you'd heard what he said back at the barn," LaRue muttered darkly.

"Well, you can tell me all about it tonight, while you work on that wet tack with some saddlesoap."

"But, Grandpa...."

"Ain't got time to discuss it, sister. If we're gonna make Drovers' Range by tonight, we'd better get movin'."

LaRue shrugged and climbed onto her own horse. She watched, bemused, as her grandfather organized the wagons and gave the drivers last-minute instructions.

What had gone wrong? she wondered. She didn't, for one minute, think the government man had outsmarted her. But she didn't understand exactly what had happened, either. All she knew for sure and certain was that they were going to be on the trail for several days. She would have countless opportunities to make up for this morning's lack of success. And she planned to take advantage of every one of them.

Overhead a few tattered clouds drifted across the broad expanse of sky, and a slight breeze stirred the leaves of the cottonwoods, making them rattle noisily. Male voices issued commands to horses and mules, and with a jangle of metal and the creak of old wood, the covered wagons began to roll forward. Before them stretched the endless green prairie.

"Move 'em out!" called Levi Tate, riding to the front of the wagon train on a buckskin pony. "Wagons ho!"

The answering shouts echoed and reechoed.

"Wagons ho!"

Chapter Four

"The prairie stretches away as far as the eye can see—
an endless ocean of waving grasses. A lovely sight!"
                    —Miss Letitia Mudd, schoolteacher,
                              Strong City, Kansas, 1876

Rafferty couldn't remember when he had ever felt so content, so smug. He supposed it was always that way when a man finally realized a boyhood dream.

Here he was, dressed in Western garb, jouncing along on horseback, crossing the wide prairie. What did it matter that the clothes he wore had been purchased three weeks ago in Des Moines, that the horse he rode had a somewhat daffy personality or that the stretch of prairie they traversed was bounded by blacktop highways? In his mind, he was the cowboy he'd always longed to be.

Rafferty's childhood could have been—should have been—much different. He'd been born in a midsized city in Minnesota, but spent part of every summer in Wyoming, at his uncle's ranch. He lived for that month each year, cheerfully grooming horses and shoveling manure, joining in the junior rodeos with more passion than skill. How he envied his cousins who actually lived on the ranch. To his way of thinking, they had paradise at their fingertips, but he was fairly certain they neither realized nor appreciated that fact. Rafferty had long harbored the wish that his own parents would someday become partners in the ranch, but that dream was shattered when his father, a biology professor at a local college, took a job with the government and moved his family to Washington, D.C.

Although the city and its environs had nurtured Rafferty's love of American history, he missed his summer visits to the ranch. Without really discussing it, he'd made plans to return to Wyoming to live as soon as he'd finished college. But then, when he was nineteen, his father had become ill. By the time Rafferty had earned his degrees and left the university, his father was an invalid. With his parents dependent upon him, Rafferty had no choice but to go to work, more or less stepping into the government job vacated by his dad. When his father died seven years later, it seemed too late to give up a secure career to go play cowboy. So he indulged his love of the Old West by reading and watching movies. He owned every Zane Grey and Louis L'Amour book ever written and had a vast collection of Western videos. And, instead of the usual Colonial decor, his Georgetown apartment boasted an expensive collection of Western art.

When his mother remarried and set off on an extended world tour with her new husband, Rafferty took on his current assignment with the Department of the Interior. But six months ago, when he was sent out to do a feasibility study on the idea of a national park to preserve some of the country's remaining prairie, he'd had no idea that it would in a roundabout way bring him close to his childhood dream. And, if for nothing else, he had LaRue Tate to thank for that.

Rafferty twisted slightly in the saddle to look back at LaRue. She was riding alongside one of the wagons, talking to the driver. Shouting, really, because the ring of the iron wheel rims on the rocky ground made it difficult to hear. She was wearing a gold-plaid shirt and jeans, and once again the gunbelt was strapped around her hips. Rafferty grinned, wondering if the gun was meant to intimidate the overland travelers and keep them in line.

Since leaving the ranch, the wagon train had been angling its way up the long slope of a grassy hill. Now the trail had leveled off and they were crossing the plateau at the top. Rafferty had never seen so much sky. It was a clear, cloudless blue that faded into the sapphire haze of hills all around the horizon. Behind them he could see the rooftops of Cottonwood Falls and its neighbor, Strong City; ahead, nothing but prairie was visible. The grass went on forever, an inland sea of green whipped into waves by the south wind.

Rafferty reined in to sit and admire the sight the caravan of covered wagons made. They lumbered up over the edge of the hill, their canvas tops billowing, their spoked wooden wheels creaking rhythmically. Most were drawn by horses, but one or two were being pulled by teams of mules.

LaRue rode past, then halted to look back at Rafferty. "Something wrong?" she asked.

"No, just looking at the wagons. They make quite a spectacle, don't they?"

LaRue nodded. "A scene right out of the Old West."

"Up here, with no electric lines or highways in sight, it's possible to see the prairie the way the first pioneers would have seen it." He gazed into the distance, his face rapt. "Imagine how it must have seemed to them—especially the ones from cities and towns."

"I'd think it would have been pretty awesome," LaRue replied. "And frightening. People used to settlements and forests must have felt very unprotected."

"I'd have to agree."

"If we had the time," LaRue said lightly, "I'd stop to build a monument."

"A monument?"

"Yes. To mark the spot where we first agreed on something!"

Rafferty laughed, and a wry smile pulled at the corners of LaRue's mouth.

They began to ride, and Rafferty, pleased by their companionability, prolonged the conversation.

"These wagon trips must be very successful. How long have you been doing them?"

"Grandpa and I got the idea about five years ago," she answered. "We usually make four to six trips a season, depending on the demand. We've had a good response so far—people from nearly every state and several foreign countries."

"I'm impressed. How do they hear about it?"

"Mostly word of mouth. People who enjoy themselves tell their friends and relatives. We have a lot of folks who take the trip every year."

"You know, this has the potential for being a fantastic money-making scheme," Rafferty commented. "Have you ever thought about doing some heavy-duty advertising?"

"No."

"Why not? A little publicity could draw in crowds from all over the country."

"We're not interested in crowds, Mr. Rafferty. We prefer to operate on a small scale."

"But why?"

"Look around," she said. "What do you see?"

Rafferty swung his gaze across the grassland and along the blurred horizon once again. "Peace," he answered. "Tranquility. Beauty...and space."

"Right. But if we brought hordes of people here to experience those same things, the tranquility and space would disappear, wouldn't they? Seems kind of self-defeating to me."

With those tart words, LaRue spurred her horse and trotted away. The square set of her shoulders said more plainly than words that their conversation had only reminded her they were on opposite sides of a touchy issue.

Rafferty sighed. She had a point, much as he would like to deny it. Score one for the prairie wildflower....

At noon they stopped for lunch beneath two hedge trees growing beside a creek bed that had left a jagged scar on the land.

"It's been a dry year," complained Levi Tate, uncorking a thermos of coffee while LaRue passed out wrapped sandwiches. "Ordinarily there'd be quite a run of water through this here creek."

Rafferty cast a sideways glance at old Mert, who stood a few yards away, calmly grazing. He could only guess what her reaction might have been had the creek actually contained water.

He suspected LaRue had caught his look, for she casually commented, "Too bad, too. The horses would have liked a good drink."

"We can water them at the pond over the next hill," spoke up Quincy, with a grin and a wink. "There'll be plenty of water there."

Rafferty couldn't fail to miss Quincy's gleeful tone nor LaRue's answering smile.

Damn, they were planning on him providing entertainment for the whole wagon train. Trouble was, he didn't know a single thing he could do to prevent it. Once Mert got a whiff of that water, off she'd go, and it'd be up to him whether or not to eject again.

Curse that little she-devil, he raged silently. He wasn't referring to Mert.

"Hope a cold lunch will hold you folks until this evenin'," Levi said to the group in general. "The cooks have gone on ahead with the chuckwagon, and I can guarantee you, they'll have a fine, hot meal ready when we arrive."

Besides Rafferty and Hollister Ames, there were eight other guests. Two of them were councilmen from Cottonwood Falls and Strong City; a third was a Kansas senator; the fourth his aide; the others were representatives of various conservation and ecological societies interested in the welfare of the prairie. All of them looked somewhat self-conscious in their new Western clothing, but their mood was amiable and they seemed to be enjoying themselves.

Two portable toilets had been set up, hidden as discreetly as possible around a bend in the deeply slashed creek bed, and following lunch, the drivers and their passengers lined up to take advantage of them.

"We can only carry authenticity so far, ya know," explained Levi Tate, with a chuckle.

As the wagon train got underway again, Hollister Ames approached Rafferty. "I'm going to walk for a while," he said. "That wagon is so rough riding, my buns are numb. God, I don't know why I let you talk me into this, J.B."

Rafferty grinned. "I'll walk a ways with you. To tell the truth, I'm a little stiff myself. I'm beginning to suspect I won't be able to get out of my bedroll in the morning."

"What will they do with us?" fussed Holly. "Leave us on the plains to die?"

"Not unless they let Miss LaRue decide our fate," muttered Rafferty.

"Hmm?" Holly was fishing in his pocket for a pair of sunglasses and his sunscreen. "My nose is going to be so sunburned!"

"Do you know what she did to me, Holly?"

"Who?"

"LaRue Tate."

"Oh. No, what did she do?"

"When she picked out my horse, she gave me one that likes to do swan dives into any convenient body of water."

"What are you talking about?"

"I'm telling you, she put me on old Mert, then told me to ride past the pond. When Mert got the smell of that water in her nostrils, she ran straight for it. If I hadn't bailed out, I'd have gone in with her. Probably have been crushed right into the mud bottom."

"What are you going to do?"

"I don't know. I can't just jump off every time we come to water. Mert has to have a drink sometime. And the hell of it is, we'll soon be at another pond. LaRue and her foreman are trying to make me look like a first-class idiot, I'm afraid."

With a sympathetic sigh, Holly uncapped a tube of rose-colored chapstick and began applying it.

"What is that?" asked Rafferty, wrinkling his nose.

"Lip balm." Hollister grinned. "It's raspberry—want to try it?"

"No, thanks. Hey. . ." Rafferty considered a moment. "On second thought, I do want to try it. Got another tube?"

"I always carry a spare. But, why? It only takes a little."

"Holly, old fellow, it may take a bit more for what I have in mind. Give me this tube and I'll owe you one big favor."

Holly handed over the lip balm. "I think I'll collect that favor tonight, if you don't mind. I'd like a thick steak and a cold martini . . . and a waterbed at the Holiday Inn."

"No can do." Rafferty smiled. "But once we get back to the city, your wish is my command."

"You were a Philistine for dragging me into this, J.B.," Holly asserted.

"You may not think so when you stop fretting and start looking around. Have you seen the wildflowers yet? Or started counting the varieties of grasses we haven't seen in a decade?"

Holly sighed. "I might as well get enthused about something. Let me get out my notebook and I'll start cataloging."

Ten minutes later Holly was flitting from one clump of grass to another, jotting down the name and condition of each particular variety. Getting to his knees, he measured the height of each plant, then finished his assessment by taking pictures, carefully noting the photograph numbers in his record.

Watching him, Rafferty had to laugh. His thin, dark-haired assistant was the only one not wearing cowboy regalia. He wore navy dress slacks and a white shirt, though he had discarded his tie and rolled up his sleeves in an effort to be casual. Whenever Holly spotted a new species of any kind, he would clasp his hands in delight, and that gesture, coupled with the big, round sunglasses perched on his nose, gave him the uncanny appearance of a giant praying mantis rushing madly about in the milkweed.

The two of them had fallen behind the rest of the wagon train, so Rafferty, walking and leading Mert, decided to take advantage of the opportunity. He had a feeble idea about preventing the disaster that was sure to occur when they cleared the next hill and came to the pond. It was a long shot, but he didn't know what else to do.

He darted a quick look over his shoulder and saw the last wagon careening along, with no one looking back at him. He patted Mert's nose reassuringly, then dug into his pocket for the tube of lip balm Holly had given him. He scanned the directions and the list of ingredients before twisting off the lid. If it was harmless enough for babies, how could it hurt a big, strong horse?

He'd just begun applying a thick line of the raspberry balm below Mert's flaring nostrils when he heard a shocked gasp.

"Good Lord, what are you doing?" Holly cried. "Have you been in the sun too long?"

"Calm down, Holly. This won't hurt her."

"I may not know a lot about the Old West, but I'm certain I've never heard of horses getting chapped lips!"

"I'm hoping the raspberry smell will block out the odor of water," Rafferty explained, applying another coat.

"And if it doesn't?" asked Holly.

"Then I'll go into the drink like a man. And when they split their sides laughing, I'll grit my teeth—if I have any left—and be a good sport. But nothing ventured, nothing gained. This just might work."

"And they say the city is dangerous," muttered Holly, shaking his head as he walked away.

Rafferty dropped the lip balm into his pocket and patted Mert's neck. "Don't let me down, girl. Did Trigger fail Roy Rogers? Did Silver make the Lone Ranger look like a fool?"

"Uh, your friends are calling you," Holly said wryly.

He pointed out Quincy and LaRue, who had ridden back to the ridge of the hill and were gesturing for Rafferty to join them.

"Guess they're anxious for the show to begin," mumbled Rafferty, swinging into the saddle. "I suppose I might as well get it over with."

"Good luck, J.B. I'll hurry and catch up with the wagons so I'll be on hand if . . . if you need me."

"Thanks. If this doesn't work, it's all over. My pretense of being a cowboy will be at an end and I'll be exposed as the biggest tin horn this side of the Potomac."

"There are worse things."

"God, I'm thankful John Wayne didn't hear you say that!"

As Rafferty rode up alongside her, LaRue called out, "Come on, the horses are ready for a drink."

Oh, you conniving female, Rafferty thought, spurring Mert forward. You devious little schemer.

"Last one to the water is an old maid schoolteacher," challenged Quincy, grinning broadly. He slapped his horse on the rump and the race was on.

Knowing the entire wagon train was watching, Rafferty concentrated on staying upright, uttering low groans each time he made contact with the saddle, hardened by its earlier dunking. The pond loomed ahead, glittering ominously in the sunshine and before he knew it, the moment of truth was upon him. Unconsciously, he pulled back, tightening his grip on the reins, and the other horses surged ahead. Mert slowed to a graceful walk, and he realized he had just cost himself the race.

Quincy, slightly ahead of LaRue, twisted in the saddle to look back at Rafferty, and in that instant, his horse stepped into a mudhole at the edge of the water and went down on one knee. With a surprised cry, Quincy slid out of the saddle and, automatically clenching his legs, found himself dangling from the horse like a human necklace as he stared in surprise right into his mount's eyes. The animal shook its head, and Quincy landed flat on his back in the mud.

LaRue's wild shout of laughter startled her own horse so much that it shied, then planted its front feet and came to an abrupt halt. LaRue flew over its head and plummeted into the pond. She came up fuming and sputtering, pouring water out of her hat before clapping it back onto her wet hair.

Barely glancing at the other horses, Mert lowered her head and took a ladylike drink, then backed away from the pond. Blessing her beneath his breath, Rafferty fondly patted her head and rode away, stopping at a safe distance to watch the spectacle.

As the wagon train drew abreast of the pond, unrestrained laughter filled the air. Some of the drivers were yelling advice, most of it designed to inspire LaRue and Quincy's wrath.

"Aw, shut up!" snapped Quincy, getting to his feet. "Jesus Christ, whose damned idea was it to race, anyway?"

"It was yours, you harebrained jackass," LaRue stormed.

"Watch yer mouth, girl," commented Levi Tate from his vantage point atop the buckskin pony. "The way I see it, yer gonna be mighty busy tonight. Now you've got to oil that gun as well as soap Mert's saddle."

LaRue's face, streaked with muddy water, settled into sullen lines as she waded out of the pond. As she stalked past Rafferty, she glared at him.

"I hope you're happy," she said from between clenched teeth.

"As a matter of fact," Rafferty replied, stroking Mert's neck, "I can't remember ever being happier. Isn't that the damndest thing?"

"Yeah," she muttered, turning her back. "It sure as hell is."

Levi Tate spat a stream of tobacco juice at the ground. "Sister, I told you to watch yer mouth. Now, let's get a move on—we're burnin' daylight."

With a grin, Rafferty urged Mert forward.

It seems things have a way of evening out, he thought. *Score one for the tenderfoot....*

Chapter Five

"A cowpoke's life ain't nuthin' but hard work, hard beds, hard luck—and beans, beans, and more beans."
—Lyle Alvarez, roper,
Cassoday, Kansas, 1881

The smell of food reached the wagons long before they topped the hill where camp would be made for the night.

With definite relief, Rafferty saw the chuckwagon and cook fire. A discreet distance away, behind a screen of scrubby hedge trees, were two more of the portable toilets. Near them was parked the Tates' old red pickup, which the cooks had used to pull their wagon away from the cottonwood grove that morning.

Had it been only this morning? Rafferty mused, stretching his arms and shoulders to test their stiffness. He felt as if he'd been in the saddle at least three days.

He slowly eased himself off Mert, pausing to give her another affectionate pat. Since she had exhibited such reasonable behavior all afternoon, he found himself more kindly disposed toward her.

Taking care of the animals was the first order of business. After the wagons were positioned in a wide circle, the teams were unhitched and the riding horses unsaddled. "An extra ration of oats for you," Rafferty promised Mert in a whisper, dropping the reins to begin unsaddling the mare. He'd done this before, but it had been so many years that he was careful to watch the others out of the corner of his eye and do everything they did.

The animals were fed, watered and curried before being turned out on the grass for the night. Levi Tate assured everyone that a simple whistle was all it would take to bring any one of the animals running.

"An old cowboy down in Texas showed me how to whistle train my horses," Tate explained, "so I taught Quincy and LaRue. Now it's the only method we use. If we get one that can't be whistle-trained, we sell 'im."

At the mention of LaRue, Rafferty looked around for her. He spotted her beside the chuckwagon, drawing a couple of buckets of water from the barrels lashed to the wagon's sides. As he watched, she knelt and began washing her hair. Rafferty smiled, recalling the incident at the pond where she'd landed headfirst in the muddy water. He'd be willing to bet that was one of the few times LaRue Tate had ever fallen off a horse.

His smile faded as he noticed the approach of Quincy, carrying another bucket of water and a couple of towels. The lanky foreman squatted beside LaRue and the two of them engaged in a brief, vehement conversation. Something told Rafferty they were plotting revenge on him, but before he had time to worry about it, Quincy had picked up LaRue's second pail and was pouring clear water over her head while she rinsed out the shampoo.

Rafferty's jaw tightened. He didn't like the implied intimacy of the scene at all, though he was at a loss to say why. He hadn't thought of LaRue in connection with a man, but of course she would be very appealing to someone like Quincy. When they were working, he'd appreciate her boyish quality and lack of feminine foolishness; when the work was done, he'd be able to see beyond the dusty face and men's clothing to the unique personality underneath.

At her age she would almost surely have paired off with some cowboy. Rafferty wondered why the fact had never occurred to him.

In the next instant he was telling himself it couldn't possibly matter less. He certainly had no plans for getting involved with LaRue Tate. He only had a slight interest in her because she was so different from any female he'd ever encountered before. He was vaguely amused, that was all—merely intrigued by what motivated someone like her.

In the next instant he forgot all his sensible arguments and simply stared. Quincy had stripped off his shirt and now LaRue, a towel wrapped around her wet hair, was washing his back for him.

That's just great, Rafferty fumed inwardly. *Very wifely. When she's done, I suppose he'll return the favor!*

As far as he was concerned, the two couldn't have chosen a better way to announce to the entire wagon train that they were . . . well, more than friendly. It was nothing short of disgusting to watch them simpering over each other.

Still, he couldn't seem to turn away until he saw LaRue draw a fresh bucket of water and disappear into the wagon she shared with her grandfather. Then, feeling somewhat more cheerful because she had gone alone, Rafferty turned away and went to wash up for supper.

Ragweed Harris and his wife, Gertie, had been doing the cooking for the overland wagon trips since the Tates had first organized them. They looked enough alike to be twins—short and scrawny, with leathery skin and cotton-white hair. They were dressed in jeans and bandanna-print shirts, and swathed in big canvas aprons. And in true Western tradition, Ragweed and Gertie ruled the roost: at the end of a long day, the last person any of the drivers or passengers wanted to offend was the cook. Not when the air was filled with the heavenly aroma of good, hot food.

Hours earlier Ragweed had buried two buckets of pinto beans in an ash-filled hole near the fire. Now the buckets had been disinterred and stood steaming on the tailgate of the chuckwagon, alongside pans of golden cornbread and a crock of home-churned butter.

Ragweed rang the bell hanging from the bow above the chuck box. "Come and git it," he yelled lustily. "Come and git these here beans!"

The line formed immediately, with the hungry travelers seizing tin plates and eating utensils to serve themselves as they passed by the food.

Nearly everyone had filled their plates when LaRue stepped into line. She had just dipped a ladleful of beans when she caught sight of Rafferty coming her way. The anger that had smoldered inside her all afternoon elbowed its way to the forefront and yet another nasty plan began to take form in her mind.

She added one more dipper of beans to the plate, then hastily dumped half a small bowl of chopped jalapeño peppers into it, stirring rapidly.

A tiny smile flickered about her mouth. *Okay, hot stuff,* she thought, *here you go!*

"Why, Mr. Rafferty," she said as he walked up beside her, "haven't you gotten your supper yet? Here . . . take this plate. I'll fill another for myself."

Rafferty looked down at her. Though obviously taken aback by her friendliness, he didn't seem suspicious.

"That's very nice of you, Miss Tate," he stated, "but I don't mind fixing my own plate. You'd better take that one and get started on your dinner."

"Oh, no, I insist. Really, it won't take a minute to dip more—"

Rafferty reached past her to pick up a plate. "Now, why should I expect you to serve me? I know darned well that you've worked hard all day. You've more than earned the right to sit down and rest."

"Lawsy," drawled Gertie. "A gentleman. Ain't that somethin', LaRue?"

"Yeah." LaRue looked down at the plate she held and frowned. She might have known the greenhorn would have manners.

Well, hell, she thought grumpily, *I can't eat this mess. I guess the only thing to do is pretend to trip over my own feet and dump the beans in the dirt.*

She executed the stumble as skillfully as possible, but as skillful as she managed to be, Rafferty was more so. He turned just in time to see her nearly fall and, dropping his own plate to the ground, caught her around the waist, putting one hand beneath her elbow to assist her back into an upright position. The plate wobbled and she contemplated releasing it anyway, but Rafferty moved quickly to safeguard her supper.

"That was a close call." He smiled, handing the plate back to her.

LaRue stared at Rafferty's untouched meal spilled all over the ground and for a brief instant considered stomping her foot and crying like a child. Nothing was going right! Why the blazes couldn't he let well enough alone?

The cowboys seated around the fire watched in anticipation—it was a well-known fact that no one got away with wasting Ragweed's cooking. They fully expected the old man to blow sky-high when he saw the disrespectful way the government man had treated his supper. Forks paused in midair as the scrawny cook set aside his own plate and rose slowly to his feet.

"I only got one thing to say," Ragweed stated. "Gertie's right. It's been a helluva long time since we've seen a real gentleman around here." He favored the men sitting about him with a fierce scowl. "A long time. Take a seat, Mr. Rafferty, and I'll fix you another plate." He reached for the ladle. "LaRue, sit down and git to eatin'. I know you've never been treated like a lady before, but that ain't no reason to stand and stare."

Rafferty and LaRue darted a quick look at each other, then obediently seated themselves on the saddle blankets scattered around the campfire. Ragweed handed Rafferty a plate, adding a second piece of crusty cornbread dripping with butter.

"I kinda favor beans fixed this way, myself," Ragweed said, returning to his own supper. " 'Cowboy beans,' they're called. When you finish those, Rafferty, jist help yourself to more. There's plenty."

LaRue looked concerned. What was going on? Ragweed wasn't nice to anyone....

Rafferty sampled a forkful of pinto beans and pronounced them delicious. Both Ragweed and Gertie beamed, fairly blooming beneath his lavish praise.

LaRue looked down at her own plate. The aroma of ham and beans cooked with onions and tomato sauce was mouth-watering, but she knew that one bite would turn her mouth into Mount Vesuvius. She glanced up to meet Rafferty's eyes. He smiled and lifted his fork.

"Better eat while your food's hot," he commented.

It'll be hot clear into next week, LaRue thought, spearing a single bean. She smiled at Rafferty and ate the bean.

"P-pass me that iced tea, will you, Grandpa?" she asked as calmly as possible. She was shocked that one tiny bean could contain so much heat. She downed half a glass of tea, all the time trying to convince herself that she was only imagining the knowing look in Rafferty's eyes. He couldn't possibly have seen her dump those peppers onto her plate . . . could he?

"What's ailin' you, girl?" Levi asked. "You know you've always liked Ragweed's beans."

"I guess I'm just not very hungry tonight," LaRue muttered, pushing the offending legumes from side to side on her plate. "I'm more thirsty than anything."

"Ragweed and I hate to see anyone pick at his food, you remember," warned Gertie.

"I remember." Glumly, LaRue scooped up a small forkful of beans and put it into her mouth, following it with a hasty bite of cornbread.

Serves you right, she told herself. This wouldn't have happened if she hadn't been trying to be mean to Rafferty.

Then she recalled the humiliation of being tossed headfirst into the pond and knew it had been worth the try.

Next time, she vowed silently. Next time he wasn't going to escape so easily.

She could feel the beans burning all the way down, and her resentment of the big-city biologist burned just as hotly.

"Got coffee and fried apple pies for dessert," Ragweed announced a few minutes later.

LaRue took advantage of the opportunity to start gathering up plates, adroitly hiding hers beneath her grandfather's. As Gertie took the stacked plates, she eyed LaRue sharply.

"Hope you ain't plannin' on no pie, miss," she said firmly. "Because we don't serve dessert to those who can't finish their supper."

LaRue sighed. "I need to get to work on that gun anyway." She walked away, apparently resigned to her self-imposed state of hunger.

When she returned to the cookfire with oil, rags and the handgun, most of the others had scattered. Hollister Ames had persuaded a few of the more energetic of them to take a twilight walk on the prairie with him; the rest were seated around a second fire, listening to one of the cowboys strum a guitar and sing Western ballads. Ragweed and Gertie were standing at the end of the chuckwagon, washing up the dishes. Only Rafferty and Levi Tate remained by the fire.

LaRue dropped down beside her grandfather and began cleaning the Smith & Wesson revolver.

Rafferty watched the efficient movements of her slim, sun-browned hands, noticing her short nails and lack of jewelry. Most of the women he knew would squeal in dismay at the mere sight of a gun, but LaRue treated the weapon as if she was comfortable with the feel of it in her hands.

"I thought only cowboys in the Old West wore guns," he heard himself saying. "Why do you wear one?"

Surprised, she looked up, and Rafferty's hand jerked, nearly spilling hot coffee into his lap.

Lord, he thought, *why did I ever think she looked like a boy?*

The last long rays of sunshine touched LaRue's head and shoulders, bathing her in gold, highlighting a prettiness Rafferty had not realized she possessed. Her freshly washed hair had been left loose, flowing down her back, and now it lifted in the evening breeze, swirling around her head in a halo of gold and bronze. Her hair might be brown, but it contained too many pale sun streaks and dark red glints to ever be considered ordinary. And the shorter hair around her face curled sweetly, as if in defiance of her usual denial of femininity.

Her eyes, deeply brown and flecked with gold, regarded him seriously. "Why are you staring?" she asked bluntly.

"Er . . . I'm not," he managed to say. "I was just waiting for you to answer my question."

"I already did," she said, clearly confused.

"You did?"

"Yes, I did. I told you that I wear a gun for several reasons. On the prairie there's always the danger of snakes . . . and if I see coyotes chasing calves, I can shoot into the air and scare them away. When I'm out alone, Grandpa likes me to carry a gun in case I get hurt or need to signal for help."

"Oh." He was entranced by the absolute smoothness of her complexion, washed with faint sunlight so gold that it almost disguised the scattering of tan freckles across her straight nose. As she spoke, his disobedient eyes followed every movement of her generous mouth with its soft, apricot-colored lips.

"Carrying a gun is more or less a habit," she murmured, made uneasy by his intense scrutiny.

Levi Tate chuckled, breaking the sudden silence. He drained his coffee cup. "She's a damned good shot, too," he commented.

"Oh, I'm sure she is," Rafferty said, struggling to pull his attention away from the woman he had previously thought so irritating. What was wrong with him?

He must have been away from home and female companionship too long.

"I'm going to have some more coffee," he announced. "Can I get a cup for anyone else?"

"Sure thing," said Levi, holding out the tin mug he'd just emptied.

Rafferty had unfolded his long legs and started to get to his feet before he realized how violently every muscle in his body was protesting. "Damn, I sat there too long," he muttered. "Got stiff as a board."

"A day in the saddle can do that to a feller, if'n he ain't used to it," Levi stated. "You okay?"

Rafferty forced a grin. Merely standing upright was agony, but it wouldn't do to let LaRue see him acting like the sissy she plainly thought him to be.

"Yeah, I'm fine. Once I work out this stiffness, I'll be good as new."

Rafferty creaked over to the chuckwagon to pick up the still-steaming coffeepot. As he poured out two cups, a shout went up from the other campfire.

"Man at the pot!" Tin cups were banged against rocks or the sides of the wagons ... anything to make noise.

"What's that all about?" Rafferty asked in surprise.

Gertie gave him a sympathetic smile. "It's an old cowboy custom. Anytime they catch someone at the coffeepot, he's expected to fill all the cups." She wiped her hands on a dish towel. "Here, I'll be glad to do it for ya, son."

"No, I don't mind. Besides, you're busy. It'll be good for me to walk around a little."

He handed a cup to Levi Tate, then, moving rather slowly, proceeded to make the rounds, pouring coffee for the others. When he finished, he returned the pot to Gertie and lowered himself by the fire once again, a rueful smile on his lips.

"I hate to think what condition I'll be in by morning."

Levi took a noisy swig of coffee. "I've got a suggestion," he said, unexpectedly. "There's some damned good liniment in my wagon—would you fetch it, sister?"

LaRue looked up from her task. She had kept her head bent in order to hide her amusement at Rafferty's obvious discomfort. At least not everything had gone his way today.

"Sure," she replied, laying aside the gun and cleaning rags.

When she returned and held out the bottle of liniment, Levi shook his head. "Tell you what. I'll soap that saddle for you if you'll give Mr. Rafferty one of your famous backrubs."

"What?" she croaked. "Are you...? *Me?* Put this on ... him?"

"He can't very well put it on hisself," the old man pointed out. "You're good at that sort of thing, and besides, it'll git you out of a heap of work."

LaRue sighed. Either her grandfather didn't comprehend the situation ... or he was being intentionally dense. "Maybe Mr. Rafferty doesn't want a backrub, Grandpa—" she began, only to be interrupted almost immediately by Rafferty's deep voice.

"I can't think of anything I'd like better right now."

She saw, for the first time, that his eyes were hazel, and she also recognized that they were sparkling with mirth—at her expense, of course.

"All right," she said, gritting her teeth, "you asked for it. Take off your shirt."

It made him nervous that she had given in so easily. "My shirt?" he repeated, doubtfully.

"Unless you're too modest," she jibed. "I can always apply this stuff right through the cotton."

He began unbuttoning his shirt. God, he hated it when she succeeded in making him feel like a little boy.

"Lie down," LaRue said faintly, wondering why her mouth had gone suddenly dry. He must've been pushing some hellishly big pencils to develop muscles like that sitting behind a desk.

"Lie down?" he echoed.

"That's what I said," she snapped. "Do you have a hearing problem?"

"No, I just wasn't sure what you had in mind."

He winced as he eased himself onto the scratchy saddle blanket and gingerly stretched out on his stomach.

"Besides, not all my working parts are cooperating, if you remember."

"Well, b'lieve I'll leave the two of you to git on with it," Levi said with a chuckle. "Got a lot of soapin' to do. G'night, sister... Rafferty." He walked away, grinning as he reached for a plug of tobacco.

LaRue decided it was going to be necessary to have a talk with her granddad. She couldn't imagine why he had placed her in this embarrassing situation and then blithely walked away. Thank heavens Ragweed and Gertie were still close by, finishing up the kitchen chores.

Kneeling beside Rafferty, LaRue didn't think to warn him before splashing his back with the cold liniment, and his tired muscles clenched involuntarily. She smothered her quick feeling of guilt and started the massage by gripping his shoulders firmly and rubbing deeply with her thumbs. After a while, she began a light pummeling with her fists.

Rafferty stifled a moan. She must be determined to kill him, he decided. Her pounding hurt like hell. He closed his eyes and concentrated on relaxing his battered body as much as he could. He bent his arms and rested his head on them in an effort to get more comfortable.

As the large muscles of his back bunched beneath her hands, LaRue's motions slowed. As difficult as it was for her to admit it, the man had a wonderful body. Applying more liniment, she lightened her touch, spreading the clear liquid across his broad shoulders and down the concise indentation of his spine. Then, moving upward again, she feathered the liniment outward toward the hard curve of his rib cage.

His skin was warm and smooth, glowing moistly in the flaring light of the fire. The sharply defined muscles tempted her fingers and she explored the hard ridges, kneading firmly, curiosity replacing roughness.

LaRue shifted restlessly, wondering at her strange reaction to this man's bare flesh. She'd had no such response to Quincy when she'd been soaping his back earlier. The sight of his lean muscles and freckled skin had aroused no sensation in her whatsoever. She might as well have been scrubbing down one of the horses. But touching Rafferty was infinitely different. Stimulating, somehow. A little flutter of excitement stirred deep within her and she was suddenly aware of her knee pressed against his jean-clad hip. She couldn't remember having moved closer to him.

Rafferty felt like moaning again, but this time from the pleasure her sure, strong hands were giving him. He didn't understand what had happened to turn the hearty pummeling into a slow, deliberate massage, but he approved, whatever it was.

The liniment had an elusive odor something like almonds, he mused. It was sweet and seductive, a balm to his tired, aching muscles. Inevitably, as LaRue's hands became more and more caressing instead of punishing, he found himself drifting to a dangerous state beyond relaxation. He felt like a deep-sea diver—one who had taken the initial plunge and survived the endless stretch of empty water to arrive at the magical world on the ocean floor. Gone was apprehension and doubt. He was left with a sense of wonder and a growing excitement. He allowed himself a huge, contented sigh, flexing his rejuvenated muscles like a big cat drowsing by the fire.

His movement brought LaRue out of her reverie, and stunned that she could have been so lost in the moment, she said the first thing that came into her mind.

"How're you feeling? All your parts working now?" She could feel the rumble of laughter deep inside him and her hands faltered.

"You could say that," he drawled.

"What I meant was, is your stiffness gone?"

He chuckled again. "Yeah." Well, it was almost true.

Night had fallen and, without her fingers heating his skin, Rafferty felt cold. He raised his head and glanced at her over his shoulder. "Through?" he questioned.

"Unless there's something else . . . ?"

Rafferty knew he'd better not press his luck. He sat up, reaching for his shirt.

"I'm fine now," he said, silently acknowledging that his most recent discomfort had nothing to do with his back. "If you'd like a massage, I'd be glad to reciprocate." He held out his hand for the liniment bottle.

"No, thanks," she said in deceptively sweet tones. "I don't get stove up riding a horse."

Touché, he thought, grinning. Well, it had been worth a try.

LaRue started gathering her things. Just as she got to her feet, her empty stomach growled loudly, embarrassing her and conjuring up an instant memory of the disastrous evening meal. She was hungry, darn it! Her stomach growled again, and she spoke rapidly to cover the sound.

"I believe I'll turn in now. Good night, Mr. Rafferty."

He watched her walk away, mystified by her sudden cool departure. For a while they'd been on the same wave length, he'd swear it.

"LaRue's a gritty one, ain't she?"

Rafferty turned to see the cook, Ragweed, standing behind him.

"You can say that again. I don't understand her."

"Don't worry 'bout it. It ain't normal to understand women," Ragweed said.

The older man stared up at the sky for a moment, then bent to lift the tongue of the chuckwagon, moving it slightly to the left.

"I'm goin' to bed now," he said. "G'night, Mr. Rafferty."

"Good night, Ragweed."

Rafferty grinned in the darkness, pleased that he had understood the cook's odd little ritual. He'd read enough Western novels to know that the cook's last duty of the night was to point the chuckwagon tongue toward the North Star, so the trail boss would have a confirmed compass heading the next morning. He wasn't a complete greenhorn, after all.

It must have been nearly midnight when Rafferty was awakened by a faint metallic clinking. He was wrapped in his bedroll, sleeping beneath one of the wagons. Holly had preferred to sleep inside the wagon, and Rafferty could hear his even snores from overhead.

The noise came again, a bit louder and accompanied by a muffled oath. It came from the nearby chuckwagon, he decided. Rafferty slipped from his bedroll and, shivering a little in the chilly night air, moved stealthily. He could see a figure standing at the tailgate of the wagon, apparently rifling the drawers of the cookbox. Briefly, he wondered if the Harrises kept money or valuables hidden there.

He crept closer and saw that the intruder was a small man dressed in dark clothing. He didn't think it was one of the Tates' hired men, and the idea of a stranger breaking into the camp angered him. He executed a running leap and tackled the unsuspecting man, who hit the ground and lay beneath him as if stunned.

"Who the hell are you?" Rafferty demanded in a low voice.

"Who the hell do you think?"

Good God, it was LaRue! She was dressed in pajamas and obviously mad enough to shoot him right between his shocked eyes. Thank heavens she didn't wear her gun to bed. . . .

"What did you think you were doing?" he asked.

"Getting myself something to eat," she rasped, wriggling her hand from between them. Her fingers were filled with crumbled cornbread.

"Well, for crying out loud," he mumbled, feeling as foolish as he ever had in his life. "Why didn't you say so?"

"What was I supposed to do?" she growled. "Wake everyone up by announcing at the top of my lungs that I was going to get a midnight snack?"

"No, of course not. But you could have...." Why did she make him feel so unreasonable? "Well, why didn't you eat your supper like the rest of us?"

She started to reply, then snapped her mouth shut.

"Hey, wait a minute," he said slowly. "You tried to give that plate to me. There was something wrong with it, wasn't there?"

She simply stared back at him, their faces only inches apart.

"Damn, I should have known. It really hurts you to be nice to me, doesn't it?"

Stubbornly she refused to answer.

"I thought we'd called a truce of sorts, at least for the duration of this trip."

"Ha!" she managed to say. Her voice was so breathless that Rafferty realized his weight was too heavy for her. Just as suddenly, he became aware of how soft and inviting her body felt beneath him. The thought was so devastating that he immediately hauled himself to his feet, unceremoniously yanking her up after him.

LaRue's next words died as she watched Rafferty brush cornbread crumbs from the hair on his bare chest. Discovering he wore nothing more than a pair of cotton briefs didn't do a thing for her sense of well-being.

They stood staring at each other, neither speaking. A log snapped in the fire and a pair of nightbirds sang throatily. From somewhere in the far distance came the faint barking of a dog.

LaRue moistened her dry lips.

Rafferty took a step toward her.

"Good night," they both choked out at the same time, turning to flee to their waiting beds.

Chapter Six

"A man can only take so much guff...then, unless
he's purely gutless, he's gotta do what he's gotta do."
—Deke Jacobs, rancher,
Alma, Kansas, 1890

As the camp stirred to life the following morning, Rafferty
found himself smiling. It had been a long time since he'd
awakened with such anticipation, anxious to get on with whatever the day might bring. Lately his life had become too dull
and predictable. This overland trip was exactly what he needed
to shake him up a little.

He dressed inside the wagon, already vacated by Hollister,
who was out photographing a herd of Hereford cattle grazing
along the next hill.

Rafferty pulled a brand-new shirt out of his duffel bag and
studied it for a long moment. It was a black Western-cut, with
a double-buttoned front placket. He'd bought it because it was
a style John Wayne had made famous in his movies, and with
Rafferty's affinity for the Duke, he couldn't resist. It was

bound to look more suitable out here than it would back in D.C.

Rafferty used a basin of cold water to wash and then shaved with a straight-edge razor. He tucked the new shirt into his jeans and pulled on his boots. He jumped from the back of the wagon to the ground and, positioning a black cowboy hat on his head, looked around with a renewed sense of satisfaction.

He'd always wanted to sleep beneath the stars, to awaken to the smell of bacon frying over a campfire. He'd imagined horses impatient to be on the trail, weatherbeaten cowhands sharing a camaraderie rife with crude remarks and cheerful laughter. He'd daydreamed about being a part of all that. He might have grown to manhood without those things, but there was a small part of his spirit that had remained unfulfilled until now. Here on the prairie, with these people, that bit of dormant spirit was learning to soar....

He heard a long, low wolf whistle and looked up to see Quincy and LaRue staring at him in amusement.

"Now, don't you look purty?" teased Quincy. "A regular drugstore cowboy."

Rafferty grinned easily. "Thanks."

"What do you think of him, 'Rue?" asked Quincy.

"He's so handsome, he hurts my eyes," muttered LaRue as she edged past him. She refused to look at Rafferty, afraid he would see that her words were more truth than taunt.

Rafferty watched the two of them walk away. Quincy didn't bother him, but he was stung by LaRue's ill temper.

Holly stepped up beside him.

"Are you going to let them get away with that?" he queried.

Rafferty shrugged. "Why not? I'm a drugstore cowboy if ever there was one, Holly. I can't get mad at the truth."

"Well, someone needs to take that LaRue Tate down a peg or two."

"Not volunteering for the job, are you?"

Holly looked horrified. "Heavens, no! She scares the living daylights out of me!"

"Me, too," said Rafferty. "Me, too."

* * *

After the animals were fed and watered, Ragweed Harris rang the bell to summon the entire company to breakfast. The morning meal consisted of cinnamon rolls, bacon and eggs, fried bread, oranges and gallons of hot coffee. The coffee tasted especially good, and Rafferty sprang up to pour a second cup.

"Man at the pot," called LaRue, holding out her cup. An immediate clamor went up and, good-naturedly, Rafferty refilled every tin cup presented to him. He wondered if he would ever remember to just sit tight and let someone else get suckered into pouring coffee. He was aware that LaRue got malicious satisfaction from seeing him caught out, though she refused to meet his eyes. He supposed she was still upset about last night. Lord, the woman didn't have an ounce of humor in her entire body.

Later, as the hands were hitching the teams to the wagons, Rafferty saddled old Mert, unobtrusively applying a thick line of the lip balm beneath the mare's nostrils. He wasn't planning on taking any unnecessary chances.

"We'll be heading down this hill toward the stretch of pasture over there," shouted Levi Tate, indicating the adjacent range where the herd of cattle grazed. "Quincy, you ride on ahead and open the gate. Last men through can close it."

The canvas-covered caravan rolled away from the camp site, leaving Ragweed and Gertie doing up the dishes and preparing to move the chuckwagon on to the location where the next night would be spent.

The senator, councilmen and ecology experts were riding in one wagon this morning, the canvas rolled up on the sides to give them a better view. They were especially interested in a closer look at the cattle herd they were approaching. Levi rode alongside their wagon, proudly pointing out the quality of the animals, as well as the thick grass upon which they were feeding. Its lushness, he explained, was the result of controlled burning early in the spring, to rid the pasture of scrub trees and weeds, allowing the grasses to push through, dense and green. When a neighboring field had not been burnt off, he told them, the difference was obvious. A haze of buck brush, weeds and young cedars would obscure the layer of grass beneath.

Holly wound a new roll of film into his camera and ventured closer to the cattle. Suddenly he called out to Rafferty. "J.B., look! Isn't that the sweetest thing you've ever seen?"

Rafferty couldn't detect a single sweet quality about the old cow—she was still in the process of shedding her winter coat, so her hide was patchy and uneven. She had one crooked horn angling out from the side of her head and a mean expression on her face.

"Sorry, Holly," he said, "but she's not my type."

"Not her! The baby...."

Hollister jabbed his finger toward a clump of bluestem and Rafferty saw the tiny Hereford calf lying there, half-hidden.

"I want to take its picture," Holly announced. "Go get it to stand up, will you?"

"Me?" Rafferty pushed his hat back and scratched his forehead. "Why not take its picture like that?"

"I want people to see all of him. Especially those spindly legs."

Rafferty's teeth clenched at the sound of Quincy's mocking voice behind him.

"What's wrong? You afraid of a little calf?"

Rafferty didn't even look around, just dismounted and walked toward the calf.

"Quince, that's One Horn's calf," muttered LaRue, watching the government man approach the animal. "She's proddy as hell."

"I know."

"But if he bothers her calf, she'll take him...."

"I know."

Rafferty moved slowly, but the calf didn't seem afraid. It simply stared at him with huge brown eyes, its flat pinkish nose twitching. When he was within six feet of it, the calf gave a frightened little cry and scrambled to its feet. Rafferty froze, and the calf stood still. Behind him he could hear the shutter on Holly's camera clicking busily.

"Oh, good gravy!" Holly gulped. "You'd better run, J.B.!"

Rafferty looked up and saw the one-horned cow lumbering his way. With her head down and her udders swinging, she gave a loud, disgruntled bellow.

Hollister shrieked a short, explicit obscenity and fled. The cow didn't spare him a glance; she kept her attention riveted on the tall man in the black shirt standing a shade too close to her offspring.

Rafferty wasn't afraid of the cow, only of the humiliation he might suffer if she actually attacked him. As he watched her, feigning indifference, his mind was frantically cataloging every Western book he'd ever read. There was something . . . if only he could remember.

Ah, yes, he thought with triumph, it was in that book *Trail Drive* by Carl Sweeny. *An old cow will never run over her calf to get to you—just keep the calf between you and its mother, and you'll be all right.*

Sure enough, when he stood his ground and didn't attempt to touch the calf again, the cow paused, sniffed her baby and then nudged it back toward the rest of the herd. She stopped once to give him a reproachful look, but it was obvious she had no real desire for revenge.

Stifling the urge to heave a relieved sigh, Rafferty simply sauntered back toward his horse. When he saw Quincy and LaRue watching him, he deduced they'd been hoping for an impromptu rodeo. The knowledge made him clench his teeth in fury.

Just as he swung back onto his horse, LaRue started to speak. "Rafferty, are you . . . ?"

"Going to shut the gate? Sure . . . stupid of me to forget."

Without a word, Rafferty dismounted and strode toward the gate. He grasped the end post and slammed it against the fence, pretending it was LaRue Tate's arrogant little neck. He dropped the wire loop over it, then walked back to Mert. Once in the saddle, he ignored Quincy and LaRue and rode toward the wagon train.

"Jesus, how'd he do that?" breathed Quincy. "It always takes two men to close that gate."

"I know," murmured LaRue, brown eyes wide.

"I figured he'd have to ask one of us for help."

"He didn't need help with One Horn," she pointed out, almost pridefully.

Quincy grinned. "Maybe we've underestimated our Mr. Rafferty."

"Yeah," said LaRue, her thoughtful gaze on the black-shirted man riding rapidly away. "Maybe we have."

Lunch was relatively uneventful, with Rafferty having to make the rounds pouring coffee only one time. He smiled and joked about it, but inside, he was starting to seethe. By God, he vowed, if he ever got caught on it again, he'd kick his own rear!

About three in the afternoon, they passed a small pond where they watered the horses and mules. Again, Mert behaved with dignity, making Rafferty proud. He silently gloated over Quincy and LaRue's exchange of puzzled looks. It was obvious that they didn't know what to make of the contrary mare's sudden disdain of water.

Ragweed and Gertie awaited the wagon train in a campsite bordered by two huge cottonwood trees. The savory smell of simmering beef wafted through the air, prompting the drivers and their passengers to hurry with feeding and grooming the horses. Rafferty had just finished tending to Mert when Quincy approached with a burlap sack.

"Go pick up some cow chips for the cook fire, will you, Rafferty? Gertie asked me, but I've still got some horses to see to."

"Sure thing." Rafferty rummaged in his saddlebags for a pair of leather gloves, and then, gripping the empty sack, wandered away from the wagons looking for the dried manure the cooks had requested. He'd certainly read about this pioneer chore often enough, but he hadn't realized cow chips were still used for fuel. Of course, there was very little wood to be found on the prairie, so he guessed it made sense.

Actually, the job wasn't as unpleasant as it sounded. The air was sweet and fresh and the wind sighed softly through the wildflowers, which spangled the grass with color—red, blue, white and yellow. The cow chips themselves were dry and surprisingly odorless. Rafferty had more than half a sack full when he arrived back in camp.

He presented them to Gertie, who looked somewhat amazed. Suddenly, aware of the circle of grinning cowboys casually lin-

gering near the chuckwagon, Rafferty knew he'd been had.
Again.

"Thanks a million, son," Gertie said loudly, taking the sack
from him. "I'd never have had time to gather them myself."

"But—"

"Cow chips add a lot of flavor to a cook fire, believe it or
not." Gertie slipped her hand, clad in a cooking mitt, into the
bag and pulled out a large cow chip, which she tossed onto the
fire. "Better'n mesquite," she pronounced, ignoring the collective gasp that went up when the cowboys saw the dried
manure crumble around the stew pot.

"Gertie," Rafferty began. "I know...."

"You best git your hands washed and pull up a plate for
supper," the white-haired woman said brusquely. "We're
havin' my specialty tonight—short ribs with cornmeal dump-
lings."

During the evening meal, as he ate a plateful of the steaming ribs, Rafferty couldn't be sure whether the warmth in the
pit of his stomach was caused by the red peppers in the food or
by the comforting feeling of having found a friend.

After supper, when Ragweed announced he was going to mix
a starter for sourdough bread, Rafferty volunteered to help
Gertie with the dishes. Despite her protests, he took off his
wristwatch, tucking it into a pocket of his jeans, tied on one of
the canvas aprons and rolled up his sleeves. After pouring a
kettle of hot water into the dishpan, he plunged muscular
forearms into the suds.

"I want to thank you, Gertie," he said in a low voice. "I
should have known Quincy was making a fool of me. God
knows, it wasn't the first time."

Gertie dipped a tin plate into the rinse water. "Don't think
nuthin' of it, Rafferty. I enjoy seein' some of Quincy's tricks
backfire on him."

"Guess I've read too many books," he said, ruefully. "I
knew the pioneers always burned buffalo chips, so I fell for it."

Gertie chuckled. "Thing is, them pioneers couldn't bring a
wagonload of wood along like we can. They didn't have ice
chests or thermoses either."

"Or pickups," Rafferty added, smiling. "Or portable toilets."

"Or smart alec hired hands with nuthin' better to do than harass them what minds their own business." Gertie fairly snorted. "Speakin' of which . . . here he comes now."

"Lookee who's wearin' an apron," taunted Quincy. "'Rue, you gotta come see this."

Rafferty dumped a handful of forks and knives into the rinse pan.

"Hey, boys," called the foreman, "Mr. Rafferty's a regular little housewife."

"Oh, leave him alone, Quincy," LaRue muttered.

"Yeah, git on outta here," snapped Gertie. "Or I'll take a frying pan to yer empty head."

"Lord, Rafferty, surely you don't need these women to defend you?"

"When I need defending, I'll handle it myself," Rafferty calmly stated.

"I hope Mr. Ames got a picture of the *ladies* at work," Quincy said, making no effort to hide his amusement.

"Very funny," flared Ragweed, coming around the end of the chuckwagon. "Why don't you git the hell out of here and do something useful?"

"He's right, Quince," LaRue put in. "Grandpa wanted us to set up the stakes for horseshoe pitching, and we've got some reins to splice."

Rafferty's jaw ground tighter, but he merely scrubbed the coffeepot with extra fervor. Damn it all! The way LaRue sounded, she didn't think he could take care of himself, either.

Thirty minutes later, dishes done and aprons folded away, Rafferty started for his wagon, determined to spend some time working on a report for the park committee. He had a few observations he wanted to get down on paper before it got completely dark. Almost everyone else was at the far end of camp, where Levi Tate was using his expertise to soundly defeat the state senator in a game of horseshoes.

Up ahead he saw LaRue talking to Quincy, who was perched on the seat of the Tates' wagon, his lap full of reins, a splicing tool in his hand. As soon as he saw Rafferty coming, Quincy began to smirk.

Rafferty realized he was getting more than just a bit tired of the cocky foreman.

"Well, if it ain't the pretty drugstore cowboy," Quincy drawled. "Back in the big city, they probably think you're a real wrangler, don't they?"

Rafferty paused, then walked on without speaking.

"But I'll bet a handsome feller like you has a string of women a mile long," commented Quincy. "You think he does, 'Rue?"

She gave him a quelling look and remained silent.

"What do ya think he does with all them women? Figure he takes 'em dancin'?"

LaRue frowned. "It's none of my business," she snapped, irritated at the foreman.

"Well, surely the man pitches a little woo," Quincy remarked with a wicked grin. "But, hell, he probably even kisses like a greenhorn."

Despite herself, LaRue had to stifle a smile as she shot a quick glance at Rafferty. Before she knew what was happening, he had whirled around to face her, and the look on his face told her he was mad. Seizing her shoulders with both hands, he slammed her backward against the broad trunk of a cottonwood tree. As he stepped up to her, he spraddled his long legs so that he could get closer to her, pressing along every inch of her body. Violently, his mouth swooped down on hers.

LaRue struggled briefly, her back scraping on the rough bark. Lord, it felt good!

No, she thought, incoherently, *the bark hurts. It's him that feels so good—his strength, his hardness—his mouth. Oh, God, his mouth!*

Her thoughts spiraled away like campfire smoke in the wind as he ground his mouth into hers. She was aware of the anger behind his kiss; he made it perfectly plain in the savage way his mouth slanted over hers, not really caring if he hurt her.

She was just as aware of the instant the anger drained away, to be replaced by some other, less-identifiable emotion. His lips gentled, warmed and softened, and her own mouth betrayed her by responding. Even her body began to stir against him, and she had to grasp the rough tree bark to keep her hands from floating upward to clutch his shoulders.

LaRue's senses fairly reeled as she opened her mouth to his, obviously inviting any intimacy he cared to bestow. She moaned faintly, uncertain whether the sound was an indication of her embarrassment or merely an expression of the sensual turbulence whirling through her.

When Rafferty abruptly ended the kiss, she couldn't decide whether to be relieved or disappointed. As he stepped away from her, it seemed the imprint of his body remained. LaRue was convinced she would feel it for the rest of her natural life.

Rafferty cocked a glance at the astonished Quincy and said, "I may kiss like a greenhorn, but your woman seemed to enjoy it."

His damned arrogance and the truth of what he'd said riled LaRue beyond all reason. She pushed away from the tree and, before she even knew she was going to do it, doubled up her fist and swung it against his clean-shaven college-boy jaw. Taken by surprise, he stumbled and went down hard on his backside. LaRue whirled and stalked off into the gathering darkness.

The cowboy on the wagon seat above him gave a shout of laughter. In an instant, Rafferty had leaped to his feet and, grabbing the man's boot, pulled him down off the wagon.

"Jesus Gawd! What the hell's the matter with you?" Quincy sputtered as Rafferty grasped him by the front of the shirt and pulled him to eye level.

"I don't like being called names," Rafferty said, punctuating each word with an angry shake.

"All right, I'll remember that," gasped Quincy. "I'll even tell the other guys."

"See that you do."

"And LaRue ain't my woman. She's my boss . . . that's all."

Rafferty released his hold on the shirt and Quincy slid to the ground in a dusty, undignified heap.

"Well, you can tell your *boss* for me that the next time she throws a punch, she'd better be ducking because, by God, one's coming right back at her."

Now it was Rafferty's turn to stomp off into the night.

Quincy sat and stared after him. "Damn," he muttered, "this is gonna be one hellaciously interesting trip!"

Chapter Seven

"As a kid, I was always disappointed when a drought year made it necessary to cancel the fireworks that our town used to celebrate special occasions. Too much danger of prairie fire, the townsfolk said."
—Jerome Wainwright, mayor,
Clements, Kansas, 1880

Rafferty awoke the next morning wondering if he was a first-class jerk . . . or a first-class fool. It was bad enough that he'd finally allowed his temper to get the best of him, but even worse, he'd kissed LaRue, complicating the situation beyond belief.

He shook his head at his image in the small metal mirror he used for shaving.

Yessir, you really showed her, he told himself, rubbing the bruise on his jaw and looking thoroughly disgusted. *She certainly learned her lesson.*

Trouble was, if she'd learned only a tenth of what he had learned during that kiss, they were both a hell of a lot smarter this morning. But smarter in ways that were going to make their relationship considerably tougher to deal with.

How was he to know that, instead of intimidating the little ruffian, his kiss would set off some well-hidden conflagration inside her? Not to mention a few white-hot fires of his own.

He'd never suspected Miss LaRue Tate's no-nonsense exterior had concealed such heat or passion. She was a seething volcano of emotion…and he'd almost be willing to bet his first-edition Zane Greys that he was the only man to ever get far enough beyond her barriers to find it out. Not that that had been his intention—it had just worked out that way.

A short time ago he'd made the hasty assumption that LaRue and Quincy were involved with each other. Now he knew better. But at her age, she had no doubt been kissed—had possibly engaged in an affair or two, though he could swear that he had been the first to really touch her. She'd responded to some indefinable something in his kiss, though she'd fought initially. What strange chemistry was there between them?

He grunted morosely, gathering up soap, razor and toothbrush to dump haphazardly into a leather shaving kit. If he had thought of it at all, he'd have anticipated that kissing LaRue would be like kissing a fencepost. Instead, it had been more like kissing a firecracker. She'd fairly exploded in his arms, sending sparks shooting in all directions. And remembering the look in her eyes just before she had decked him, Rafferty was convinced that she was just as shocked and dismayed by her reaction as he had been.

He didn't really understand what had happened. One minute he had been mad enough to strangle her, the next he had found himself marveling at the warmth of her mouth beneath his, at the softness of her skin. And instead of leather and horses, as he'd imagined, she'd smelled of floral-scented soap. That fact alone had delivered almost as much punch as her small, hard fist.

The past two days had presented him with some real surprises. He'd discovered that LaRue, though at times as mean as a prairie rattler, could also be human. And she was pretty, a fact his subconscious had previously ignored. Then, to top it off, not only had he kissed her, he'd enjoyed it! Things were definitely getting more complicated.

LaRue braided her hair, all the while mentally *upbraiding* herself. She thought of Rafferty again and gave the strands of hair she held such a vicious twist that it made her eyes water.

Although it had been a reflex reaction, she should have socked him twice as hard . . . and, Lord help her, while she was at it, she should have punched herself.

How could she have done such a stupid thing? And how was she going to be able to keep her distance from Rafferty for the rest of the trip? It was devastating to know she had practically swooned in his arms like a poleaxed heifer. And even more devastating to admit he knew it, too.

If nothing else, LaRue was painfully honest, and now she accused herself of knowing exactly what she had been doing when she'd taunted Rafferty. All along, she had known he wasn't the weak sissy she'd tried to believe he was. No, Rafferty might not be the cowboy he pretended to be, but there was a tough core about him that belied the vain, city-bred image she had attempted to thrust upon him. Because he was neither the kind of man she was used to nor the type of man she had hoped he would be—the kind most easily despised—she didn't really know what to make of him. That fact alone was enough to account for her reluctant interest in him. The thought brought her back to the admission that she had stood by and let Quincy goad him, almost hoping Rafferty would react the way he had.

You wanted him to kiss you, LaRue Tate, she told her reflection in the piece of broken mirror propped against the wagon seat. *Giving him that backrub got you all hot and bothered, I suppose. But why did you have to act like some oversexed rodeo groupie?*

She tied the end of her single braid with a leather thong and flipped it back over her shoulder. With a sigh and a promise to herself that she would avoid J. B. Rafferty at all costs, she put on her hat and went to breakfast.

Breakfast consisted of fried ham, eggs and blueberry coffeecake. Rafferty and LaRue tried to ignore each other all through the meal, but just before it ended, Rafferty looked up to see her pouring a second cup of coffee and couldn't resist calling out, "Man at the pot!"

Amid the chuckles and amused glances, LaRue obligingly made the rounds, filling tin mugs. When she came to Rafferty and he handed her his cup, she kept her head lowered until, when he took the cup back, his long fingers closed around hers, refusing to release her. Warily she raised her eyes and met his, wondering if he was trying to further ridicule her in front of the others. But he merely favored her with a slight smile and a nod.

"Thanks," he said, trying to convey to her that he regretted his impulsive action the night before.

"You're welcome," she replied, convinced that he was reminding her he now had something incriminating to hold over her head, should she step out of line again.

This time when LaRue tried to pull her fingers away, Rafferty let them go. She turned and walked off; he took a hasty swig of coffee and burned his tongue.

Rafferty sighed. Surely things were easier back in the days of the real wagon trains. Then people only had to worry about simple matters like Indians, dust storms and flash floods. . . .

"I've got half a dozen Band-Aids under these argyle socks," complained Holly, climbing aboard the wagon. "And so many blisters my feet will never be the same again."

Rafferty grinned up at him. "But think of the story you can write for...say, *National Geographic* about this trip. It'll all be worth it, trust me."

"Trust you? That was my mistake in the first place," Hollister grumbled. "Of course, I have gotten some fabulous pictures. Maybe I could write an article. . . ."

"Why don't you rest your feet today? And while you're riding, feel free to use the lap-top computer to work on your story."

"I just may do that." Hollister glanced up at the sun, then unfolded his dark glasses and put them on, reaching into his pocket for the tube of lip balm.

"Oh-oh," muttered Rafferty, "that reminds me. . . ."

Leading Mert to the back of the wagon, he unobtrusively brought forth the tube of raspberry-flavored wax Holly had loaned him and began applying it to the area between the horse's long nostrils and upper lip.

"By God, I've never seen anything like that," said a male voice. "You ain't one of them fellers that'd rather kiss his horse than a woman, are ya?"

Rafferty whirled, guiltily, to see Levi Tate standing there, a huge grin on his whiskery face.

"I, uh...."

"No need to explain—I was jist joshin'." Levi laughed outright. "Anyway, I reckon I know what's goin' on. Now I see why Mert has been such a landlubber the last two days. That stuff sure has a powerful odor! Cain't say as I'd have thought of somethin' like that."

Rafferty shrugged. "I couldn't believe it would work, but it did."

"There's an easier way, though. Jist put your hands over Mert's eyes when you're approachin' water. She'll still smell it, but she won't run if she cain't see where she's goin'."

"That sounds simple enough."

"LaRue should never have give you such a cantankerous horse," Tate said, his grin disappearing. "I'll make her trade with ya, if you'd like."

"No need," Rafferty said easily. "I'll try your suggestion with Mert, and if it works, I shouldn't have any more problems."

"Well, I admire the way you outwitted my granddaughter."

"Don't know how long I'll be able to keep ahead of her," Rafferty commented.

"Somehow, I think you'll manage. Oh, I came to tell ya that we're headin' for the Circle C Ranch today—I'm anxious for you to meet Bill O'Conner and his sons. You'll enjoy seein' their ranchin' operations, I think."

"I'm looking forward to it."

"Guess we'd best git started, then." As Levi walked away, he pulled his hat low over his eyes and spoke, just loud enough for Rafferty hear.

"By the way, after what Quincy told me, I knew ya wasn't the type to prefer horses when it came to kissin'."

Rafferty could swear he heard the man chuckle.

The wagon train crossed onto Circle C land shortly after lunch. The heavily grassed pastures were filled with a mixed herd of fat, healthy cattle, but careful observation on Rafferty's part brought him to the conclusion that the ground wasn't overgrazed.

The O'Conner ranch house was set at the edge of the property near a gravel road. The house itself was a long, modern ranch-style built to incorporate the original limestone homestead. Behind it were two huge metal barns and between them, a circular pond surrounded by young cottonwood trees, with a grassy dam and a picnic area. The wagons were parked just beyond the pond, where the Harrises' chuckwagon was already located.

Rafferty swiftly covered Mert's eyes as he rode toward the water, and she seemed perfectly content to amble to a stop with the other horses. As soon as he dismounted, Rafferty led the mare to the edge of the pond for a drink. When she'd had her fill, he unsaddled her and turned her into a small corral with the others. Although they were whistle-trained, Levi Tate pointed out, Mrs. O'Conner wouldn't be pleased to find them trampling through her garden.

Bill O'Conner and his two married sons spent the afternoon showing Rafferty and the other men their extensive farm and ranch operation. The younger son, Jason, showed them how he used a computer to keep business records. Within minutes, he could find receipts for machinery or hired labor, calculate the interest on a loan or determine when and for what disease any animal on the place had last been vaccinated. Information about taxes and insurance was stored on separate diskettes, readily available.

From the office, the group moved outdoors into the rather surprising heat of the afternoon. They toured the barns and stables, and then the elder O'Conner son, Matt, took them for a drive through some of the family's outlying properties, explaining improvements they were planning to make as time and money allowed.

When the group returned to the ranch in the early evening, Mrs. O'Conner graciously invited the members of the wagon train to make use of the two showers in the house while she and the Harrises broiled steaks over charcoal in the backyard.

Rafferty couldn't quite remember a hot shower ever feeling so good. Only the thought of a T-bone steak lured him from beneath the refreshing spray. He slipped into a pair of clean jeans and a striped Western shirt and joined the others in the yard.

Accepting a tall glass of iced tea from Mrs. O'Conner, he folded his lanky frame into a lawn chair and, as casually as possible, watched LaRue help the O'Conner daughters-in-law put supper on the table. She, too, must have showered, for her hair, pulled back into a thick ponytail, was still damp and slightly curly. She was wearing a sleeveless cotton blouse and softly faded blue jeans. Rafferty found himself thinking that she looked fresh and clean, pretty in a natural way, completely without artifice.

An occasional cool breeze stirred the heavy air, providing a respite from the unusual heat. Far from concerned about the weather, Rafferty was fascinated by the way the gentle wind molded the thin fabric of LaRue's blouse against her breasts.

It was with a definite feeling of relief that he heard Ragweed Harris ring the dinner bell and advise everyone to take seats at the picnic tables. He'd almost forgotten how hungry he was....

The tables were loaded with platters of grilled steaks and bowls of fried potatoes, sweet corn and salad. As the food was passed around and plates filled, the conversation was pleasant, relaxed. The environmentalists and the ranchers had found they were of one accord—both wanted only to preserve the land around them. Discovery of the common goal fostered an easy fellowship, and for the first time Rafferty knew they were all communicating on the same level.

He glanced up to find LaRue's eyes on him, her expression vaguely puzzled as if she, too, was analyzing the presence of the new amity. Her high cheekbones colored and she looked away, turning her attention to Smoky, one of the overland drivers. At her murmured comment, she and the young cowboy laughed. Rafferty smiled, too. For once he didn't sense that her laughter was directed at him.

With surprise, Rafferty decided he liked her voice. It was rough, almost raspy—the type sometimes described as a whiskey alto. But it was unsettling, to say the least. He wanted to make himself believe its effect on him was irritating, like that created by the screeching of chalk on a blackboard. However, in all honesty, he had to admit that it more nearly had the effect of fingernails being raked lightly down his spine in a moment of blind passion, just before he—

My God, he thought, stunned. *I can't go around thinking things like that!*

He ran a hand through his hair, thankful the falling darkness masked his agitation. He forced his gaze away from LaRue and out across the hills that sloped gently upward from the back of the O'Conner ranch. Only a faint rim of twilight was left along the horizon. The rest of the sky was black, the stars ominously obscured by a layer of thin clouds.

By the time the dessert of homemade ice cream and fresh strawberries was served, a chilly wind had gusted to life and vivid slashes of lightning were beginning to light up the night. Everyone pitched in to clear the tables and return the remaining food to the kitchen.

"Don't look like we'll git much rain, though," Levi commented, eyeing the clouds. "Just a lot of thunder and lightning."

Rafferty watched the electrical fireworks overhead, awed by the power and unpredictability of nature. It was one of the things that had drawn him into the field of science in the first place. A loud crack of thunder exploded around them, and he felt the massive tremors through the soles of his boots.

"Grandpa," LaRue shouted. "Look!"

She was pointing to a bright red glow that suddenly danced along the top of a not-too-distant hill.

"What is it?" cried Mrs. O'Conner.

"The lightning must have started a fire," replied her husband. "And a pretty good-sized one, it looks like."

"That's over on the Adams place, Dad," spoke up Jason O'Conner. "It has to be. This late in the spring, nothing else is dry enough to burn like that."

The red glow had spread, and a line of flame was now visible.

Bill O'Conner turned to the watching conservationists. "He's right, I'm afraid. The land belongs to an elderly widow who only lives there a few months each year. She hasn't pastured that land for I don't know how long and refuses to rent it out so that someone else can take care of it."

"With the wind out of the northwest like this, that fire could sweep right up to Mrs. Adams's back door," said Matt O'Conner. "We'd better get over there."

As if his words were some prearranged signal, the O'Conner men went into action. "Mother, call the fire department," ordered Bill. "Matt, you and whoever else is willing to help, get out on the hill. Jason and I will take a couple of chemical sprayers over and set backfires behind the Adams house."

"What about Mrs. Adams?" questioned Levi.

"Can you go warn her? Take that truck parked by the barn...keys are in it. Make sure she understands the danger and get her out of that house." Bill shook his head. "The old woman probably won't want to leave, Levi. She never has listened to reason about anything. That's why her pastures are in such bad shape."

"I'll persuade her," Levi promised with a wry grin, scuttling toward the pickup.

Matt backed a big truck out of one of the barns, and some of the others loaded a couple of barrels filled with water onto the back. Armloads of burlap feed sacks were tossed onto the truck bed, as were buckets and shovels. The men climbed on as the truck lumbered out of the yard.

Matt drove across O'Conner land on a narrow road that skirted the hill and angled toward the fire. Twice he had to stop while someone opened gates, but they were soon approaching the glowing heart of the prairie fire.

The flames, feeding on dry, dead grass and old buckbrush, flared skyward, filling the night with thick white smoke and showers of red sparks. When Rafferty saw most of the others pull bandannas out of their pockets, soak them with water and tie them around their noses and mouths, he followed suit. His throat was already starting to feel tight and dry, and his eyes were smarting.

Matt had parked the truck upwind of the fire, out of immediate danger, and now the men scrambled down out of the back, soaking wet burlap sacks in their hands. Positioning themselves along the creeping line of fire, they began to beat at the flames, slowly spreading out to cover a larger area.

They were gaining ground, smothering the worst of the fire when, unexpectedly, the wind whipped up, sending billows of smoke high into the air. Sparks exploded, scattering the flames randomly, and the pasture was filled with dozens of new fires.

Rafferty dashed back to the truck to douse the burlap sacks in the water buckets, then took up his position on the line again. Brittle, blackened grass crunched beneath his feet, sending up an acrid stench and puffs of cooling black smoke. Where the fire had already burned, the devastation was complete.

"Over there!" called out a voice, and Rafferty turned to see LaRue pointing to a new outbreak of flame. Her face was partially covered by a now-dry bandanna, her hair stuffed up into a cowboy hat. Her clothes were grimed with dirt and soot. Rafferty could only allow himself a split second of surprise at seeing her there, battling the fire as determinedly as any of the men. Then he had to deal with the tongues of flame threatening to spread the fire outward into a wider arc of destruction.

Above them, the lightning flashed and thunder rumbled, but there was no rain. There was only the fierce wind, driving the fire on inexorably. Even a small creek the men hoped would help slow the fire was useless—the wind simply hurled the flames across to the other bank, where they went on greedily consuming the dry vegetation.

Quincy was the first to notice the approach of flashing red lights over the pasture road. Glad shouts greeted the arrival of two tank wagons and a sheriff's car. With swift efficiency the volunteer firemen responded to nature's challenge.

Propped against a tree in the O'Conner yard, Rafferty wasn't sure he could ever move his arms again. They hung at his sides, weak and aching. Still, when Mrs. O'Conner handed him an icy can of beer, he was pleased to find he could summon the energy necessary to reach for it. He tipped back his head, letting the cold, slightly bitter liquid slide over the dryness in his mouth and throat. Despite the handkerchief, he'd swallowed more than a little smoke.

"You boys did a hell of a good job putting out that fire," observed Bill O'Conner, taking a drink of his own beer. "We were lucky you were all on hand."

"And we were lucky the fire brigade made it out here so fast," added Matt. "With the wind, it was touch and go."

"Well, it made a believer out of Mrs. Adams, I can tell you," stated Levi. "When she looked out and saw that fire prett'near in her backyard, she liked to have panicked. I think, Bill, if you'd talk to her about rentin' her pasture in the real near future, you'd be surprised at how willin' you'd find her."

"We've tried to tell her how dangerous neglect can be. Even if she doesn't want to rent her land to us, maybe she'll at least let us include it when we burn off the pastures next year."

"Hey, anyone want to cool off with a swim in the pond?" asked Matt. "It'd sure feel good to wash away some of this soot."

"You bet," agreed Quincy, pulling off his boots. "Best idea I've heard all night."

"We've got a few extra swimsuits at the house," said Mrs. O'Conner. "Come on up if you're interested."

Some of the older men followed her to the house, while the younger ones either dived into the pond wearing only their jeans or hurried to the covered wagons to put on their own swimsuits or cutoffs. One or two bolder ones simply shucked off their jeans and went into the water in their underwear.

Rafferty watched LaRue vanish inside one of the wagons and wondered if she would return. Something about the set of her shoulders hinted that she was tired and, it seemed to him, somewhat dispirited. Of course, the fire was out, so it didn't make sense for her to be worried or depressed. He must have been mistaken. . . .

In a matter of moments, she was back, dressed in a one-piece white swimsuit. She paused at the edge of the pond for a few seconds, then executed a graceful dive and disappeared into the dark, rippling water.

Rafferty realized he was holding his breath as he waited for her to emerge again. When he finally saw her surface, he forced himself to relax. To his way of thinking, he was spending too much time lately being concerned about LaRue Tate.

With a groan, he got to his feet and dropped his empty beer can into a trash container. He started along the path that led over the dam, past a row of shadowy willows and cottonwoods. He'd thought he only wanted to get to bed, but suddenly, he realized how hot and sweaty he was. A swim would feel good, he reasoned.

Having neither cutoffs nor swim trunks, Rafferty decided his Jockey shorts would have to do, and he entered the pond under cover of the drooping willows. The water was cold against his heated skin, but after the initial shock, it became invigorating.

Rafferty swam a few slow laps—he was too tired to do much more than that. No way did he care to join in the roughhousing going on at the other end of the pond. He turned, floating lazily on his back, and caught sight of LaRue only a few yards away. She was treading water as she watched him, a curious expression on her face. He used a sidestroke to propel himself closer to her.

"Getting cooled off?" he asked quietly.

She nodded. "You, too, I see."

"Yeah, it feels good."

She raised one hand and gently scuffed the surface of the water. He thought it was an excuse to keep from having to look at him.

"What's wrong, LaRue?" Even he was surprised at the gentleness of his tone.

She shook her head, refusing to look up.

"Are you still upset by the fire? Your grandfather assured me there wasn't that much damage."

"I know. It's just that . . . well, why did something like that have to happen while you were here to see it?" Her eyes finally met his and he was taken aback by the depression he saw within them.

"What do you mean? What difference could it make that I was here?"

"I guess it will look good on your report to the government committee, won't it? I mean, what a perfect opportunity to point out a landowner's failure to protect his property. A fire that needn't have happened...."

"Is that how you saw tonight's events?" he questioned.

"Of course not. But I know it must have occurred to you."

She started to swim away, but Rafferty reached out to grasp her arm. "Listen to me, LaRue. I didn't have a single thought along those lines. As a matter of act, I was too damned impressed by the way the fire was handled to worry about whose fault it might have been in the first place."

"You . . . you were impressed?"

"I sure was. Do you realize the organization that went into fighting that fire?"

"Well," she said with a slight smile, "it isn't as if we haven't done it before."

With an answering grin, he said, "No, I suppose not. It was evident every man there knew exactly what to do."

"They do work together well, don't they?" LaRue's tone was a bit lighter.

"What about you?" he asked. "You were right in the middle of everything, working just as hard as anyone there."

"So were you."

"Yes, but that's to be expected. Most of the women I know wouldn't risk breaking a fingernail."

"I guess I'm not like most women," LaRue muttered. "Some things seem a lot more important than hair or fingernails or clothes. At least, to me."

Rafferty took a long, hard look at her upturned face, entranced by the droplets of water that sparkled on her thick lashes. He reached out to grip both her arms and moved closer.

"I—I'm . . ."

"What?" she prompted breathlessly.

He grinned again. "I was going to tell you that I was sorry about last night—sorry that I'd kissed you. But I can't do that...."

"Why not?" she whispered.

"Because I'm not sorry."

He slipped his right hand up her arm and along her shoulder, bringing it to rest against the side of her neck. Her skin felt silky and warm beneath his touch. After a long moment, his lean fingers moved again, cupping her jaw to tilt her face upward. His mouth rubbed softly against hers, his lips gently molding themselves to the shape of those beneath them. LaRue shuddered slightly but did not move away. Instead, she clutched his shoulders to steady herself, and Rafferty's free arm slipped around her waist, lifting her against him.

He liked the feel of her cool, slippery body resting along the length of his; he liked the contrasting warmth of her face and lips. But most especially, he liked the straightforward response he was getting from the usually complicated woman he was holding. At first she had met his kiss with a hesitant shyness, as if testing her feelings. Then, just as he pulled her against him, he thought she must have decided she liked the experience, for she suddenly began to participate. Her mouth stirred beneath his, again offering all its sweet softness with a generosity that made Rafferty's heart hammer in his chest.

In the darkness, they were virtually hidden from the other swimmers. They were two next-to-naked adults wrapped in a potentially passionate embrace and the night wind was seductively whispering wicked suggestions into their ears.

In the same situation with any other woman, Rafferty was sure that, at this moment, an easily-awakened desire would begin to course through him, prompting him to hasten matters to their natural conclusion. But for some strange reason, he didn't want it to be that way with LaRue.

Oh, it wasn't that she didn't inspire lustful thoughts—she was managing that very nicely. It was just that, somehow, despite the thundering of his pulse, Rafferty felt more compelled to protect LaRue than to take advantage of her. It was a new sensation to have a woman—especially one as stubborn and independent as LaRue Tate—put herself into his hands with such trust, such earnest innocence.

Damn, I'll hate myself in the morning, thought Rafferty.

It was echoed by the thought that maybe that would be better than having LaRue hate him. Their relationship was fragile, at best, and he didn't want to do anything to damage it at this point. Exactly what he did want from a relationship with her was something he would shove to the back of his mind, to be considered later.

Reluctantly, he eased his mouth from hers and drew back to look into her face. "I guess I'm taking my life in my hands, aren't I?" he teased.

Her eyes were enormous pools of fathomless darkness as she gazed up at him. "W-what do you mean?"

"Remember what happened last time I kissed you?"

Her lips curved upward. "This is different," she said in a low voice. "This time you didn't kiss me—we kissed each other."

For an instant he regretted his own damnable honor. Staring down into her upturned face, he was intrigued by the spangles of water that flashed like jewels in her wet hair, bemused by the sweet, inviting look of her. If they lingered like this any longer, he might renege on his decision to respect her trust.

A burst of muffled shouts from the far end of the pond roused him from his thoughts. The wind soughed through the cottonwoods, and though the thunder and lightning had long since faded, a handful of icy raindrops was flung from the sky, briefly roughening the water before dying away.

"Well," he said with forced heartiness, "we'd better get out of here before we get any more waterlogged."

LaRue smiled and nodded, almost with relief. "It's not going to rain, but I think you're right, anyway. I'd really like to go to bed now."

It took all of Rafferty's remaining energy to summon enough composure to ignore both LaRue's unthinking remark and the stricken look on her face. He loosened his hold on her waist and moved away from her. As he did, she began to sink more deeply into the water and, realizing she couldn't touch bottom, tightened her grip on his shoulders, dragging him down with her. They both slid beneath the choppy surface of the pond, then came up spluttering and laughing at the incongruous end to their brief moment of passion. In silent, mutual agreement, they began swimming back to shore.

Just as Rafferty stepped out of the water, LaRue called his name softly. He stopped, turning.

"Thanks for helping fight the fire, Rafferty," she said.

"You're welcome."

"Good night." Unexpectedly, she went up onto her tiptoes and pressed a brief kiss against his lips. Then she disappeared into the darkness.

Surprised, Rafferty watched her go.

It's been quite a day, he thought. *Quite a day!*

With a pleased smile on his face, he slipped into his jeans and boots and went in search of his bedroll.

Chapter Eight

> "It ain't so important that a man knows everything.
> It's jist important that what he does know is right."
> —Lester Mullins, postmaster,
> Wonsevu, Kansas, 1877

On the following day, the wagon train didn't leave the Circle
C Ranch until after lunch. Because his guests as well as his hired
men had responded so valiantly to the previous night's prairie
fire, Levi Tate was in a benevolent mood. He had allowed
everyone who wanted to sleep later than usual to do so, and
breakfast had been long and leisurely.

At midmorning, some of the men had driven up into the
burned pasture to evaluate the damage. Though the fire had
spread over nearly fifty acres of grassland, there was minimal
destruction because no domestic animals or buildings had been
in its path. All things considered, the fire could have been much
more disastrous.

LaRue found herself in a curiously cheerful frame of mind,
though she suspected it had very little to do with the fire and

much more to do with the new understanding that seemed to have sprung up between her and Rafferty.

Just before lunch she had seen him sitting at one of the picnic tables, wearing his reading glasses, a small portable computer in front of him. He appeared to be making notations, and she assumed he was committing his observations about the fire to the machine's memory. It surprised her that she wasn't more worried about what he was writing, but after all, he had told her his viewpoint last night and she saw nothing threatening in his opinions. A few days ago, LaRue thought it would take nothing short of a miracle to sway Rafferty from his support of the government park. Now, suddenly, she wasn't so sure.

Hours later, Rafferty was again making notes as he and Hollister followed the wagons, measuring stands of bluestem and Indian grasses. He couldn't help but be distracted by the myriad of colorful wildflowers, and soon found himself listing the names of those with which he was most familiar.

"Purple milkweed... verbena... daisy fleabane," he murmured, scanning the rolling meadow that spread out before him. "Prairie rose...."

The roses were growing close to a misshapen chunk of limestone jutting out of the stony ground. The petals glowed deep pink against the dark leaves and the pale mellow gold of the rock, making an eye-catching composition. Rafferty stopped to study it for a long moment. Somehow, it reminded him of LaRue—fragile loveliness surviving in a wild and unexpected place.

But, he acknowledged, that fragility is just an illusion, because both LaRue and the rose have tough roots that reach deep into this soil and cling tenaciously.

Because he was thinking of her, his eyes automatically moved over the wagon train ahead, searching for LaRue. When he found her, she was tying her horse to the back of her grandfather's wagon. To his sudden pleasure, he realized she was coming over to talk to him.

"What are you doing?" she asked, falling into step beside him. "I don't think I ever saw a man so interested in flowers before."

Rafferty could tell by her tone of voice and the way she carefully avoided his eyes that she was shy about what had happened between them the night before. Perhaps she was regretting the fact that she herself had initiated that final kiss. Still, he had to admire the way she was extending the proverbial olive branch.

Apparently she was ready to bury the hatchet, Rafferty thought, trying out the phraseology LaRue would have used. He had to chuckle silently. He knew very well that there had been a time she would have considered burying it in his skull! Looking at her now, he was glad that time seemed to have passed.

"I'm just cataloging the different species of plants and flowers we're seeing out here. Actually it's rather impressive."

"Oh?"

He laughed. "I'm a biologist. I'm supposed to be impressed by things like that."

"Aren't these flowers gorgeous?" enthused Hollister Ames, rushing up to join them. "Look what I've made." He held up a wreath woven of flowers and grasses. "Try it on, LaRue."

"Holly," scolded Rafferty, "what do you think you're doing? You've destroyed a part of the ecosystem by picking those flowers."

"Only a tiny part," Holly defended himself. "And it will make such a wonderful addition to my photographic essay that I couldn't resist. Take off that hat, LaRue."

With an amused glance at Rafferty, LaRue shrugged and removed her battered Stetson. Seizing it, Holly handed the hat to Rafferty and then demanded LaRue unfasten her ponytail.

When her dark hair was sufficiently tossed by the wind, Holly settled the floral wreath on top of her head and stood back to eye it critically.

"Perfect," he announced with a satisfied nod. He reached for the camera hanging around his neck. "This is going to make a heck of a picture."

Rafferty had to agree. As a matter of fact, he couldn't remember ever seeing a more appealing sight than LaRue as she now looked.

The misted haze of green-and-blue hills formed a soft, watercolor background for the portrait's vivid subject. The bright blues, yellows, purples and pinks of the floral wreath contrasted with the golden-brown streakiness of her hair and the glowing, sun-tinted skin. Though it was obvious LaRue was trying to be a good sport about the situation, her eyes reflected a certain self-consciousness, and Rafferty sensed she was one of those people who dislike posing for photos. Silently, he blessed Holly for his inventiveness in getting her to pose for this particular one, because he never wanted to forget how LaRue looked at that moment.

A strand of hair blew across her face, and as she lifted a hand to brush it back, her eyes met Rafferty's. He grinned and winked, and she smiled back—a sudden, lovely joyfulness lighting her face. Rafferty felt his heart jolt alarmingly in his chest at the same instant he heard the *snap-whir* of Holly's camera. It was a sobering thought to know that whenever he looked at the picture his friend had just taken, he would be seeing LaRue at the exact moment he had realized he was in love with her.

Not falling *in love,* he mused, *but actually, undeniably, irrevocably* in love.

The pleasure the thought gave him was shortlived. No halfway measures for him—when he made a mistake, he made a colossal one. As staggered as he was to discover his feelings for LaRue, Rafferty never for a second doubted that it was a mistake. How could it be otherwise? Despite what he felt for her or hoped she might learn to feel for him, the reason he was there...and her reason for fearing and resenting his presence...was still an insoluble problem between them. As far as he could see, there was no way to resolve the matter successfully.

It didn't change the way he felt.

It didn't alter the fact that he wanted nothing more than to pull her into his arms and take up where they had left off the night before.

I love her, Rafferty thought, feeling as if he had lain down on the prairie and allowed every last covered wagon in the train to run over him with all four wheels. *I don't know how it happened, but I love LaRue Tate.*

He thought of all the sophisticated, silk-and-satin women he had known in Washington. Why had he ever thought they were beautiful? Or interesting? Or even worth a second glance? With his fascination for the Old West, he should have known he was destined to fall for a modern-day Annie Oakley.

Hell, he reminded himself with some asperity, *I didn't even know there was such a thing as a modern-day Annie Oakley.*

He was out of his depth and out of his element. And he didn't like it much.

"That ought to do it," said Holly. "I knew it would be worth destroying a little nature to get those shots. Thanks, LaRue."

"Nothing is worth destroying nature," Rafferty groused, shoving LaRue's hat into her hands and walking off. "I just hope none of the others noticed. You'd better keep that photo to yourself."

LaRue and Holly looked at each other, surprised by his unaccountable hostility. Only a moment earlier he had been all smiles.

Holly shrugged. "Maybe he's got chiggers in his skivvies," he chortled.

LaRue laughed, too, though she couldn't help but think the problem was more serious than that.

"I swear, Holly, I just don't understand that man."

But, in compliance with her new determination to get along with Rafferty, LaRue hurried to catch up with him.

"Holly didn't really do anything so wrong, did he?" she asked quietly. Again, Rafferty was stricken by the powerful effect the huskiness of her voice had on his nerves.

"It seems harmless enough, doesn't it? Pick a few wildflowers—who could possibly object? On the other hand, might as well say cut a few trees, dam a few rivers, shoot a few eagles..."

"All right, you made your point." She frowned up at him. "But I think you were pretty nasty to him. Surely it couldn't have been because you really wanted to be nasty to me?"

"I'm perfectly capable of being nasty to you if I want."

She gathered her flying hair in one hand and stuffed it up beneath her hat. "I suppose that's true."

"You're not denying that you're equally capable of being nasty to me, are you?"

"Not at all," LaRue replied. "In fact, I honestly feel very badly about . . . well, about the things I did, or tried to do, to you."

"You mean like Mert?"

She studied the ground passing beneath her feet as she walked. "That was a terrible trick to play on you, wasn't it?"

"Terrible," he agreed.

"When did you figure out that she had a certain fondness for water? And how on earth did you manage to control her so well?"

"I don't think I want to reveal that secret. I may need to use it again someday."

"My grandfather must have been the one to tell you how to keep her from running into the water. He hasn't said much, but I definitely got the feeling he was upset with me."

"It doesn't matter now. Mert and I get along all right."

"But I guess I do owe you an apology. Not just for that, but for . . . well, all the other things."

"No problem."

They walked in silence for a time, then LaRue spoke again. "The reason I got so mad at you was because I overheard you telling Holly that this trip wouldn't make you change your mind about the prairie park. I—I had hoped we could prove to you that the landowners were taking sufficient care of things, you see."

Rafferty heaved an audible sigh. "I have to admit that I started this trip with a negative attitude. But I've already learned a lot."

"Then you agree that the people in the Flint Hills are doing a good job?"

"I agree that they're doing better than I expected. However, a great deal still could be done. Look around you—what you are looking at is the only prairie of this kind left in America."

Dutifully, she let her gaze scan the smooth, green hills that rolled away into infinity. Its emptiness disrupted only by an occasional tree or grazing cattle, the landscape seemed the epitome of peacefulness.

"Surely the fact that this prairie remains intact is enough to convince you that we are safeguarding it," LaRue pointed out.

"That might be a more effective argument if we didn't both know that the only reason this particular land hasn't fallen under the plow is because the soil is too thin and rocky."

"Oh, all right," returned LaRue, "maybe we can't take credit for preserving it originally. But at least the people of the Flint Hills recognize the value of their property and are working to maintain it."

"But is that enough?"

"It has to be," she argued. "You can't turn families out of their homes in order to put the property in a big glass case...to be admired from afar."

"It would become a national asset."

"Or a national disaster." LaRue's tone was dry, causing Rafferty's eyebrows to quirk upward in question. "I mean," she continued, "that if you attempt to make this into a tourist spot, you'll have to improve the roads, build parking lots and restrooms...trailer parks and campgrounds. Pretty soon, it will be just like all the other overcrowded, litter-strewn points of interest this country is so fond of creating. Tell me, Rafferty, who needs it?"

"It wouldn't have to be like that."

"It always is."

He was torn between the desire to throttle her and a need to take her hand, pull her close to his side and match his steps to hers. To feel her against him...where, unreasonably, his mind was insisting she belonged.

"Look, LaRue," he said finally, "there's no need for us to hash this out right now. Can't we just manage to get along with each other for a while and enjoy the beautiful day?"

He liked her quick smile and the decisive nod of her head.

"Okay. Tell me about the flowers and grasses you're listing. What's the purpose of that?"

"To have some kind of record of what is growing and flourishing here. When we get back to D.C., we can check our list against the master list to see what plants have failed to survive or determine if there are any species not previously known to adapt to the prairie. If—if the government ever has access to this land, they might choose to gather flower or grass seeds to use in rebuilding other prairies.''

''If they can rebuild, why do they need this particular land?'' LaRue couldn't resist asking.

''A prairie facsimile can be grown in five to ten years,'' Rafferty answered, ''but to actually reconstruct the complicated prairie ecosystem would take nearly two hundred years. Some scientists argue that it would take more like five hundred. Some say it already has become impossible.''

''Why is the reconstruction so important to scientists?''

''I suppose it's the same impulse that makes society renovate historic buildings or trace family genealogies. It's a connection with our past, with something more enduring than mere mankind.''

''Is that supposed to make sense to me?''

''LaRue,'' he said gently, ''are we about to quarrel again?''

She grinned and looked away, pointing to a field dotted with white flowers. ''What do you call those?''

''Achillea millefolium.''

''I beg your pardon?''

''Milfoil,'' Rafferty simplified.

''Strange. My grandma always called it yarrow.''

''Yes, that's another of its common names,'' he said. ''When I think of plants, I tend to think in Latin. An old habit from school.''

''What's the Latin name for those?''

''Chrysanthemum leucanthemum,'' he stated.

''Ox-eye daisy,'' they said in unison.

Rafferty laughed. ''So you know about flowers?''

''Not really, only what my grandmother taught me when I was young. I don't know any Latin, I assure you.''

''Surely you remember something from high school biology?'' he teased.

LaRue gave him a quick look, then angled her face away from him. ''I expect I'd better go see if Grandpa needs me to do anything,'' she said abruptly. ''We're almost to the spot where we're going to spend the night.''

She strode away, leaving Rafferty staring after her, puzzled by her sudden mood change. He wondered if he had said something to offend her, but feared it was more likely that she had simply tired of his company.

As Holly hastened to catch up with him, Rafferty shook his head and announced, "I swear, Holly, I just don't understand that woman."

Holly grimaced. "Frankly, I don't understand either of you."

Rafferty ate his supper of beef stew and sourdough bread with little enthusiasm. He was sure now that there was something wrong with LaRue. She was back to avoiding him, and even when he forgot and absentmindedly got up to fill his coffee mug, she hadn't bothered to call out the usual refrain. He went over their conversation in his mind, but for the life of him, he couldn't recall anything that should have annoyed her.

"What is your view on the proposed national park now, Mr. Rafferty?" asked one of the conservationists, a man named Baxter who headed up an organization called Green Kansas. "After seeing the condition of some of the land, I mean."

Rafferty hesitated. He really didn't want to get into any discussion of the government project. That topic was almost certain to cause LaRue to be further displeased with him. Still, the man had asked a straightforward question and deserved an answer.

"I haven't made a complete evaluation yet, of course," he said carefully, "but I am impressed with what I've seen. This is prime grassland, all right."

"Does that mean you're swayed more toward the park or the present method of keeping the land?" queried the state senator with interest.

Rafferty darted a look at LaRue and found her watching him intently. Why did he get the feeling that he was already standing with one foot in quicksand?

"In all honesty, I can't say exactly what it means right now. All the pros and cons are worthy of consideration. And I do hope to see something more of the local means of conservation before this trip is finished."

"You're crawfishing, Mr. Rafferty," LaRue said bluntly. "Why don't you just admit that your mind was made up before we ever left Sin Creek?"

"Maybe the past few days have changed my mind," he said quietly. "About a lot of things."

Good Lord, man, he thought with sudden self-disgust. *What are you thinking of?*

There was no need to give the circle of people sitting around the campfire any more to think about than he and LaRue already had.

"What about this idea of releasing herds of buffalo and antelope in the park?" asked Ned Jackson, another of the men. "Do you think that's a good idea?"

"It might be nice to see the prairie populated by the animals that once lived here," Rafferty hedged.

"What about disease?" put in Quincy. "Surely the government doesn't expect the ranchers to sit back and let their herds be exposed to brucellosis and the like without saying a word?"

"There's no need to assume that—"

"Come on, Rafferty," cried LaRue. "Even you have to admit the government park service doesn't have a very good track record when it comes to containing the animals on their land— usually due to inadequate fencing, inadequate food and inadequate manpower."

Nettled, he snapped, "I suppose you picked up that theory in your local ag college?"

LaRue's eyes fairly blazed. "Actually, I've read about the problem in farm and ranch magazines. And I've also read that it isn't feasible to attempt an inoculation program for wild animals. Therefore, some diseases are inevitable. Could you guarantee they wouldn't be spread to our cattle?"

Rafferty bit his tongue. Okay, so he'd been wrong. He didn't love her. Probably even her mother hadn't loved the little brat. He couldn't remember anyone ever making him madder.

"You're pretty young to be such an expert," he ground out, seeking retaliation in any form. "Where'd you get your degree?" The expression on LaRue's face told him his words had stung.

"You know, Rafferty," she said, "I may not have a college degree like you, but that doesn't make me a complete simpleton. I can read and reason...and use my brain." As she talked, he was aware that she was building up quite a head of steam. It looked as if they were destined for a real fight this time.

"I didn't say you were..."

His words trailed away as he realized he was speaking to her back. Astonished, he watched as she marched resolutely out of sight into the darkness.

"What in the hell did I say now?" Rafferty fumed, hands knotting into fists as they dropped to his hips. Had it been only that afternoon he had entertained thoughts of a serious relationship with her?

Nearly an hour later, when most of the travelers had wandered off to bed, Rafferty found himself alone at the campfire with Levi Tate. He had a strong hunch the old man had delayed turning in for the night because he wanted to talk to Rafferty about something. There was little doubt that something was his granddaughter.

"Son," began Levi, shifting the wad of tobacco he chewed into the other cheek, "I think there's somethin' you ought to know about LaRue...somethin' that will help you understand her a mite better."

"I can use all the help I can get," acknowledged Rafferty. "Just when I think we're making progress, we butt heads over some new issue."

"I've no doubt most of it can be worked out, but 'Rue is pretty touchy about this education business."

"Education?" Rafferty echoed in surprise.

"Yep. Ain't you ever noticed anythin' odd about my granddaughter?"

"Such as?"

"Such as her habit of speakin' like a cowhand...and then, right in the middle, rippin' off some of the fanciest three-dollar words you ever heard."

"I'd have to agree that she does sound well-educated...most of the time."

"Well, that's jist it. She ain't educated at all. Not past the eighth grade, that is. Anythin' LaRue knows is what she learnt in grade school or taught herself from her everlastin' readin'."

"What are you saying?"

"That 'Rue never finished school."

"But, why? My God, why would such a bright kid leave school?"

"Because that bright kid had a dad without a lick o' sense. When her ma died, Lonnie—my son—sent LaRue to live with me and her grandma. He never was much for ranchin', but he'd try to come see LaRue ever six or eight months. He'd hang around for a while, then go on back to the rodeo circuit. Lonnie was a champion rider, till his drinkin' took over.

"When LaRue was thirteen, her daddy decided he wanted her to live with him. So he took her outa school and dragged her from state to state on the circuit."

"And she never completed her education?"

"Oh, she kept her nose in a book ever' chance she got, and once she came back to Sin Creek to live, she went in and got her GED. But it ain't the same to her. She's real ashamed that she never graduated, never went to college. That's why she liked to have bit yer head off this evenin'."

Rafferty groaned. "Can't say that I blame her. Lord, why did I keep bringing up schooling? I just assumed she had gone through high school and then on to a university."

"I've tried my best to git her to enroll in a college, but she's dead set against it. Too old, she says."

"That sounds like the obstinate little twit." Even Rafferty was aware of the indulgent note that had crept into his voice. "What was her life like when she lived with her father?" he asked.

"It's up to LaRue to tell you about that, if'n she wants to. She don't talk about it much. She'll probably have my hide for tellin' what I have."

"Well, however she feels about my knowing, I do owe her an apology. Do you have any idea where she is now?"

Levi chuckled. "Reckon you'll find her down by the creek. You'll see the lamplight...."

As Rafferty stepped out of the light from the campfire and into the darkness, he could see the faint flare of a lantern some distance away. Like a beacon in the night, it drew him. Or, rather, he admitted, the angry woman keeping her lonely vigil was drawing him. Drawing him to her like no one else ever had before.

Rafferty sensed that the next hour could change his life in important ways, though he didn't have a clue as to what to expect. When had he ever, with LaRue? The only thing he did know was that seeking her out now was something he had to do, even if it scared the living hell out of him.

Chapter Nine

"On the prairie, a cowboy soon learns to check his bedroll before crawlin' in. The general rule is: if it's got fur, claws or rattlers, don't sidle up next to it."
—Earl Bekins, trailhand,
Elmdale, Kansas, 1882

Rafferty tripped over a tuft of grass and cursed himself for not bringing a light. It'd be just his luck to fall and break a leg.

No, he thought, envisioning LaRue's Smith & Wesson, *better not give her the chance to put me out of my misery.*

He paused long enough to let his eyes begin adjusting to the gloom, then walked on. The lantern he was using as a guide was located farther from camp than he'd realized. He was somewhat surprised that LaRue would be brave enough to venture such a distance from the others, but then, he reminded himself, she was no stranger to the prairie.

Nevertheless, there was a tinge of fear in her voice when he heard her call out softly, "Who's there?"

"It's me . . . Rafferty."

Her silence told him that that was precisely what she had been afraid of. He gritted his teeth and forged on.

"What do you want?" she asked as he stepped into the wavering circle of light cast by her kerosene lantern.

"I want to talk to you," he replied easily, dropping down beside her. She had been lying on a quilt, head propped against a pillow, reading, but now she sat up and inched away from him.

"What about?"

"About the apology I owe you."

"I don't want any apology from you, Rafferty."

"Well, you're going to get one anyway," he said firmly. "I didn't mean to insult you."

"Why do I have the awful feeling my grandfather opened his cussed mouth and told you things that were none of your business?"

"He was only trying to protect you, LaRue. He didn't want me to keep on making stupid remarks that . . . that hurt your feelings."

Her head came up. "My feelings were not hurt," she protested. "Do you think I'm some kind of baby?"

"We're all babies about one thing or another," Rafferty said quietly. "It's only natural for you to feel insecure about . . ."

"About my ignorance?" she supplied.

"Don't be a little ass," he snapped. "You are one of the least ignorant people I've ever met."

She looked at him as though she would like very much to believe him, but didn't quite.

"Levi told me about you going to live with your dad. I realize it would have been impossible to keep up with an education."

"Yeah—every month we were in a different state," she said flatly. "I tried enrolling in school, but after the first town or two, it didn't seem worth it."

"So, how did you spend your time?" he asked, his question too earnest to be rude.

"Cooked...kept our trailer clean. Did the laundry. Took care of the horses when my dad was too drunk to get off the couch."

Something inside Rafferty's chest clenched tightly, touching him with very real pain. "Why did you stay with him, LaRue?"

"Because he needed me so much," she said fiercely. "Because he was my dad and I loved him. Because he was like a little boy...and there was no one else to take care of him."

Between one beat of his heart and the next, Rafferty had put his arms around her and pulled her into his embrace. At first she resisted, the heels of her hands pressed against his chest, but suddenly, all the fight seemed to go out of her and she let her hands fall, clasping them loosely about his waist. Her head fit naturally into the curve of his shoulder, and he could feel her resigned sigh.

He rested his cheek against her hair, murmuring, "You're not very good at this, are you?" He immediately felt her stiffen.

"Good at what?"

"At allowing someone to take care of you. At just letting down and letting go."

"I don't like to let down," LaRue said. "It's weak...and I won't be a weak person."

"Relaxing your guard once in a while isn't exactly being weak," he told her. "Besides, every man wants to comfort his woman occasionally. It makes him feel strong."

She leaned far enough away from him to look up into his face with a scowl. "I'm not your woman, Rafferty."

He grinned back at her. "I thought that would stir you up."

"Hmph," she snorted, "it would take more than that to stir me up."

"Sometimes I wonder what it would take," Rafferty mused aloud.

"You'll never know," she vowed.

"Think not?"

Before she could form a retort, he lowered his head and captured her mouth with his, gently but firmly, brooking no argument.

Far from giving him an argument, LaRue found herself totally without recourse. Oddly, she was more than willing to simply surrender herself to the haven of his arms, the solace of his lips—despite her brave words.

Besides, it was obvious that Rafferty already knew how to stir her . . . probably had since the first instant he'd decided to kiss her. A man like him would know instinctively what a woman required to make her abandon all resistance to his charm. And there was no denying Rafferty had charm in abundance.

But some small perversity in LaRue's nature was upset that his caresses had been prompted by sympathy for her. Suddenly she wanted him to see her as a woman. And she wanted to determine just what it would take to stir him as a man.

Her hands were only too happy to accommodate the impulse, she discovered. They moved upward, over the broad muscles of his back, along the steely ridge of his shoulders and into the thick hair that brushed the collar of his cotton shirt. She arched her back so that her fingers could travel higher, and found that her breasts were now pressed firmly into the barrier of his chest.

LaRue turned her head a bit to one side, fitting her mouth more closely against his. She was rewarded with a sound somewhere between a gasp and a sigh that was wrenched from Rafferty's parted lips.

"Oh . . . LaRue, sugar," he murmured against her lips, his arms tightening around her.

LaRue found that, in experimenting with what stirred Rafferty, she was becoming increasingly aroused herself. Her reaction to him was exactly the same as it had been when he'd first kissed her, and the knowledge that it hadn't just been a fluke was frightening. In the past, she'd been more than capable of maintaining a cool disdain for the romantic fumblings of ardent cowboys. Even the one time she had allowed herself a semi-serious relationship, she had kept a respectable distance from real emotion. It had been easy enough then. What was going wrong now?

What was there about J. B. Rafferty that attracted her so? How could he anger and frustrate her one minute, then make her forget her hard-won principles entirely in the next?

If anyone had told her, the first time she faced the man on the dusty side street in Cottonwood Falls, that she would soon find herself clasped in his arms beneath the stars, she would have laughed until she was sick. Back then, it hadn't even been a remote possibility—right now, it was a stunning reality.

What is happening to me? she thought, somewhat incoherently. It seemed she was becoming all weak and wobbly, sagging backward onto the quilt, drawing Rafferty down with her.

In a moment, she silently promised herself, *I am going to push him away and put an end to this. In a moment....*

They stretched out full-length, with Rafferty shifting her body so that she was lying slightly beneath him. One of his arms was under her shoulders, the other rested casually across her hip. Her own hands had slipped forward to clutch the front of his shirt, and her fingers felt the intense heat of his skin right through the fabric. Despite the alarms sounding in her head, she nestled closer to him, and he responded by draping one leg over hers. His free hand went to her hip, pulling her even more tightly into his embrace.

LaRue felt surrounded by Rafferty—but it didn't strike her as threatening in any way. In fact, his actions seemed designed to shield and protect her. She knew it was ridiculous to feel safe with this man—he could bring disaster to so many areas of her life with so little effort. It was unwise to trust him, and she knew it. She just didn't seem to be able to do anything else.

"Will you stop analyzing this and simply enjoy it?" Rafferty admonished softly, lifting his mouth from hers to gaze steadily into her wide eyes.

"I'm not analyzing—"

"Yes, you are. I can feel it. Your suspicious mind is sifting and sorting, trying to come up with suitable reasons for me to be kissing you and logical explanations of why you're letting it happen."

His assessment of her mental scurryings hit so close to home that she couldn't meet his eyes. Instead, she buried her face against his shoulder and her feeble protest came out muffled and vague.

"People don't always have ulterior motives for the things they do, LaRue. Maybe the reason I'm kissing you is because I find it extremely pleasant being with a pretty girl under a sky full of stars." He dropped a soft kiss on the corner of her mouth. "I really don't like you thinking I'm only after the deed to the ranch."

His lips drifted along the line of her cheekbone, nuzzling into the disorderly curls in front of her ear, sending tiny electrically-charged thrills down the tender skin of her neck. She raised her own mouth to touch his ear and felt him tense. Pleased, she rubbed her lips softly upward to his temple, then downward. He turned his face, letting her mouth fall upon his, and the ensuing kiss was both piercingly sweet and insistently erotic.

Rafferty stroked her ribs, brushing the underside of one breast. As their kiss grew bolder, his hand curved around the breast, his gently nudging thumb inspiring the nipple to impudent life. LaRue's fingers curled around his wrist, but whether to stop him or urge him on, she didn't know.

At her touch, his movement stilled, but with a small whimper of protest, LaRue let her hand fall away, signaling her permission for him to continue his daring quest. Rafferty glanced at her, glimpsing the shy confusion in her eyes before she lowered thick lashes. Tremors of excitement coursed through his veins, addling his thoughts and sharpening his sensual perception of the woman and the night.

The woman was soft, warm and unbelievably compliant. This was a new and different LaRue, her mood as rare as pigeon-blood rubies. The warm fragrance of her hair and skin drifted upward to ensnare him, to entice him to touch her more intimately. His fingers slid across the roughness of her shirt, to the cold metal snaps, which he undid, one by one. Then, with deliberate slowness, his fingers moved over the heated silkiness of the flesh beneath, and he heard her sharply indrawn sigh of pleasure. As his hand invaded the plain white cotton bra she wore, LaRue arched her body, pressing her breast invitingly against his wide palm. Her low moan of encouragement was caught by the night wind and carried away.

Rafferty half raised himself, studying her. The pale golden light from the nearby lantern washed over LaRue, picking out the hidden gold in her hair and eyes. Long strands of hair spread out on the pillow beneath her head, giving her a delicately wanton look heightened by her eyes, now wide open and vulnerable. The enlarged pupils made deep black pools that reflected her passion; the fringe of dark lashes shadowed them with mystery. Her lips were slightly parted, making her mouth delectably irresistible. Rafferty stole a lingering kiss before continuing his leisurely survey.

His eyes caressed the satiny perfection of her skin, from the taut cheekbones, down the slim line of her throat, to the point where her shirt lay open to reveal the stark white bra and the hint of full, feminine breast beneath.

There was a wind-born sweetness in the air that was either the scent of night-blooming wildflowers or the product of Rafferty's overcharged imagination. Either way, the fragile aroma worked its way through his consciousness, a powerful aphrodisiac. But again, instead of merely inciting him to blind passion, it instilled in him a desire to adore and worship her. No other woman had ever affected him this way. He felt awe-stricken, humble.

"Rafferty?" she whispered, capturing his attention. He gazed into her eyes and sensed her impatience, her dismay at his slow pace. He smiled, deeply pleased by her obvious want.

He watched his fingers push away the material of her undergarment, freeing one rounded breast. The aureole was dark apricot in the lantern light, provoking his need to taste her. She whispered his name again and he moved to kiss her, his lips and tongue capturing the tightly budded nipple that rose to meet his touch.

"Oh, Rafferty," she cried softly, as though the words had been drawn from her by some exquisite torture. Her arms went around him, her hands restlessly stroking his back. The last shreds of Rafferty's common sense were rapidly disintegrating.

His mouth returned to hers, his tongue gently teasing the sensitive inner softness of her lower lip. LaRue wriggled beneath him as she pulled him down into her arms again, and suddenly, the kiss became explosive in its impact.

Rafferty's initial impulse was to give in and go with the flow. To simply let their mutual passion sweep away reason and reality. He longed to express the love he was more certain than ever he harbored for this woman; he needed to learn something of the feelings she had for him in return. But with the last bit of rationale he possessed, Rafferty realized he couldn't permit this thing to happen, no matter how badly he wanted it. It would be a mistake, not just for him but, even more importantly, for LaRue. Everything about her proclaimed her absolute trust in him, and he knew he couldn't bring himself to betray it.

He brought one hand up to rest against her overheated cheek and purposely softened the kiss they shared. He forced his mind away from dangerous thoughts of fulfillment, striving for a lighter, more playful mood.

He lifted himself away from her, settling to one side and drawing her close against him.

"What's wrong?" she murmured fretfully.

His hand stroked her shoulder and arm soothingly. "We'd better slow down, LaRue."

"No," she protested, turning her face so that it rested against his neck, muffling her words. "I don't want to."

He chuckled softly, regretfully. "Believe me, neither do I. But later you'll be glad we called a halt while we still could."

"That's just it. I don't think I can," she moaned, twisting restlessly within the circle of his arms. "Damn it, Rafferty, you big tease!"

His laugh was louder this time. "That's supposed to be the man's line, isn't it?"

They lay quietly, as if gathering strength. Gradually, breathing slowed and pulse rates dropped back into the range of normalcy. After a few minutes, Rafferty was aware of a cooling breeze stirring around them, dispelling the tension.

Some time later, LaRue released a huge sigh. "What happened to us, Rafferty?" she asked.

"I don't know," he replied. "I guess it had something to do with two sets of healthy hormones meeting up in the dark."

"I've never... been affected like that before," she said quietly.

"To tell you the truth, neither have I."

She turned on her side to study his face. "Come on, Rafferty. You don't expect me to believe that?"

"Why not?"

"Surely you left some woman back in Washington?"

He ran a finger along her cheek, down to her chin.

"Yes, there's a woman. But right now... I can't seem to remember her name." He caught LaRue's chin between thumb and forefinger and tilted her face upward to meet his kiss. LaRue's laugh broke softly against his lips.

"We just stopped this sort of thing," she whispered. "Remember?"

"Yes, damn it, I remember."

Rafferty rolled onto his back and LaRue nestled close to his side, her head on his shoulder.

"Look at that sky," he said, after a while. "Have you ever seen so many stars?"

"There must be billions of them...."

Overhead, the sky resembled a jeweler's case, with thousands of polished diamonds flung across black velvet. The Milky Way was a swirl of stars that seemed to melt and run together, while the Big Dipper was a series of sparkling individual stars. Rafferty pointed out the visible constellations until, gradually, LaRue had completely relaxed. Then he turned the conversation in another direction.

"What were you reading before I disturbed you?"

In the dark, LaRue smiled at his choice of words. If only he knew how very much he had disturbed her!

"*The Ivy Tree* by Mary Stewart," she answered. "It's one of my favorite books—I've read it five times."

"Five times? You *must* like it. What's so special about it?"

"Surely you know that Mary Stewart is a wonderful writer? And this is a very romantic book."

"Romantic, huh?" He grinned. "I didn't know you were a romantic."

LaRue chose to ignore him. "Another thing I like is that the heroine pretends to be something she isn't . . . only, in the end, it turns out she really is what she's pretended to be all along. It's more complicated than that, of course, but that's the simplest way to put it."

"Maybe the reason you like the book so well is because the heroine is a lot like you."

"What do you mean?"

"I mean that you think you're a phony...pretending to be something you're not."

"What is it you're trying to say?" she asked, her voice becoming ominously quiet.

"Now, don't get huffy," he warned, knowing all too well how thin the ice on which he was treading had become. "You feel you have to pretend to be intelligent and educated because you think you're not. But, LaRue, you're wrong...really wrong."

"Oh?" Her tone was positively frosty, her body stiff and unresponsive against his encircling arm.

"What I mean is, you *are* what you think you have to pretend to be. No one can talk to you for more than a few seconds and not realize you're a very intelligent woman. How you got to be that way, I'm not sure. You claim you didn't have any sort of education, but obviously, you got one from somewhere. I suspect you've always read so much that you've taught yourself."

LaRue was silent for a long moment, and when she spoke, her voice was hesitant. "You don't think I'm...ignorant?"

"I'll tell you as many times as it takes," he said patiently. "You are a very intelligent woman. Too damned smart for your own good, if you want the truth."

She had to laugh. "All right, I'll admit I know some things. But I don't know everything I want to know."

"Who does? When a person gets to the place he thinks he knows it all, he's got to be the world's biggest fool."

"But I'd like to have learned all the things someone...well, someone like you must know."

"Simple enough. A few years in college should do the trick."

"It may sound simple to you, but it isn't always that easy."

"There isn't one reason in the world you can't get a college education."

"I can think of several," she said flatly. "The two main ones being I'm too old and Grandpa couldn't spare me from the ranch that long."

"Not good enough, LaRue. Lots of people older than you are attending college these days. And your granddad already told me that he's tried to persuade you to go back to school."

"All right," she said tensely, "those aren't the real reason. But you'd never understand if I told you."

"Try me."

"There is no way you'd be able to see that . . . that trying to compete with kids six or eight years younger than me would be really humiliating. They've been in school, learning the things they're supposed to learn. I've spent too much time on that damned rodeo circuit . . . too much time on the ranch . . . too much time away from the classroom."

"I hope you don't expect me to buy that flimsy excuse."

"It's not an excuse. It's the honest-to-God, rock bottom truth of the matter. There are so many gaps in my education that I would be embarrassed to sit in a class with other students."

"It doesn't matter whether you've been in a classroom all these years or not. You've been learning. Hell, you probably know a lot more than most of those kids. You may not know how to conjugate French verbs or dissect a frog, but I'm willing to bet you've got a great deal of practical knowledge that most of them could really use. Don't sell yourself short, LaRue—because that would be the first truly dumb thing you've done since I've known you."

"You don't think it was stupid of me to put jalapeño peppers in your beans? Or fall on my head in the pond when I goaded you into a horse race?" She smiled ruefully. "Or risk breaking your neck by giving you a loco horse to ride?"

"Well," he said, deliberating, "maybe those things weren't exactly the result of rational thinking, but they don't prove you're stupid. They only prove you're bad-tempered where I'm concerned. Obviously your problem with me transcends your good sense."

"Is that supposed to be a compliment? Remember, you're talking to a hick from the back hills."

"I'm talking to a coward who hides out on an isolated ranch," he corrected, giving her a gentle squeeze. "A scared little cowgirl who's afraid to take a chance."

"I am not!" she returned, fire in her voice.

Rafferty once again cupped her chin and turned her face to his. "Let's not fight, LaRue," he murmured, dropping his mouth onto hers.

Initially, LaRue seemed to enjoy the interruption of their conversation, but suddenly she twisted within his grasp and tried to pull away.

"What's wrong?" he muttered.

"Stop tickling me," she gasped, giggling softly.

"What?"

"Stop tickling my leg—I hate to be tickled!"

His perplexed silence warned her.

"It's not you? Oh, my God!"

In a single movement, both Rafferty and LaRue raised their heads to look down at their feet. There, nestling close to La-Rue's bared ankle were two tiny animals, their spotted coats looking soft and cuddly in the glow of the lantern.

"Kittens?" whispered Rafferty, surprised.

LaRue answered, being careful to move only her lips. "No . . . civet cats."

"What?"

"Civet cats! Their mother must be nearby. Keep still."

"Wait a minute," Rafferty protested, his mouth close to her ear. "I thought civet cats lived in Africa or somewhere."

"I don't know about that, but *civet cat* is what we call spotted skunks."

Rafferty tensed. "Skunks?"

"Exactly."

"Do they—? Can they—?"

She turned her head so that her lips brushed his ear. "You'd better believe it."

He groaned. "Great."

"Shh, here's their mother. Keep as quiet as you can."

The female skunk approached the edge of the quilt, her nose twitching busily. She sniffed LaRue's discarded boots, then her ankle and then the two babies. She must have communicated her concern for them with some animal telepathy, for when she turned to waddle away, her youngsters obediently followed. Clutching each other, Rafferty and LaRue stifled their laughter and watched the civet cats disappear into the surrounding darkness.

"Whew, that was a close call," breathed LaRue, after several minutes had passed with no recurring sight of the intruders.

"We'd never have lived it down if she had sprayed us," Rafferty pointed out. "We got lucky."

"We sure did. And I think we'd better get back to the wagons and not press our luck any further tonight."

"I expect so, though this has been very pleasant. And I do intend to continue our . . . conversation at the first available moment."

"I'll keep it in mind," LaRue said dryly, pulling on her boots.

Rafferty got to his feet and folded the quilt, while LaRue gathered up her book, pillow and the lantern.

They walked back toward the circle of wagons, both reluctant to end the evening, yet knowing they needed a breather. They had to have time to adjust to the new dimension in their relationship—time to reflect on their feelings for each other and how swiftly those feelings were undergoing a dramatic change. And what, precisely, that change was going to mean.

Chapter Ten

"When a stranger comes to town, it's only natural that
he wants to see all the sights. It's my job to make sure
he ain't disappointed."
                    —Monette LaBeau, bawdy house madam,
                              Florence, Kansas, 1878

Rafferty's breakfast of pancakes and sausage the next morning was interrupted by the arrival of a dented blue pickup
bumping across the uneven pasture. As the thin, redheaded
driver jumped out, he was greeted by Levi Tate.

"What's up, Jed? Problems of some kind?"

"Naw, just a message for J. B. Rafferty. Seems some feller
from Washington's been callin', tryin' to git ahold of 'im."

"Do you know who it was?" Rafferty spoke up, setting his
plate aside.

Jed drew a wrinkled slip of paper from his shirt pocket.
"Uh . . . feller name of Terence Whitelow."

"Head of the Tallgrass Committee," Rafferty commented
absentmindedly. "Wonder what he wants?"

"Wants to talk to you right away is all I know," replied Jed. "I thought maybe I'd better come and git ya."

"I appreciate it."

"You can ride back to the ranch with Jed," said Levi, "and when you're done with your phone callin', he can bring ya back." He turned to the other man. "Since we traveled into Morris County yesterday, we oughta make the crossin' by this evenin'. Reckon you can find us there."

"What's the crossing?" Rafferty inquired.

"Place where wagon tracks from the old Santa Fe Trail can still be seen. I figure these folks are gonna want a look at that."

"Sounds good," Rafferty said. "I just hope I'm not going to hold you up."

"No problem. We usually like to stay a couple of days around Council Grove. Sometimes we take the overland passengers in town for a look-see. Lots of history there. So you jist take as long as you need—we'll be here."

"It okay if'n I send a list of food supplies with 'em?" Ragweed Harris asked. "There's a few things I'm needin'."

"Get your list ready, then." Tate beckoned to his granddaughter. "Sister, I 'spect you'd better go along. You mind doin' the grocery shoppin' while Rafferty's makin' his call?"

LaRue shook her head, unable to resist a darting glance at Rafferty. "No, I don't mind," she said.

Maybe a break in the routine was exactly what she needed to get her feelings for Rafferty under some kind of control. Traveling with the wagon train was like being caught in a magical world somewhere between the past and present. And in the last few days, Rafferty had become a part of the magic. He had her imagination stampeding unrestrainedly, filling her with all sorts of thoughts and ideas that would most likely disappear once she had a chance to examine them in the cold light of reality. Back at the ranch, she would be reminded of her priorities and everything would fall into place again.

Rafferty stood up and dusted off the seat of his jeans.

"You need to go into town for anything, Holly?" he asked, silently hoping his assistant would decline.

"Not if you'll leave my film somewhere to be developed. A couple of days ago I'd have jumped at the chance to return to civilization," Hollister admitted, "but now I want to see the wagon ruts . . . and the old treaty oak at Council Grove. How could I write a magazine article without mention of them?"

Rafferty's grin was broad. "You couldn't." He was unashamedly glad that he and LaRue would have the day to themselves. "Well, get me that film and we'll be on our way."

He walked around behind the pickup with its Keep the Grasslands Free bumper sticker, and held the door for LaRue.

A change of pace is just what we need, he was thinking. *If I can manage to keep LaRue away from the others for the day, maybe I'll be able to break down her reserve and really get to know her.*

Rafferty was silent for most of the trip back to Sin Creek. He enjoyed sitting next to LaRue, listening to her and Jed discuss events at the ranch while he let his eyes roam over the countryside through which they traveled.

Once back on the Tates' property, Rafferty was amazed that he hadn't noticed the elegance of the house before. When he and Holly had arrived to join the overland trip, he had admired the three-story limestone barn—of obvious historical value—but he had failed to pay much attention to the house. Now, actually approaching it on the cedar-edged lane, he was properly impressed. It was a masterful example of the ornate architecture so popular in the 1880s. Rearing upward for three stories, the house was of mellowed limestone, its squared towers topped by red mansard roofs, its balconies and porches trimmed with fanciful white gingerbread.

"What a marvelous old place," he commented in a respectful voice as he jumped out of the pickup. "I had no idea you lived in a museum."

LaRue laughed and, thanking Jed for the ride, led the way to the house. "That's exactly what it looks like, isn't it? From the outside, at least. But you'll soon find that it's a bit more lived-in looking on the inside."

They entered the back way, through what LaRue called a "mud porch," a long, window-lined room with washer and dryer, old-fashioned stone sink and modern shower stall. This adjoined the kitchen, a room decorated in blue and white, with pine cupboards and blue-checked wallpaper.

LaRue introduced Rafferty to the round, black-haired woman who was just taking a pan of cookies from the oven of a white enamel cookstove. "This is Mrs. Mendoza, our housekeeper. Dozy, this is J. B. Rafferty."

"How do you do, Mr. Rafferty?"

Rafferty sniffed the air with appreciation. "I think I may have died and gone to heaven."

"Ha," the woman said with a pleased smile, "if you think the smell is good, just wait till you taste them. They're my specialty . . . oatmeal-pecan."

LaRue picked up the half-full cookie jar and offered it to Rafferty. "How come you're baking today, Dozy?"

"Nothing else to do. It sure is quiet with everyone gone. Besides, I figured you might come in with Jed and Mr. Rafferty, so I decided to make you all a treat."

"Glad you did," commented Rafferty, his mouth full. "These are delicious."

"As always," added LaRue. "Thanks for thinking of us. Come on, Rafferty, phone's in here."

"Glad to have met you, Mrs. Mendoza." Like a little boy, he flashed her a charming smile as he seized a handful of cookies and followed LaRue down a short hallway.

"This is Grandpa's office," she was saying, opening the door to a tidy, masculine room dominated by a huge walnut desk. "You can use that phone. I'll go on upstairs and get ready to go to town."

Rafferty sat down in the high-backed swivel chair, gazing in approval at Levi's collection of Western artifacts. A glass-fronted cabinet against one wall contained Indian arrowheads and pottery, and there was a case filled with a variety of antique guns. Rafferty struggled to control his envy as he reached for the phone and dialed the operator. After giving her his credit-card number, he munched oatmeal cookies and waited for the call to Whitelow to go through.

When he announced his name to Whitelow's secretary, the woman said, "Oh, Mr. Rafferty, I have a message for you. Mr. Whitelow said that if you called, I was to tell you he had to make an unexpected trip up to Boston and won't be back until sometime tonight. He said for you to leave a number where you'll be and he'll call you as soon as he gets back. I'm afraid it may be very late.''

Instead of being annoyed, Rafferty found he was delighted by this latest turn of events. ''No problem,'' he assured the secretary and proceeded to give her the Tates' phone number. ''I'll wait to hear from him. 'Bye now.'' He replaced the telephone receiver and heaved a big sigh.

''Trouble?'' LaRue was standing by the door, digging a set of car keys out of the shoulder bag she carried. She had changed clothes for her shopping trip and was now wearing a blue denim skirt and a summery blouse of white handkerchief material, with a tiny bunch of blue flowers appliquéd on the square collar. Her hair had been released from the usual ponytail, and it fell to her shoulders in deep, shining waves.

''No, no trouble,'' he replied, unable to stop smiling. ''Whitelow had to go out of town unexpectedly, so he can't return my call until late tonight.''

''Oh.''

''Is that a problem for you? I mean, do you mind waiting around?''

''No, I don't mind, but I wouldn't want Grandpa to worry about us. Maybe I'd better let him know what's going on.''

''How can you do that?''

''I'll call the sheriff in Morris County and see if he'll send someone out with a message. They'll know where the wagon train usually camps.''

LaRue made the call, advising the deputy to tell Levi that it might even be morning before they returned. ''No sense in starting out at midnight,'' she said defensively as she hung up the phone and met Rafferty's amused eyes. ''There's no telling how late your call will be.''

''That's right,'' he agreed. ''Well, since that's all settled, do you mind if I go into town with you?''

''Not at all. I'll be glad for the company.''

And to her surprise, LaRue realized she meant it.

Rafferty got a surprise of his own when LaRue backed the car out of the garage. In contrast to the beat-up old pickup he had always seen her driving, she now sat at the wheel of a sleek black Chrysler New Yorker.

He shook his head in amazement and grinned. Would he ever learn what to expect from the redoubtable Tates of Sin Creek Ranch?

Cottonwood Falls was a small town, the high-fronted buildings along its brick main street reflecting a Western heritage. At one end of Broadway Street was the Cottonwood River and the falls that gave the town its name. Standing in isolated grandeur at the other end was the Chase County Courthouse, a beautiful structure built in the French Renaissance style. Its clock tower, silhouetted against the deeply blue sky, seemed an appropriate symbol of the town's unique relationship with the past.

As she pulled into a parking space, LaRue noticed Rafferty's apparent fascination with the old building. "Would you like to have a look inside?" she asked. "It's almost always open for tours."

He grinned at her. "Sure, why not?"

They were walking up the sidewalk toward the tall courthouse of hand-cut limestone when Rafferty suddenly reached out and took LaRue's hand. Though it was clear she was somewhat startled, LaRue didn't pull away. Instead, she favored him with a sharp, inquisitive glance.

"Oh, did I forget to mention that today we're starting over?" He raised one black eyebrow, as if challenging her to refute his plan. "While we're away from the wagon train, we're going to be just plain LaRue and Rafferty. No more angry cowgirl, no more pushy government man—no more feud. Today we're friends."

"Seems the government man is still a bit pushy," she stated, wryly.

"You're not going to give me grief over this, are you?"

She shook her head hard enough to send her brown hair swishing about her shoulders. "No, no grief. If friendship is what you want, friendship is what you'll get."

Rafferty tightened his grip on her hand. "I didn't say it was what I wanted—I just indicated that I was willing to settle for it." They started up the front steps of the courthouse. "At least temporarily."

They had to step aside for a small group of people just coming out the door, and LaRue was grateful that she was saved from having to reply to his absurd statement. The inherent threat behind his words both thrilled and frightened her.

"Good morning, LaRue," said an attractive, white-haired lady standing in the main foyer. "You bring your friend to see our courthouse?"

Friend? Well, it was his word, after all.

"I sure did, Cora. This is J. B. Rafferty." She turned to the man beside her. "By the way, what does J.B. stand for?"

"I'll tell you some other time," he said evasively. "It's pretty gruesome."

"Sounds interesting," laughed Cora. "Why don't you two sign the guest book? And then I'll give you the grand tour."

It gave LaRue an oddly pleasant feeling to see Rafferty's name scrawled beside her own on the guest register. And this time, when he took her hand, she gave him a dazzling smile and curled her fingers around his broad palm.

They followed Cora to the circular walnut staircase that spiraled upward for three floors with no central support. At each level Cora paused to tell them more of the courthouse's history.

"When construction was finished in 1873, the residents of Chase County threw a grand ball here in the second floor courtroom to celebrate. They set up tables for food back there in the old jail." Cora pointed overhead. "Be sure to notice the original embossed tin ceilings."

On the third floor, they stepped around massive bookshelves to the few steps that provided access to a high, recessed oval window that faced the main street below.

"In the old days, people could climb out this window and walk on the wide ledge around the roof," Cora explained. She shuddered. "It gives me the willies just thinking about it."

"It's a long way down," Rafferty commented.

"Yeah, but I always wanted to come here and go out on the roof." LaRue chuckled. "Especially after hearing Grandpa brag about how he and his friends used to do it."

"Fortunately, the window no longer opens," Cora informed her. "I expect the insurance company had something to say about daredevils like you and your granddad."

When the tour was completed, Rafferty thanked the friendly guide and tucked a ten-dollar bill into the donations box. "This courthouse is quite a showplace," he said. "And I think your town has done a wonderful job of keeping it up."

"Well, we're pretty proud of it," Cora told him. "It's something no one else has, so you can bet we're going to take care of it. You all come back and see us sometime."

From the courthouse, they walked along the main street of the town, nodding and speaking to nearly everyone they met.

"I like your town, LaRue," Rafferty said. "The people are genuinely nice."

"Why shouldn't they be? You have a guilty conscience or something?"

"Ah-ah," he warned, shaking a finger at her. "None of that now."

"Sorry."

"You know, I've never seen you contrite before. You look cute...."

"Shoot!" LaRue's chin shot up, but she couldn't hide a faint smile. "I've never looked cute in my life!"

"That's your opinion. Hey, is there anyplace we can get something to eat around here? I'm starving."

"Our one and only café is right down this street, just past the drugstore."

"Good. Go get us a table while I drop off Holly's film."

"You're getting pushy again, Rafferty," LaRue dared to say before she hastened away, skirt swaying with each lively step. Rafferty watched her for a long moment before ducking into the drugstore, which looked as if it had changed very little in the last fifty years.

Ten minutes later when he walked into the crowded café, he caught sight of LaRue waving to him from a corner.

"Sorry, but this is all that was left," she said, indicating the one-sided booth stuck at the end of a row of more ordinary ones. "I didn't realize this old place filled up so fast."

"This is fine with me," he announced, sliding in beside her. "Very cozy."

That's putting it mildly, she thought, edging toward the corner. "Not too crowded?"

He gave her a positively wicked grin. "Is it possible to be *too* crowded?"

LaRue was relieved to see the waitress approach with two battered menus and a couple of glasses of ice water.

They ordered cheeseburgers and fries, then sat back to wait. With only the wall to look at, Rafferty promptly turned his full attention on LaRue, who began to fidget. She moved the silverware back and forth, rearranging and fussing over it. Finally, she gave him a desperate look.

"Please stop staring at me," she half whispered.

"What else am I supposed to stare at?" he asked, amused. "You're far better-looking than the wall. And there's really nothing else in my line of vision."

"It makes me nervous," she confessed, her brown eyes wide and serious.

"Why?"

"How should I know?" Realizing she sounded more than a little testy, she cleared her throat and began again. "Okay then, let's talk. What other errands do you have to do in town?"

"I'm all finished, I guess. How about you?"

"I have to get the groceries for the Harrises and that's it."

"We're going to have a lot of time to kill," he remarked, taking a sip of ice water. His eyes met hers over the rim of the glass. "What shall we do?"

"Do?" LaRue thought her normally husky voice sounded like a very sick frog. "I—I have no idea."

"Fortunately, I have several."

"I'll just bet." The words were out before she could stop them. Rafferty looked interested. He leaned closer to her. "Why do you say that?"

"It was only a comment. I didn't mean anything by it."

"Good. For a second there, I got the definite impression that you thought my intentions were less than honorable."

She managed a weak laugh. "Oh, heaven forbid!"

"LaRue, why do you keep inching away from me?"

His audacious question caught her so by surprise that she blurted out the first thing that came to mind.

"It just seems safer to keep some distance between us!"

He laughed aloud. "Safer? Sugar, you're the one who wanted to live dangerously! Remember the window onto the courthouse roof?"

Before she could form a reply, the waitress appeared with their cheeseburgers.

When they got back from town, they carried in the groceries, and then Rafferty suggested LaRue give him a tour of the ranch.

They strolled through the huge barn and past the wellhouse and chicken houses, also constructed of limestone.

"My great-great-grandfather started building the ranch in 1881." LaRue went on to tell the story of how Sin Creek got its name. "Once he'd married Faith and fathered a son, he decided he wanted something special to pass on to his descendants. Over the years, he became something of a cattle baron."

"And ended up with quite a legacy for his children, obviously. How much land does Sin Creek actually encompass?"

"About twelve thousand acres," LaRue answered. She wondered if he was calculating its value to the national park committee, but she didn't give voice to her thoughts. Instead, she stopped to lean against the rail fence that enclosed the lawn and let her gaze roam over the man beside her.

Rafferty leaned over to pick a stem of foxtail grass and, with a jaunty smile, stuck the end of it in his mouth. Booted foot resting on the bottom rail, he gazed out over the prairie that rose behind the ranchhouse. LaRue thought he looked much less tense than he had when he'd first arrived in Cottonwood. He seemed more relaxed and . . . happier, somehow.

He tucked his thumbs into the rear pockets of his jeans, and his tapered shirt pulled tight across his chest, hugging his back and ribs. He had the kind of muscular-yet-spare body that was made to wear Western clothing. It was ridiculous how good a pair of tight denim jeans looked riding low on his lean hips. Or how masculinely appealing his tanned forearms were in rolled-up sleeves. Just a glance at the tufts of dark chest hair and the strong neck revealed by the open shirt collar was enough to send LaRue's pulses racing.

Nothing and no one had ever affected her this way before. It was both exciting and scary. And totally unexpected. Who would ever have believed the man who frustrated her more than anyone else in the world ever had, would also be the one who made her yearn for things she had never before desired?

She realized Rafferty was looking at her as though he could read her mind. Quickly she turned away to hide the blush that colored her cheeks and said, "Come on, I want to show you something." She strode away, leaving him no choice but to follow.

The path they took crossed the pasture for about a quarter of a mile before climbing upward along a stony hill. There, on the windswept crest was a small stone building with shutters and a belfry.

"It's the old Sin Creek schoolhouse," LaRue said, shouting to be heard over the wind. "Want to see inside?"

Rafferty nodded. She took a key ring from her pocket and, finding the appropriate key, unlocked the door.

The one-room schoolhouse had been restored to its original condition, with old-fashioned desks and blackboards. There were shelves of books beneath a row of long, narrow windows, and LaRue pointed out faded copies of *McGuffey's Reader* and *First Primer for Kansas Schoolchildren*.

"I love this place," she declared, running her hand over the smooth wood of the teacher's desk. "It's kind of a hobby for me, I guess. I like to go to sales and try to find things for the schoolhouse...like this hand bell. Or this old globe. I bought that at an auction in Strong City. The portrait of Lincoln belonged to my great-grandfather...and my grandmother sewed the curtains from feed sacks. They're pretty, aren't they?"

She looked up from the green-and-white curtains to see Rafferty watching her, arms folded across his chest. Self-consciously, she wondered what he was thinking.

Rafferty was thinking that, for the first time, he was seeing a side of LaRue she usually kept well hidden. Her fond delight in the schoolroom showed in her glowing eyes and softly parted lips and the reverence with which she touched polished wood and crumbling pages. No one could mistake her love for home and history; her sincerity reached out and drew him like a magnet.

"Come here." Rafferty's low words seemed to vibrate through the room as he lowered himself into the highbacked chair at the teacher's desk. He took LaRue's hand and tugged her toward him, pulling her down onto his lap.

She laughed uncertainly and tried to push away, but he curled one steely arm around her waist and pressed her against the length of his chest. His other hand came up to rest alongside her face, lifting her mouth to his.

His kiss was more expressive than words could have been at that moment. It coaxed her to relax, to trust him—to surrender her emotions, her fears, her dreams . . . *everything* to him. The sweet, warm touch of his lips told her that he cared about her, that he would care for her. That he would protect and defend her, march into battle for her, if necessary. *Just ask me,* he was saying. *Ask anything you want and it's yours.*

At that moment he seemed certain there was nothing not within his power, and he conveyed that certainty to her with the gentle caress of his hands and mouth. And she believed him, reassured by the steady beat of his heart beneath her fingers. Reassured by the solemn promise she saw deep in the eyes that gazed lovingly into hers.

"Oh, Rafferty," she breathed, snuggling closer and raising her lips to meet his again. "Oh, Rafferty. . . ."

Outside, the wind keened and moaned, clawing at the stones but leaving them as untouched as they had been for the last century.

Cradling LaRue in his arms, his cheek resting against her soft, fragrant hair, Rafferty allowed himself a small flight of fancy. To him, this sturdy little schoolhouse symbolized the kind of love he and LaRue were going to have—the kind that would stand forever, undamaged by the winds of time or adversity.

Chapter Eleven

"Out here, it ain't always healthy to inquire too deep into another man's past. We try to think his life began the day he rode into our town."
—Murphy Hodgens, sheriff,
Diamond Springs, Kansas, 1874

LaRue pulled the plug in the old-fashioned bathtub and stood up, reaching for a towel. She dried quickly, then slipped into a robe and padded barefoot into her room.

Bemused, she opened the closet door and stared unseeingly at the neat row of clothing. Her mouth curved into an indulgent smile as she recalled how Rafferty had held and kissed her at the old schoolhouse, and how they had walked home, hand in hand, through a meadow of wildflowers. Just before they had gotten within sight of the house, he had pulled her into the shade of a hackberry tree and, picking a long-stemmed daisy, tucked it behind her ear, kissing her soundly.

LaRue had laughingly reminded him of the lecture he had once given Holly about destroying the ecosystem, and with mock threats, he had chased her all the way to the ranchhouse. When they flung themselves into the kitchen, Mrs. Mendoza was waiting for them with iced tea, cookies and a broad, beaming smile.

LaRue knew that Dozy was entertaining thoughts of romance where she and Rafferty were concerned. Heaven knew, ever since she had come to work for the Tates several years ago, the woman had fondly nagged LaRue to find a boyfriend. "A woman needs someone to look pretty for," Dozy had scolded. "Someone to take care of her."

Independent to the core, LaRue had never thought being taken care of sounded especially appealing—not, that is, until this afternoon, when a certain handsome, dark-haired government man had put his arms around her and cradled her like a baby. Suddenly, the importance of having someone strong to lean on didn't seem such a puzzle to her. With Rafferty, it all made perfect sense.

LaRue had never been in such a pleasant, dreamy mood. All she could think about was the long evening that stretched ahead of them. Dozy had declared her intention of fixing dinner before she left to go home to her husband and, she confided to LaRue, she was planning an elegant candlelit meal to be served on the screened-in porch. Embarrassed, LaRue had protested, but she was secretly pleased when the housekeeper stubbornly refused to be thwarted.

Now LaRue found herself wanting to look nice for her dinner with Rafferty. Just this once, she had decided to let him see her as someone other than a cowgirl in blue denim. She needed to be at her best, to be able to tell by the way he looked at her that he thought she was pretty. . . and desirable.

She didn't own many frilly clothes, and for the first time, it seemed like an oversight. With his big-city background, Rafferty was probably the kind of man who liked silks and satins— it worried her that she could offer only calico.

Dozy had outdone herself. A small round table covered by a gold cloth and set with the heavy, old-fashioned Tate silver sat on the screened porch that ran along the northwest corner of the house. In the center of the table was a pale yellow candle in a hurricane glass, surrounded by a ring of fat, brown-and-yellow pansies from the flower bed. Gold-rimmed white china caught and reflected the gilded rays of the dying sun.

LaRue stepped onto the porch hesitantly. Rafferty was already there, standing at the screen watching the sunset's fiery display. His head was bare, his hair still damp from the shower and curling over his collar in back. He'd had clean clothes in the car he and Holly had left at the ranch, and now he was wearing a pair of crisp poplin slacks and a knit shirt in olive green. Unexpectedly, he wasn't the Rafferty she had grown accustomed to seeing. The tall cowboy with the five o'clock shadow and faded jeans had been replaced by a sophisticated stranger from the city. Suddenly LaRue felt shy and awkward. If he hadn't heard her and turned, she wasn't certain she wouldn't have just silently slipped away.

"Hello," he said in a deep, almost reverent voice. "Lord, but you look pretty."

She was wearing a full-skirted sundress of cinnamon-checked gingham, with a scooped, peasant neckline and a tight waist. It looked cool against her tanned skin, its color complementing tawny eyes and skin the color of summer peaches. Her hair had been swept up, revealing delicate hoops of braided gold wire in her ears.

"I take it back," Rafferty said after a long moment. "You look *beautiful*."

"Thank you," she murmured, pleased and alarmed all at once. How could she maintain any kind of poise with him looking at her that way?

Rafferty cleared his throat and took a step toward her. At that instant, Mrs. Mendoza bustled through the back door, carrying a tray.

"I hope you two are ready to eat," she said in a cheerful voice. She placed salads at each plate and left a carafe of chilled white wine, promising to return with the main course in fifteen minutes.

Rafferty held LaRue's chair and, as she slipped into it, he rested a warm hand against the curve of her neck for a few seconds, squeezing lightly, before taking his own seat.

As if he sensed her shyness, Rafferty kept up a running commentary on the mishaps that had befallen him and Hollister as they traveled through the Midwest. By the time Dozy reappeared, LaRue was laughing easily, her earlier reticence forgotten.

The main course was chicken, breaded and rolled up around thin slices of ham and Swiss cheese. Tiny whole potatoes and green beans from the garden, and hot, buttery crescent rolls accompanied the chicken.

"Dozy, you shouldn't have gone to so much trouble," said LaRue, as the plump housekeeper set down the steaming plates.

"No trouble, 'Rue. Besides, I wanted to serve something nice for a special occasion like this."

"But this isn't a special occasion," LaRue protested.

"Oh, I think it is. You just wait and see." With a wink at Rafferty, Mrs. Mendoza waltzed away to the kitchen.

Ignoring his delighted smile, LaRue began asking questions about life in Washington, D.C., and about Rafferty's life in particular, though she purposely avoided issues she deemed too personal. His answers were casual and relaxed, but heavily laced, she thought, with pride and affection for the city he called home. It wasn't any surprise, so she had to wonder why she felt mildly depressed by his responses.

"LaRue and I can take care of the dishes, Dozy," Rafferty said when Mrs. Mendoza served the dessert of strawberry tarts. "Your husband is probably wondering what's keeping you."

"Are you sure you don't mind?"

"After the wonderful meal you cooked for us?" cried LaRue. "Good gracious, the least we can do is straighten up the kitchen."

"Well, then, have a terrific evening, you two." And with another wink, she disappeared through the back door.

They cleared the table and while LaRue put away the leftovers, Rafferty rinsed the dishes and stacked them in the dishwasher. LaRue had just added detergent and started the washer when the phone rang.

"That may be your call," she said, drying her hands and reaching for the wall phone. "Hello?"

"Is this the Tate residence?" asked a cool, female voice.

"Yes."

"I'd like to speak to J. B. Rafferty, please. Tell him it's Louise."

LaRue had an ungovernable urge to slam down the receiver, but she reminded herself that, for all she knew, Louise might be Rafferty's sister.

"It's for you," she said, holding out the phone. "Someone named Louise."

The look on Rafferty's face told her quite clearly that the woman wasn't his sister.

"I'll take it in Levi's office," he said tersely, loping out of the room.

She heard a click, then Rafferty asking, "Louise? Is something wrong?"

"No, dear heart," the silky voice drawled. "But you haven't called me in over a week now . . . and I missed you. Have you missed me?"

There was a slight pause. "Of course I missed you."

LaRue's fingers closed so tightly over the receiver that she thought it might snap in two. Jealousy was an ugly emotion, she decided, quietly hanging up the phone.

Forcing herself to keep busy and not speculate about Rafferty's relationship with the woman, she removed the centerpiece from the dinner table and folded the tablecloth, then wiped the kitchen countertops and hung the dishcloth up to dry. Finally she stepped into the small bathroom adjacent to the kitchen to tidy her hair. Solemnly, she met the gaze of the young woman staring back at her in the mirror. It was a LaRue Tate she didn't know—at least, not very well. She wasn't at all certain what this LaRue's hopes or fears or dreams for the future were. She only knew that at this moment, she was feeling dangerously vulnerable.

She waited twenty minutes before going to check on Rafferty, convinced he would be off the phone by then. But just as she stepped into the doorway of the office, she heard his rumbling laugh and knew she was wrong.

"You should see her," he was saying. "Her name is LaRue, of all things. And the first time I saw her, I thought she was a boy!'' Unaware of LaRue's presence, he smiled as he listened to whatever comment Louise was making.

"No, but sometimes she carries a gun," he went on. "I tell you, Lou, she's a regular little prairie wildflower...." His words trailed away as he looked up to see LaRue standing there. "Oh, hell," he muttered.

"Sorry," LaRue said faintly. "I thought you'd be done...."

Rafferty started to rise, then remembered the phone in his hand. As she walked quickly down the hall, LaRue could hear him speaking to Louise again. She went through the kitchen and without pausing, out the back door. At the bottom of the porch steps, she grasped the railing and took several deep, painful breaths. Then she began walking as fast as the darkening night would allow.

How could she have been so mistaken about Rafferty? At what point had she become so gullible as to start believing he might really care anything about her?

He'd thought she was a boy? Her cheeks burned at the memory of his humiliating description of her. It hurt to think he would laugh about her with the smart, sophisticated Louise. And she had no doubt whatsoever that Louise was sophisticated and elegant and everything else that epitomized the world from which Rafferty came. In her mind's eye, LaRue could see the woman—glorious hair, beautiful eyes, milky complexion. Tall, lithe and glamorous, fitting into Rafferty's life in Washington with an inborn ease.

She found herself hating both Rafferty and the unknown Louise, but most of all, she discovered she hated herself. She hated being plain, rustic LaRue Tate. She hated being inexperienced and uneducated . . . and too naive and trusting to know better than to believe a fast talker who was good at emotional con games. But mostly, she hated not being all the things she knew Rafferty would want in a woman.

Her feet recognized the path, even in the darkness, and in a few minutes, she opened a gate and stepped into one of her favorite places on the ranch. Surrounded by a picket fence that tended to sag, the old family burial plot lay at the foot of a steep hill. It was a place that never failed to offer refuge.

There had been no burials in the cemetery for the past fifty years, so LaRue had never known any of the Tates laid to rest there. But somehow, the dozen or so stark and stately headstones, smothered with climbing roses and trumpet vines, had always represented stability and security. The carved names were her link with the past . . . a past that bound her to a family, a heritage. Whenever she felt lonely or uncertain, she could come here and sit on the stone bench beneath the gnarled catalpa tree and regain her sense of self-worth and belonging. These men, women and children had struggled to tame the land and survive the elements. In essence, they had provided her with the life she now enjoyed. Coming here helped to remind her that she, too, owed something. Her life might seem dull and uneventful at times, but what she was doing had purpose. She and her granddad were constantly working to improve Sin Creek for the next generations, and they were making sure the wonderful history of this land was not forgotten.

That was important, damn it. A lot more valuable than being charming and ornamental so some hulking lump of masculine arrogance would look twice at her.

She didn't know he was there until he spoke. "LaRue? What in the world are you doing hiding out here in the dark?"

"I'm not hiding," she said quietly.

"Then what are you doing?"

His hands were on her shoulders, turning her to face him. They tightened involuntarily the instant he saw her tearstained face. She heard his sharply indrawn breath and tried to pull away. He held her firmly in place. "I didn't mean to make you cry, you know."

"I'm not crying."

"You are and it's my fault. I'd like the chance to explain what you heard me saying on the phone."

"Rafferty," she said stiffly, "it really couldn't matter less."

"You're wrong. It couldn't matter more. To me, at least."

"Well, it doesn't matter to me, so let's just skip it, okay?"

"Sorry. This is one misunderstanding I mean to clear up."

LaRue couldn't free herself from his grasp, so she merely turned her face away from his stern gaze and waited for him to have his say.

SILHOUETTE®

 **PRESENTS** ❤️

A
Real Sweetheart
of a Deal!

**PEEL BACK THIS CARD AND SEE
WHAT YOU CAN GET! THEN...**

Complete the Hand Inside

It's easy! To play your cards right,
just match this card
with the cards inside.
Turn over for more details...

Remember! To win this hand, all you have to do is place your sticker inside and **DETACH AND MAIL THE CARD BELOW.** You'll get four free books, a free gold-plated chain and a mystery bonus.

BUT DON'T DELAY!
MAIL US YOUR LUCKY CARD TODAY!

If card is missing write to:
Silhouette Reader Service, P.O. Box 609, Fort Erie, Ontario L2A 5X3

Business
Reply Mail
No Postage Stamp
Necessary if Mailed
in Canada

Postage will be paid by

SILHOUETTE READER SERVICE ™

P.O. Box 609

Fort Erie, Ontario

L2A 9Z9

Canada Post
Postes Canada
125

"As soon as I saw you standing in the doorway, I realized it must have sounded as if I was making fun of you. Honey, that's the last thing I ever intended."

LaRue's chin rose sharply.

"I know you don't believe me," he went on, "but it's true. Louise...the woman on the phone...was, *is* a friend of mine...."

"The one whose name you couldn't remember, I suppose?" LaRue said acidly, though she hadn't meant to speak at all.

Rafferty chuckled softly. "That's right."

It angered her that he could find anything in the situation to laugh about. "How dare you make fun of me to—to someone like her? I may be an amusing little country bumpkin to you, but that doesn't give you the right to joke about me behind my back."

His lean face grew serious again. "That isn't what I was doing, LaRue. I was trying to explain things to the lady."

"What things?" she snapped.

"Things like why I haven't called her lately—why I no longer have plans to rush back to see her."

"You were breaking off your relationship with her? Yeah, right," LaRue scoffed. "You told her you missed her!"

"What did you expect me to say? That I've barely thought of her at all in the past two weeks? That I have to think twice before I can come up with her name...or remember her face?" He gave her a small shake, almost as if he was angry. "Was I supposed to tell her I don't know what her voice sounds like anymore because yours is so damned sexy it kicks the breath out of me each time I hear it again? That I don't know if her eyes are gray or blue, but that yours are the deepest, clearest gold I've ever seen? Did you want me to tell her I've suddenly decided red lipstick is an abomination after—" he inhaled deeply "—after seeing...and kissing your sweet mouth?" He dragged her against him and captured that mouth with his own, his hands stirring restlessly over her back, pressing her into the heated curve of his body.

LaRue was too shocked to do anything but hold on, weathering the sudden storm of passion that seemed to have blown up between them. When Rafferty released her, she could only gasp, desperately pulling air into her needy lungs.

Rafferty's voice was quieter now and more caressing. "How on earth could I tell her that, after seeing your hair streaming in the prairie winds, hers was just ordinary blond?" He raised a hand and began plucking the pins from LaRue's hair, letting it fall softly onto her slender neck and shoulders. Almost instantly, the night wind caught and lifted the strands. "When I touch your hair, it's like running my fingers through layers of silk. And when you're in the sun, it catches the light and reflects every autumn color nature ever invented. It's brown, it's bronze—it's gold and nutmeg—" He broke off, giving her a slow, lopsided smile. "Listen to me! I sound like some poor, demented poet babbling away in a dark asylum somewhere." He smoothed her hair back from her face. "You've made me crazy, LaRue, and God only knows what I'm going to do about it."

Her eyes were wide and disbelieving as she returned his gaze. Her brain didn't seem able to accept the words he was speaking.

"What are you trying to tell me?"

"I'm trying to tell you that I care far too much for you to have been making fun of you to Louise. I was attempting to make her understand what had happened, how some little midwestern farm girl had, without even trying, pushed her way into my mind, leaving no room for anyone else."

"You laughed at my name."

"I did not. I merely meant LaRue was an unusual name. Surely you can't deny that?"

"It was my mother's maiden name," she said in a small voice. "That's not unusual. And did you really think I was a boy that first day?"

He grinned broadly. "Hell, yes. Why do you think I kept calling you sonny?"

"You called me a hayseed."

"I called you a prairie wildflower," he corrected softly. "And I meant it as a compliment."

"Oh, sure." But he was winning her over, and they both knew it.

"You're different from any woman I've ever known. You're natural, fresh and untouched. You aren't world-weary or blasé. Best of all, I never know what to expect from you. One minute you're roping dogies," he teased, cupping her head with one large hand and brushing his thumb along her cheek, "and the next you're on your way to town in a fancy car, wearing a skirt that shows off the best-looking legs I've ever seen."

She had to smile. "And I'll bet you've seen a lot of legs, haven't you, Rafferty?"

"Absolutely." His hand moved to tip up her chin, and he grazed her lips with a kiss. "Can I take it that you've decided to believe me?"

"Let's just say I'm willing to think about it, all right?"

"All right."

He studied her for several moments, thinking how natural she looked standing in the middle of the old cemetery, surrounded by a past that never seemed very far distant. Instinctively, he knew that she could never survive in any other environment. Life in a city like Washington would stifle and intimidate her. Without knowing it, he heaved a frustrated sigh.

"What's wrong?" she inquired.

"Nothing. I was just thinking how perfect Sin Creek is for you. I can't imagine you being happy anywhere else."

"I can't, either. I certainly wasn't very happy the years I lived away from here. I don't think I'll ever have any other home."

It wasn't a new thought, so there was really no reason for Rafferty feel her words like painful blows to his midsection. He'd known from the beginning that they were from two different worlds. What he hadn't known was that it would begin to matter so much. Suddenly he wanted to find some way to breach the gap...at least for a time. For as much time as fate was going to allow.

"It's late," he said. "I suppose we'd better go back inside."

He slipped an arm around her waist and led her back toward the house, wishing he could think of some acceptable way to prevent their day together from coming to a close. Not that spending the rest of the night making love to her wasn't acceptable to him; he was afraid it might not be the best move to make right now. He had no idea where they were headed or what was going to happen to them. Something like that could create hopeless complications.

LaRue showed him the guest room where he was to sleep, and all the while, both of them were intensely aware of the silence. Though there were a dozen ranch hands sleeping in the nearby bunkhouse, for all intents and purposes they were alone in the house. It was a tempting thought, but Rafferty had already decided he was not going to take advantage of the situation.

He walked LaRue to the door of her room where she hesitated, her hand on the doorknob, and said, "I hope my stupidity didn't ruin the evening for you. Dozy fixed such a nice meal and—"

"The evening was great, right up until that damned phone call." He reached out, running a finger along the elasticized edge of her neckline. "But after we straightened out a few things, it got better again." His smile turned devilish as he hooked his finger beneath the cloth and slowly pulled the blouse down to reveal one bare shoulder. "There is one thing, however, that would help the evening end on a positive note." He placed a heated kiss on her shoulder, letting his mouth drift deliberately along her collarbone. "Mmm, this is something I've thought about doing countless times in the last hour."

LaRue closed her eyes, enjoying the thrill of his touch. She put her arms around his waist and stepped closer to him, lifting her face in an invitation that he readily accepted. But when she attempted to deepen the kiss, he reluctantly drew back.

"I'd better go to my own room," he murmured, "while we're still thinking rationally."

Her disappointment was not well hidden. "I guess you're right. Good night, Rafferty."

"Good night...."

Rafferty set aside the Western novel he'd been reading and was just getting ready to switch off the lamp when the bedside phone rang.

"Hello?"

"Rafferty, you're a hard son-of-a-gun to get hold of."

"What's up, Terence? Problems?"

"Not really, but the other committee members are hassling me for some word on the Tallgrass Park. I need to know when you're going to be able to get an evaluation to me."

"It shouldn't be much longer. I'm in the middle of an intriguing study right now that ought to wrap up next week. Can you give me that long?"

"I'll try to hold them off... but your findings had better be convincing. Care to give me any hints as to your frame of mind?"

"I would if I could, Terence, but damned if I'm not more confused about the issue than ever." Of course, it wouldn't do to tell the man that the issue was being clouded by the most interesting woman Rafferty had ever met. "There's a real need to preserve the prairie, but in most ways, the ranchers are doing a hell of a fine job. There are one or two more areas I need to check out, and then I'll get back to you."

"Fair enough. I'll wait for your report... just don't be too much longer."

"I won't. 'Night, Terence. I'll call you next week."

Hanging up the phone, Rafferty slipped into a short terrycloth robe and stepped into the hall, intending to go down to the kitchen for a glass of water. When he saw a light coming from beneath LaRue's door, he wondered if she had been disturbed by the late phone call and tapped lightly.

Instead of calling out to him as he'd expected, she opened the door and stood facing him. In that instant, Rafferty was lost.

The glimpse of the bedroom behind her was both surprising and revealing. It was not at all what he had imagined. Instead of a plain room full of trophies and Western memorabilia, it had a fragile, feminine look. The ceiling was slanted, the walls printed with old-fashioned nosegays of violets tied with blue streamers. The bed, with a tall brass headboard, was smothered with pillows and an eyelet bedspread that matched the sheer white curtains at the windows. His gaze dropped to the deep blue carpet, then moved to her bare feet and slowly, admiringly traveled up the length of her body.

LaRue stood still beneath his survey, a tiny frown marring the smooth skin of her forehead. Rafferty sensed that she wanted to please him, and only wished there was some way to tell her how very much she did.

She was wearing a thin lawn nightgown gathered beneath her breasts, the narrow straps and low neck laced with mint-green ribbon. The fabric, lovingly clinging to every curve and hollow of her slender frame, was nearly transparent in the faint golden glow of a bedside lamp. As she took a step backward, her long hair whispered against her shoulders.

"Hi," she said with a smile. "Would you like to come in?"

Rafferty was too bemused to even reply. He walked into the room and shut the door behind him.

Chapter Twelve

"In this territory, stealin' a lady's virtue is a hell of a lot easier than stealin' a horse. Trouble is, either is liable to git you a life sentence—or a noose around your neck."
—Wilbur Catt, president of anti-horsethief association,
Cedar Point, Kansas, 1889

LaRue drew a deep breath and faced the truth. She wanted Rafferty. She wanted him here in this room, in her arms—she wanted him to spend the night.

Reason told her there was a good chance the call had been made to summon him back to Washington, D.C. He had been on the road for a long time, and perhaps the committee was getting anxious for his report. Or some other problem could have arisen. It didn't matter. What did, was that Rafferty could soon be gone, disappearing from her life as quickly as he had entered it. The past few days had brought her to the realization that, though his departure was inevitable, she was not going to welcome it. And the day they had just spent together had brought her to the equally shattering awareness that before he left, there was something she wanted from Rafferty. She wanted this night.

LaRue let her gaze wander over him, from the half-puzzled, half-sultry look in his eyes to the oddly intimate sight of his bare feet. He stood against the closed door, suddenly looking uncomfortable, his hands jammed into the pockets of his robe. She admired the display of lean, athletic legs delineated by crisp, dark hair. She took a step toward him and saw his hands curl into fists beneath the fabric of the pockets. She grasped his wrist with both hands and tugged one fist free, closing her own fingers around it.

"LaRue?" he whispered, his voice sounding rusty. "What—"

One by one, she was releasing his fingers from the tight fist he had made, smoothing and straightening them with gentle strokes of her fingertips. As her nails lightly grazed his palm, he shuddered violently.

"What am I doing here?" he croaked, trying to draw away. "I'd better get back to my room."

"Please don't go," she murmured, her gold-flecked eyes raising to his. "I'd like you to stay." She moved even closer and laid his hand against her breast. "Please."

Rafferty swallowed deeply and though his hand felt scorched, he couldn't find the energy to remove it. He was intensely aware of the soft swell of flesh beneath it, the insistent prod of the nipple that had blossomed beautifully at his touch.

"Sugar," he moaned, "if I don't go now, I may not have the presence of mind to go later."

"It's all right. I want you to stay," she said, her voice small and earnest. "I want you to spend the night with me." Her eyes filled with sudden alarm. "I mean...if you want to...." Her words trailed away in doubt.

Rafferty felt his good intentions disintegrating as he withdrew his other hand from his pocket and pulled her into the circle of his arms.

"Want to? God, yes, I want to," he muttered against her hair. "There's nothing I want more. But I don't like taking advantage of you."

"You're not. I swear you're not." LaRue stepped back to look up into his face. "If anyone is taking advantage, it's me. I just want to know what—what being with you is like...."

He closed his eyes, as if fighting for control. "LaRue...."

She lifted her hand, needing to touch him. As she brushed her fingertips across his lips, he opened his eyes to look into hers. She played her fingers along the curve of his jaw and upward into the thick, springing black hair.

His skin was bronzed, fine-pored and smooth, stretching tautly over the clean line of jawbone and throat. His eyebrows and lashes were clearly etched, shadowing the hazel eyes where mysterious fires were beginning to leap and burn.

"I want you to make love to me," she whispered. "Make love *with* me."

At her words, the fire in his eyes burst into flame and they both knew there could be no turning back.

"Would you...just this once, could we pretend we really love each other? That we met today and it was love at first sight?" She shook her head, as if amazed by her own words. "Do you think I'm crazy, Rafferty?"

"No, sweetheart," he murmured. "It's never crazy to want to be close to someone."

LaRue cupped his head in her hands and drew it downward. "Then...let's pretend." Lightly, she rubbed her lips back and forth across his, as if memorizing their shape, their taste.

She wanted to savor this night, to store up memories that would remain with her when Rafferty was gone. She wanted to imprint him on her heart, mind and body...forever, if she could.

As his mouth responded to her sweetly tempting kiss, Rafferty was cautioning himself to go slow. He wanted this woman more than he'd ever wanted anything in life, but even unreasoning desire couldn't protect him from making a regrettable mistake. Their backgrounds were too different and their goals clashed terribly. They had started out as enemies—but what had they become? Unless he backed off right now, in a few more minutes they would be lovers. But would that be enough to overcome their earlier problems? God help him, he didn't know. What was worse—in that seductively supercharged little wrinkle in time, he really didn't care.

Suddenly nothing seemed more important than her softness pressing into him, her delicious mouth working such devastating magic on his own. His hands gripped her waist, dragging her against him.

LaRue gave a tiny gasp and wriggled closer, her arms going around his neck. "Does this mean yes?" she asked, smiling up at him.

He lifted her so high that her toes actually cleared the floor. "Yes," he whispered, then laughed with abandonment. "Yes . . . yes . . . yes!"

He clasped her to him, his lips descending upon hers with purpose. Gone was his indecision, his worry. He had made up his mind. He would love her tonight as he wanted to—as if there were no obstacles, no worries about tomorrow, no problems. He could bare his soul to her under the pretext that he was playing a role. If he were to blurt out how he really felt, he had no doubt she would run like a scared rabbit. It was safer this way.

Safer, but less honest, he reminded himself. That bothered him . . . almost as much as the swift, butterfly kisses she was spreading across his eyelids. She did make it difficult to think.

"LaRue, there's something I have to confess," he finally whispered, letting his own lips travel up the side of her neck to her ear. She shivered beneath his touch and he nearly reeled with the sense of power her reaction gave him.

"Mmm, what is it, Rafferty?"

"I—I really do love you."

There. The words had been spoken. They were out in the open, for better or worse. One thing about it, she couldn't exactly run away while he held her captive in his arms.

"Thank you," she murmured, pressing her cheek to his. "It's nice of you to play my silly game."

"I'm not playing a game," he replied. "I love you."

He sounded so sincere that LaRue found herself wanting to believe him. There was real danger involved in this, and it was her fault. She forced a laugh. "You're a great actor—but there's no Oscar for this role. Sorry."

His amused but exasperated sigh was cut off by LaRue initiating a kiss that grew scorching by slow degrees. Heat, intense and flaming, roared through him, casting out the desire for anything other than their mutual satisfaction.

When he let her feet touch the floor again, it was only for the length of time it took him to wrap an arm about her knees and swoop her up into his arms. Slowly, he walked across the room, relishing the feel and look of her nestled so closely against him.

LaRue lay her head on his shoulder, lightly brushing her lips against his throat. She liked the clean, soapy fragrance of his skin—the subtle aroma of after-shave. She thought he must have borrowed her grandfather's razor to shave, for there was a tiny nick on his cheek. She kissed her forefinger and touched it gently to the cut.

The unexpectedness of her action caught him unaware, overwhelming him with the same rush of tenderness he had experienced in the old schoolhouse. He sat on the edge of the bed, cradling her, kissing her with lips that cherished and adored.

Far from content to be passive, LaRue shifted positions and deepened the kiss. Her lips opening to his, and the gentle exploration of her tongue laced the kiss with such innocent eroticism that Rafferty's heart skipped several beats. He might like to think he was holding an angel, but her actions plainly told him she was earthbound. The pressure of her thinly-clad buttocks stirring against his lap caused his last rational thought to flee, and with a ragged groan he surrendered himself to her.

Softly, sweetly, she practiced a form of witchcraft that seared his soul, branding him as hers.

They lay back upon the bed and her hands went to the tie of his robe. Her eagerness filled him with almost unbearable excitement, and he helped undo the knotted belt, his hand looking large and masculine next to her smaller one. He watched, bemused, as her hand pushed the robe aside and off his shoulders, one at a time. Her fingers then traced the swirl of hair on his chest and lower to the matching one around his navel. He caught his breath as she slipped one fingertip beneath the elastic waistband of his Jockey shorts and looked at him, one eyebrow raised questioningly.

"I'll take them off," he muttered, getting to his feet. He reached for the switch on the bedside lamp.

"No, don't," she half whispered. "I want to see you." She got on her knees in the middle of the bed and gave him a beseeching smile. "Please?"

He never knew what to expect from her. She was as different from any woman he had ever known as black is from white. But seeing her in the surprising role of seductress intrigued and pleased him. His answering smile was an equal mixture of manly pride and boyish shyness. He hooked his thumbs in the waistband of his shorts and pulled them off, kicking them aside.

"My God, Rafferty," she breathed. "You're beautiful!"

"Men aren't beautiful," he said self-consciously.

"You are."

LaRue meant it. It had never been her experience to see a body so perfectly proportioned, so muscularly athletic yet lithe, promising strength and graceful agility. His shoulders stretched wide, his torso tapered to a hard, lean waist and narrow hips. He *was* beautiful, from his handsomely chiseled face to the soles of his feet. A quick glance told her that even the evidence of his gender, surging forth so boldly, was mysteriously beautiful.

Had his skin been ruddier and his hair longer, Rafferty would have looked like one of the Indian athletes in a painting her grandfather had hanging in his office. Standing naked before her, he seemed to exude the same exciting and primitive savagery of the men in the picture. Somehow, the idea of Rafferty shedding his civilized ways to race the prairie wind pleased her. LaRue had a curious need to race with him. She held out a hand to him and felt his warm fingers close over hers.

Rafferty put one knee on the bed and leaned toward her, his hands cupping her shoulders to draw her near. He bent his head to place a slow, lingering kiss upon her mouth, his tongue deliberately stroking the outline of her lips, the softness where they met . . . the honeyed moistness where they parted to invite him inside.

Rafferty's hands grew restless, roaming from her shoulders down the slenderness of her back to frame her hips and press her even closer to his aroused body. His breathing ragged and shallow, he ended the kiss to rest his face between her breasts, dragging long draughts of air into his lungs. He felt as though he had been running a hard race that left him weak and winded. But her lips moving along his temple, her fingers stroking his back, created new energy inside him. He moved his face to nuzzle one of her breasts through the sheer material of her nightgown, catching the nipple lightly between his teeth. LaRue's body twisted within his arms, as though a jolt of electricity had streaked through her. He heard her gasp his name, felt her fingers tighten upon the ridge of his shoulders.

He brushed the straps of her gown aside, letting the flimsy garment slide downward to her waist. Her breasts were golden in the lamplight, round and high and tipped with apricot. Rafferty could no more have resisted touching them than he could have gotten off that bed and walked out the door.

Gently, he pushed her backward into the nest of pillows, and, after whisking away the nightgown, settled down beside her. He caressed her shoulders, covering her breasts with swift, feverish kisses that left her gasping in delight. As she arched toward him, he swung one long leg over her body, tucking her halfway beneath him. Then, leaning over her, he delivered a kiss that ravaged her senses, inspiring her to frantic urgency.

"Rafferty, please...."

With a placating murmur and a smile, he grasped her writhing hips and rose above her. Briefly, he studied her as she lay flushed and waiting. Again he was stricken by the sheer beauty of the woman he had once thought a dusty tomboy. LaRue ran her hands up his arms, from his wrists to his elbows, impatiently. He chuckled, dropped a quick, burning kiss on her mouth and united their bodies with one strong, slow, smooth motion.

She cried out in surprised pleasure, then surprised him in turn by curling her legs around his hips, holding him intimately. When he rocked against her, she slipped her arms about his waist to stroke and massage his back. She loved the feel of his powerful muscles bunching and stretching beneath her hands.

With each shattering thrust, Rafferty whispered into her ear unintelligible murmurings that made no real sense, but whose fervent tone whipped her emotions into a fury of passionate response. She pretended he was pledging eternal devotion, confessing undying love, and she wished she dared utter declarations of her own. She did, she feared, love Rafferty terribly. Had for some time now—against all logic and reason. Fortunately in this moment of pretended affection, she could say it aloud and he would be none the wiser.

"I love you," she breathed.

Rafferty's whole body jerked in stunned reaction before he could remind himself that she was making believe, only playing at love.

"I love you, too, sugar," he replied, nettled by the charade but convinced he had to abide by her rules...at least for the time being.

The words lingered in the room, spurring them from deliberate, rhythmic movements to a frenzied, driving pace that culminated in an explosive, shuddering climax that left them weak and gasping, clinging tightly to each other.

As their harried breathing slowed, peaceful oblivion washed over them. Passions sated, limbs torpid and heavy, they gave themselves up to the night and sleep.

The old walnut clock in the hallway chimed three times, and LaRue drifted out of a sound sleep. With Rafferty's arm across her waist and his legs entangled with hers, she felt enveloped in incredible security. She turned her head on the pillow and met his warm gaze.

"Can't you sleep?" she asked softly.

His teeth gleamed in the darkness. "Uh-uh. Too keyed up, I guess." He kissed her chin. "How about you?"

"Yeah, me, too."

She felt his searching glance. "LaRue? What's wrong, honey? You sound depressed." He paused, but when she didn't answer immediately, he went on, "You aren't sorry about tonight, are you?"

She shifted closer to him. "No, of course not. I could never be sorry about that."

"Then . . . what's the matter?"

"Nothing. Really, I'm fine." She drew a deep breath. "Actually, I wake up about three in the morning lots of times. Habit, I suppose."

Rafferty slipped an arm beneath her, curling it around her shoulder, and she turned to rest her face against his chest.

"What kind of habit?" he asked quietly.

The long silence was finally filled with LaRue's heavy sigh. "A habit from when I lived with my dad. Three is about the time of night he'd come home...if he was coming home at all."

Rafferty didn't say anything, but his hand moved to gently stroke her hair. In a few seconds, she spoke again.

"You see, after a competition he'd hang around with the other cowboys at whatever bar was handy, drinking and blowing off steam."

"And when he didn't come home . . . ?" Rafferty prompted.

"It usually meant he'd picked up some rodeo floozie and gone home with her." LaRue's tone was flat, as though she had long ago become bored with the subject. Rafferty sensed the pain beneath the boredom.

"You were just a kid—what did you do when he didn't come home?"

"Kept the doors locked. Kept a gun close by."

"A gun? Jesus, LaRue, what were you doing with a gun?"

"I knew how to shoot it," she said, laughing a little. "My granddad taught me when I was nine years old. And by the time Daddy came to get me, I'd been handling guns for at least four years. Grandpa didn't think the circuit was anyplace for a kid, so he insisted I have some means of protecting myself. Guess he knew my dad pretty well... ."

"You had a rough time of it, didn't you, honey?"

Even in the dark he knew her chin had risen proudly. "It wasn't so bad, most of the time. Lonnie Tate was a real champion for a while, you know. And when he was riding well and winning and had a steady girlfriend, things were good. Then he got hurt and started drinking again. When Madeline—she lived with us for a year or so—got fed up and walked out, he just sort of went to pieces."

"And that left no one but you to try to pick them up again, right?"

"Right. But I didn't mind, really. Those were good years, as well as bad ones. When my dad was sober, he was great . . . I loved him. And when he was drunk...well, I just stayed out of his way. He'd usually throw a few things, yell a lot, then stomp off to find one of his drinking buddies."

"And you'd creep out of hiding and . . . do what?"

"Straighten up the trailer and fix a good meal. I knew he'd be back sooner or later...sick and apologetic. He didn't mean anything by it, Rafferty. He just couldn't help himself."

"Poor little girl. I don't enjoy thinking of you on your own like that. I'll bet it nearly killed your grandparents."

"I wrote and called them as often as I could. And I always knew they'd be there if I really needed them. The idea of them waiting for me back at Sin Creek . . . that was what kept me going sometimes. That, and my books." She gave another short laugh. "I knew every used bookstore between here and Omaha."

"What finally happened, LaRue? When did you come back here?"

"I guess I must have been about seventeen. I woke up one morning in Sioux City and my dad was gone. He called a week later, told me he'd married some former rodeo queen named Shanna, and they were on their way to the Dakotas for a honeymoon. Said he'd send me some money when he got established in the circuit out there and I could join them. Two weeks later I hadn't heard from him again and I knew he wasn't going to send for me. So I borrowed enough money to get me home, hitched up the trailer and drove back to Sin Creek. I've been here ever since."

"God damn the man," Rafferty swore, his voice thick and growling. "How the hell did he expect a seventeen-year-old kid to handle something like that?"

"He knew I could do it," she said simply. "I'd been older than him all my life."

Rafferty hugged her to him. "Living is a hell of an unfair proposition sometimes."

"I was only trying to explain about my habit of waking up in the night," she said softly. "I didn't tell you all that to make you feel sorry for me. It was only four years out of my life—the rest of it has been good. Real good, in fact. I don't have any complaints, Rafferty."

"Then you're one in a million," he remarked, realizing the truth of that statement was something he had known all along.

Idly, his hand caressed her bare shoulder. "LaRue?"

"Hmm?"

"I've got an idea...."

"What?" She raised her head to look up at him, and smiling, he slid down in the bed, bringing their mouths to the same level.

"Since we did such a great job earlier—pretending to be lovers and all that—why don't we prolong the fantasy for a while and pretend we're always going to be together? That way, when you wake up in the night, I'll be there to...occupy your mind."

"Sounds interesting," she conceded, smiling back at him. "And just how would you go about doing that?"

"I'd start like this..." He touched his lips to hers, lightly, with an aching tenderness that filled her with yearning, with a longing that this could be a reality. After years of awaking alone and afraid, she wished she never had to be alone again. She wished she could count on Rafferty to always be there beside her.

It won't happen, she told herself, *but for now, for tonight...I'll make believe.*

Her thoughts were disrupted by the thrilling sensation of Rafferty's warm hands moving over her body, demanding the enraptured response he wanted and which she was all too glad to give.

This time he made love to her with a gentle passion that left her bound to him, heart and soul, for all time. With an incongruous sense of joyousness, she realized she was never going to love any other man the way she loved Rafferty. Smiling, she resigned herself to fate and then fell asleep in his arms.

Holding her, trying in vain to recover from their soul-searing lovemaking, Rafferty, too, knew the truth of it. In the vernacular of the prairie folk, he was roped and branded.

And don't forget 'hog-tied,' he told himself with a grin. He pulled the blanket up around their shoulders. *As hog-tied as a man can get.*

Rafferty woke at exactly five-thirty. It was a trick he had taught himself so long ago that he never needed an alarm clock. A psychology professor who had been a friend of his father's had once told him the human mind was amazing and could do any task a person was confident enough to expect of it.

"For instance, before you go to sleep at night," he'd told Rafferty, "just tell yourself when you need to wake up, and presto, you've got a built-in alarm."

The method worked like a charm, and Rafferty was glad. He knew he needed to be out of LaRue's room and back in his own before Mrs. Mendoza appeared for work.

He eased out of bed, careful not to wake LaRue. Slipping into his bathrobe, he stared down at her for a long moment, then tiptoed out the door.

The sky was awash with every shade of pink, gold and mauve imaginable, and Rafferty lingered at his window watching it for a time before crawling into his bed. How he would have loved to watch the sun come up with LaRue!

Next time, he promised himself. *Maybe next time.*

Chapter Thirteen

"Indians have always communicated with nature—
with the fox, the buffalo, the wild hawk. The only animal the white man hears speaking is the eagle on an
American gold piece."
                    —Chief Coyote Eyes, Osage Indian,
                         Morris County, Kansas, 1873

If Mrs. Mendoza noticed anything unusual at breakfast, she
didn't let on. Ignoring Rafferty's sheepish grins and LaRue's
guilty glances, she bustled about the kitchen serving waffles and
fresh fruit, keeping up such a constant stream of chatter that,
fortunately, they weren't called upon to do more than mutter
an occasional response.

LaRue was relieved. She'd been certain the events of the
night would be written all over her face for the world to see. It
had been hard enough to meet the warm, intimate look in Rafferty's eyes. How could she endure knowing everyone else was
perfectly aware of what had happened between them?

When they had thanked Dozy and told her goodbye, they went in search of Jed. As they stepped into the dim interior of the barn, Rafferty paused, taking LaRue's arm and pulling her against him.

"I wish our time together didn't have to end," he said, wrapping his arms around her waist.

"We'll still be together," she said, secretly pleased to know he, too, regretted leaving Sin Creek to rejoin the wagon train.

"Don't pretend that you don't know what I mean," he chuckled. "Once we're back with the others, I'll never have the chance to touch you or kiss you . . . like this." His smile faded and he bent his head, his eyes dark with intent. LaRue's mouth was already anticipating the feel of his. She stretched upward to meet him.

"Miss LaRue! Where are you?"

"Oh, damn," she muttered.

"Damn it to *hell*," Rafferty added.

Reluctantly, they moved apart and turned to face the cowboy coming their way.

"Oh, there you are," said Jed, unaware of the tension in the air. "Dozy said you was lookin' fer me. You ready to go back out to the train now?"

Rafferty and LaRue exchanged frustrated glances. "Yes, I guess we are," she answered.

While they loaded the groceries into the back of the pickup, Rafferty was ever alert, looking for a chance to steal a swift kiss. But Jed inadvertently robbed him of the opportunity at every turn. In the end, Rafferty had to settle for the inadequate comfort of LaRue next to him in the pickup, her shoulder and thigh pressed tightly to his. Rafferty quickly discovered that, after last night, it wasn't nearly enough. He hated not being able to shout his possessiveness to the world at large. It made him feel like a child who'd found a fifty-dollar bill but was afraid to tell anyone for fear they'd take it away from him.

The wagon train was just leaving the campsite when they arrived.

"We decided we'd move on and leave Ragweed and Gertie to wait fer ya," Levi said, giving them a sharp look.

Rafferty felt a prickle of unease along the nape of his neck. Could the old man possibly know what had transpired between him and LaRue? For the first time he thought how Tate might take the news. It was yet another complication he had overlooked. *Ignored* was more like it.

"Sorry it took us so long to get back," LaRue said lamely. "Dozy insisted on cooking a huge breakfast, as usual."

"Yeah, I know how it is, tryin' to get away from a pushy woman." Levi let fly a stream of tobacco juice, then wiped his mouth on the sleeve of his jean jacket. "Sister, why don't you help the Harrises stash them groceries away and then take Rafferty out to see the crossin' before you come after us? We'll be stoppin' at noon. You oughta be caught up by then."

"All right, Grandpa. That's a good idea. Is it okay with you, Rafferty?"

"It sounds great," he replied, with an enthusiastic grin.

Once again, Rafferty caught the shrewd look Levi gave him before turning away to yell, "Wagons ho!"

When the supplies had been unloaded from the pickup, Jed left to return to the ranch, and Rafferty and LaRue assisted the Harrises in putting the groceries away. Then Ragweed hitched the chuckwagon to the old red pickup, and he and Gertie prepared to head off toward the next camp site.

"We'll see you two later," Ragweed said, racing the engine. "Don't git into no trouble now."

Rafferty laughed, indicating the open prairie surrounding them. "How are we supposed to get into trouble way out here?"

Ragweed pulled his straw hat forward to shade his eyes. "Oh, there's ways," he said.

With that cryptic comment, he wheeled the pickup around, heading for the nearest road that would lead them to the evening's designated meeting place.

"Well, here we are, alone at last," Rafferty murmured, his hazel eyes gleaming with amusement. "Just you and me and these two horses."

LaRue couldn't prevent the blush that tinged her cheeks with color. "Rafferty, did you think Grandpa looked...well, funny? I mean, do you think he suspected anything?"

"Naw," Rafferty assured her. "He was just anxious to get underway." He studied her for a few seconds, a slow, half smile lighting his face. "Come here, cowgirl," he commanded softly, "and give me a kiss."

Just as LaRue stepped into his open arms, Mert whickered impatiently and, tossing her head, gave Rafferty a shove from behind. He stumbled, only preventing LaRue from falling by grasping her about the waist.

"I think Mert is trying to tell you something," LaRue laughed, straightening her hat.

"She must have missed me." Hands on hips, Rafferty eyed the mare, who returned his gaze with calm regard. "Okay, you old bag of bones, we'll get started. But let it be known I can outfox you anyday."

Once he and LaRue were in their saddles, Rafferty maneuvered Mert close to the other mount. "Now, where were we?" He reached over to put a hand on LaRue's waist. She leaned toward him and at the same moment, Mert sidestepped; LaRue would have taken a spill had it not been for her death grip on the saddlehorn. Mert's low whicker sounded suspiciously like horsy laughter.

"Face it—she's jealous," teased LaRue. "You won't get within three feet of me all day."

"Oh, yeah? Want to bet?"

"Yeah," she threw back, lightly spurring her horse.

Rafferty took up the chase with a loud shout and they galloped across the grassy stretch of prairie. When he caught up with her, LaRue pointed to the northeast.

"That's where the old trail crossing is," she called out.

"Lead the way."

Permanent ruts had been worn into the ground where thousands of covered wagons had rumbled over the Santa Fe Trail on their way to and from the Mexican frontier.

"About four hundred miles of the Trail were in Kansas," LaRue explained as they reined in and observed the historic wagon tracks. "Traders started out separately or in small groups from Franklin, Missouri, and later, Independence and Westport. But when they made it to Council Grove, they formed big caravans."

"Safety in numbers, huh?"

"Yes, something like that. Up to this point, the Kansa and Osage Indians the wagon trains encountered were unlikely to commit any worse crime than petty thievery. But after Council Grove, the traders had to pass through lands belonging to the Comanches and Pawnees, who were more inclined to make war. Then they needed all the protection they could get."

"This is really impressive," Rafferty stated. "I hope Holly got some good pictures."

"When we get back to the ranch, I'll show you some aerial photos a neighbor of ours took. You get a much better view of the Trail from those."

"You know, Miss LaRue," Rafferty drawled, a teasing glint in his eye, "you sure do know a lot about Kansas history for an uneducated person."

She made a face at him. "Are you making fun of me?" she demanded sternly.

"Not in a million years. Not when all I can think about is hauling you out of that saddle and making love to you."

"Right out here in broad daylight?"

"Yeah, how does that sound?"

She laughed. "Pretty nearly impossible . . . with old Mert being so jealous and all!"

"Woman," he growled, "now who's making fun of whom?"

"Would you listen to the college boy?" she taunted. "Of *whom*?"

"That does it!" He urged Mert closer to LaRue's horse, and before LaRue could ride out of his range, snaked out an arm to seize her around the waist. He lifted her free of the saddle, pulling her onto Mert.

LaRue squealed in mock terror, thrilled by Rafferty's purposeful strength. She could feel the jarring thud of his heartbeat against her back, and when he spoke, his warm breath tickled her neck.

"Hold still, sugar, or we're both going to end up on the ground."

Obligingly, she stopped wiggling and leaned against him. Rafferty carefully shifted his weight, sliding backward to sit on Mert's broad back. LaRue settled comfortably into the saddle, Rafferty's arm wrapped securely about her. With his free hand, he gave the reins a snap and Mert began ambling on across the prairie. With a puzzled look and a faint snort of protest, LaRue's horse followed behind, stopping occasionally to sample an appealing clump of grass.

"This is nice, isn't it?" Rafferty whispered, dragging his lips along LaRue's neck in softly nibbling kisses.

"Mmm, very. But did you know we're going the wrong way?" she asked.

He glanced about. "Which way are we supposed to be going?"

"South. Our overland trip goes north to Council Grove, then loops back south again. It's only a matter of time now before we're all back at Sin Creek."

"I wish it didn't have to end," he sighed, "especially now that we've found out we don't dislike each other."

"All good things . . ." she quoted lightly.

"Shh, don't say it," Rafferty warned. "It's too beautiful a day to be depressed."

He let his hand drift upward along her ribs, settling firmly over one breast. At his touch, LaRue was filled with such a flood of memories from the night before that she felt weak and sagged against his arm. She twisted around to look over her shoulder; Rafferty attempted a kiss that fell short of its mark and landed on her cheek.

"This isn't very satisfactory, is it?" he grumbled.

"It's the best we can do, under the circumstances," she consoled.

Rafferty refused to be that easily appeased. "Oh, no, it's not. I'm going to hang on to you, honey, and you turn around and face me."

"What?" she gasped. "I can't do that!"

All the time she was objecting to his suggestion, LaRue was gingerly lifting one leg over Mert's neck, then slowly pivoting. She managed to position her legs on either side of Rafferty, bringing them face-to-face.

He pulled her thighs over his, his hands cupping her bottom to slide her closer to him. Her hands went to his waist, to cling to the belt loops of his jeans.

"This is perfect," he proclaimed, slipping his arms about her. "I'm going to get my kiss at last."

"Yes," she whispered, arching toward him, "you are very resourceful."

His big hands splayed across her back as his mouth caught hers in a trembling caress that deepened and intensified almost immediately. Her lips shaped to his heated demand, her hands moved to stroke his muscular upper arms. He lifted her onto his thighs, holding her tightly against him as his mouth devoured hers.

"God, LaRue," he groaned, trying to catch his breath, "this is a damn fool thing to be doing on horseback...."

"As long as Mert hasn't figured out what's going on, we're okay," LaRue replied, resting her head against his chest. There had never been an experience in her life to equal this. Rafferty certainly had a knack for doing things in his own, unique way.

He rubbed his palms along her shoulders, filling her with delicious, shivery sensations. Feeling drugged, she looked up at him and, slowly, his eyes on hers, he began to undo the buttons on her blouse, one by one. He thrust the fabric aside to place a burning kiss on the curve of flesh above her bra, and she caught her breath.

"Oh, Rafferty," she panted. "My God!"

"You liked that, did you?" he queried, his lips still brushing her skin.

"Rafferty." Her voice seemed suddenly strained and her fingers tightened convulsively on his arms. "Rafferty!" she hissed. "You've got to stop!"

He raised his head. "But, love, no one can see us...."

"That's what you think," she said tersely.

He followed her shocked gaze, and felt as if someone had kicked him in the stomach.

"What the hell?"

They were surrounded by a dozen Indian warriors on horseback, each magnificently attired in full battle regalia. Even their faces were streaked with brilliant warpaint.

LaRue moaned and hastily began buttoning her blouse. Unmindful of safety, she swung around in the saddle, facing away from him.

"What's going on?" he asked. "Is this some kind of joke?"

"How should I know?" she mumbled miserably.

He patted her hip. "Where's that damned gun when you need it?"

One of the men, wearing a chief's headdress and long braids, rode forward. He raised a hand in the traditional Indian greeting.

"It is good to see you again, LaRue. And nice to see you enjoying . . . nature this way."

His tone was bland, his face carefully devoid of any amusement or emotion.

"Loping Wolf?" she exclaimed. "Is that you?"

"It is."

"I didn't recognize you with all that warpaint."

"You know him?" asked Rafferty, unsure whether to be relieved or not.

"Yes, I know him. And probably most of the others, too." LaRue fixed her gaze on the Indian again. "What are you doing, Wolf?"

"Beside freezing my conchos off, you mean?" He grinned and flicked the row of silver disks that adorned the loin cloth he was wearing. "Well, surely you recognize a fierce raiding party?"

"Raiding party?" Rafferty echoed. Was he dreaming this or what?

"What's there to raid out here?" LaRue asked.

"To be truthful, we're not exactly on a raid," Loping Wolf admitted. "It's more like a kidnapping."

"Get serious," laughed Rafferty. "Do you expect us to believe grown men still dress up in costume like big, bad warriors and go around kidnapping people?"

"Believe what you like," Wolf said smugly. He raised his head and intoned two words, *"Wabaunsee choctaw."*

Instantly, the others closed the circle around Mert, and Rafferty and LaRue found themselves staring at a row of befeathered spears.

"Us?" croaked LaRue. "You're kidnapping us?"

Loping Wolf nodded. "Well, actually we're after Mr. Rafferty. I guess you're just a bonus."

"Wait a goddamned minute," Rafferty began, but his words trailed away as he felt the sharp prod of a spear between his shoulder blades. These crazies weren't joking, after all.

"You will come with us to our camp now," the chief stated. "Virile Warrior, you take LaRue."

"What are you guys? Some kind of amateur Savage Society or something?" ranted Rafferty. "Whoever heard of an Indian named Virile Warrior, for God's sake?"

But the instant he saw the young brave approaching on horseback, Rafferty conceded that he *could* be called Virile Warrior with no stretch of the imagination. And looking at the sun-bronzed muscles, he knew it could be unhealthy for any man who dared scoff at the title. Or favor the notion that he might be amateur at anything.

As the Indian leaped down from his horse, Loping Wolf said, "Do not mock Virile Warrior. He has earned his name, and he is a proud brave."

Judging by the brevity of his costume, Rafferty was fairly certain he knew what the man was so damned proud of.

The man kept his sternly handsome, large-featured face totally impassive as he clamped his hands on LaRue's waist and lifted her from Mert's back, out of Rafferty's reach. At the sight of her tucked against the Indian's nearly bare body, Rafferty exploded in rage.

"Get your hands off her," he yelled, starting to dismount. Again, the spears poked at him and he froze. What the hell was going on?

"Take her," Loping Wolf commanded, and Rafferty surged forward in the saddle once more.

"Rafferty," gasped LaRue, "that was just a poor choice of words. Relax! This is some kind of joke, believe me." She didn't struggle as the brave tossed her up onto his horse, then swung up right behind her. She looked steadily at Loping Wolf. "Did my grandfather put you up to this?"

"Your grandfather has nothing to do with our desire to kidnap the government man."

"I wish I could believe that," she sighed.

Wolf pointed to her horse, grazing peacefully a few hundred yards away.

"You will be convinced of Levi Tate's innocence when we send the ransom note. We will tie it to your horse's saddle and one of my men will lead him into the white man's camp."

"Ransom note?" she repeated, stunned. "Then…Grandpa really didn't send you?"

"He knows nothing of this." Loping Wolf issued brief orders and one of the braves went after LaRue's horse, while the rest fell into a loose formation around Rafferty. *"Tishcohan minnehaha!"*

"I may not know anything about Indians," Rafferty shouted in frustrated anger, "but I know enough to realize that you're not really speaking a legitimate language."

Loping Wolf grinned, his teeth white against the rust-colored warpaint. "None of us were taught to speak Sioux, the language of the Plains Indians, so we decided to devise a simple speech of our own. We think it gives us a little more credibility."

The word Rafferty muttered was far from socially acceptable, so he wasn't surprised when the chief ignored him and rode on.

They traveled at a leisurely pace for about twenty minutes before they came upon a village of tepees.

Several women dressed in buckskins or calico skirts watched their arrival with curiosity. One with gray braids scolded the two spotted dogs who barked in shrill excitement. The camp might have looked like something from a movie set, except that there was no bustle of activity—no children and no smoke emerging from the tepees. Beyond a small corral of horses were two pickups and a van, looking wildly out of place.

"Dismount," cried Loping Wolf, "and deal with the prisoners."

Before he could determine what was going to happen, Rafferty had been dragged from his horse and securely tied to a somewhat wobbly stake. LaRue was bound to a similar stake just inches away, and he wished he could touch her, if only to reassure himself she was okay. She looked okay, although wary and somewhat tense. At first he'd thought this whole thing was one of those schemes thought up to amuse tourists, but now he simply didn't know.

"Sequoyah gitchigoomie," Loping Wolf called out. "Time for the ceremony." His tribe gathered in a ring around their prisoners, all but the chief sitting cross-legged on the ground. When everyone was settled, Wolf raised his head and gave an unearthly howl. From the nearest tepee stepped a tall man swathed in a blanket and buckskin leggings. Twisted ropes of beads hung about his neck and heavy, beaded earrings decorated each ear. But the most unusual thing about his appearance was his hair. His head had been shaved except for a shock of black hair on the crown; from this hung three long, thin braids that swung crazily with each step he took. In his hand was a wooden pipe, hung with beads, feathers and what looked like bear claws. The man stopped in front of Rafferty and fixed him with a somber glare.

"This is Singing Antelope, our priest—what you would call a medicine man," explained Wolf, retreating to join the others. "Our treatment of you and your woman will depend on how closely you listen to what he has to say."

Singing Antelope carefully laid aside his blanket, revealing a square, beaded bag hanging over a thin chest that had not yet seen much sun. A faint blue tattoo of an anchor on his upper right arm read U.S. Navy.

He clapped his hands twice and called out, "Prepare to light the ceremonial fire."

Three young women came out of his tepee and proceeded to neatly arrange sticks and dry grass in a ring of stones. Then they stepped back and allowed Singing Antelope room to kneel before the fire ring and rummage through the bag around his neck. He came up with two flint rocks and, for the next few minutes, worked diligently at striking them together, with little success. Finally, heaving a disgusted sigh, he flung the flint aside.

"Magic fire rocks suck," he declared.

With a giggle, one of the women handed him a cigarette lighter and, in a matter of seconds, he had the fire burning.

"Can you believe it?" Rafferty muttered to LaRue. "A medicine man who flicks his Bic."

She smiled, then shook her head in warning. She knew these people and was positive they couldn't have anything sinister in mind, but she didn't want to take any chances until she knew what was really going on.

Singing Antelope took up the pipe and, walking slowly around the cleared circle, lifted it high, pointing it in each of the four directions. Then he addressed the elements, reaching into the bag for handfuls of dried herbs that he tossed about as he spoke.

"Be with us, O Spirit of the Earth! Guide our feet and sustain our bodies.

"Come to us, O Spirit of the Wind! Take falsehood and scatter it to the corners of the earth, so that only truth is heard today.

"Stay near us, O Spirit of the Water! Cleanse our souls and give us strength of purpose.

"Rise about us, O Spirit of the Fire...." Here the medicine man faltered, thought a second, then pulled a piece of paper from his medicine bag and quickly scanned it before continuing. "Warm our hearts and inflame our determination."

Rafferty rolled his eyes heavenward. Singing Antelope stuffed the paper back into the beaded bag. "Well," he said defensively, "it's not easy to remember all this stuff, you know."

Next, he raised the pipe over his head and intoned, "Oh, Great Spirit, be with us. Accept our invitation to sit in council. Guide us in the ways of peace."

He approached Rafferty, waving a sheaf of hawk feathers in the air and singing some unlikely chant. Then, head back, he began an obviously rehearsed soliloquy. "Many moons ago this land belonged to the Red Man, from the hills that rimmed the prairie to the clouds that rimmed the sky. The Red Man revered the land and its inhabitants. Then came the White Eyes to take the land from us, to kill or drive away its inhabitants. There followed a time of sorrow for our people, but we have learned to survive in the White Eyes' world.

"Now many of us have left the reservation to come back to the Flint Hills where the White Eyes are finally content to let us live as we please. We have found peace here, for we are free to search out the ways of our forefathers.

"But tomorrow more White Eyes come to destroy this peace. The Great White Father in Washington wishes to take our land a second time. He says he wants to preserve the prairie, but he makes a joke, for by his method of preservation, the land will be destroyed."

LaRue's face suddenly registered comprehension and she began to smile.

"You, Rafferty," continued Singing Antelope, "were sent by the Great White Father, and when you return, he will listen to all you have to say. As peace-loving Native Americans, we command you to tell him he has no need for this land. Tell him the Red Man wishes the prairie to stay free."

"So that's what this is all about," said Rafferty, visibly relaxing. "Lord, man, couldn't we have just sat down somewhere and discussed it sensibly?"

"Sometimes that which is discussed sensibly is soon forgotten," Singing Antelope replied. "We wanted to make a more lasting impression."

"Well, you did," Rafferty assured him. "You sure as hell did."

"Will you carry our message to your chief in Washington?"

Rafferty let his gaze wander to LaRue, who was watching the whole scene with real amusement. She was close enough that he could almost feel her body shake with laughter. The floral scent of her bath soap taunted his nostrils, the ends of her hair teased his cheek. He tried to summon anger at her obvious enjoyment of his situation, but he couldn't do it. Even tied to a stake, she was a tempting distraction.

"Rafferty?" prompted the medicine man, impatiently.

"Huh? Oh...oh, yes, you were issuing an ultimatum, weren't you?"

"Not exactly an ultimatum. Just a simple request."

Rafferty couldn't suppress a grin. "Look, you've certainly made your point, and now I'd like some time to think about it. And to get a few more details from you."

"You're willing to talk?"

"Sure, but how about untying me so we can sit down and discuss it like civilized men?"

Singing Antelope looked askance at Loping Wolf, who finally nodded. "We will sit at council in my tepee," he announced.

Fifteen minutes later, LaRue having been banished to another tepee with the women, Rafferty found himself in the middle of a strange fellowship. Loping Wolf had lit the peace pipe and now it was traveling from man to man. When it came to Rafferty, he paused.

"You aren't smoking anything illegal, are you?"

Loping Wolf chuckled. "No, it's only a special blend of Dutch tobaccos that Slithering Lizard brings back from Amsterdam."

"Amsterdam?" Rafferty's black eyebrows quirked up.

"He's a pilot," Wolf said by way of explanation.

Rafferty choked on the puff he had just taken on the pipe.

"Does that surprise you?" queried the highly amused Indian. "It shouldn't . . . Twisted Serpent is a doctor, Old Dog a shoe salesman. Virile Warrior is a gym instructor, I'm an accountant, and Singing Antelope runs a saloon in Emporia. That's why he can get away with the hairdo. The rest of us have to fake it." He pulled off his headband and his two long braids came with it, revealing an everyday haircut.

Rafferty shook his head. "Then you really are just ordinary people."

"Ordinary people who happen to have Indian ancestors," Wolf said. "We're just a bunch of guys who got so tired of being caught up in the modern world that we decided to try to get more in touch with our heritage. So we formed a group and we get together on weekends . . . and sometimes, like this, for a week-long camp out."

"I'll be damned."

"We know we aren't very good at it yet," put in Singing Antelope, "but we figure we can have fun while we learn."

"And we don't get all bent out of shape if we aren't one hundred-percent accurate," Old Dog added. "We're from several different tribes, actually, so we tend to combine customs. Take our tepees, for instance. . . ."

"Yeah, I wondered about that," said Rafferty. "Didn't the Plains Indians live in grass huts?"

"Yes, but we got a special deal on these tepees from the Ranchers' Co-op," explained Loping Wolf. "And they're easier to put up and take down."

Rafferty jumped as a loud and unexpected roar sounded not far from the tent where the men were sitting. "What in the—"

"The women have started up the generator," answered Slithering Lizard, glancing at the wristwatch he wore, camouflaged by a feathered bracelet. "It's one o'clock, time for their soap opera. They won't come camping with us if we don't let them bring a TV along."

"Times sure have changed," groused Loping Wolf. "In the old days, squaws were obedient and hard-working. Now the White Eyes have taught them equal rights." He winked broadly. "Just one more grievance...."

"What's your real name?" Rafferty suddenly asked.

"Does it matter?" Wolf took the pipe from him. "Would it make you take us any more seriously to know my name is Sam Walker or that Virile Warrior is really Rocky Armstrong?"

Rafferty groaned. The guy would have a name like that!

"No, I guess not," he conceded.

"Hey, we're here to talk business," Singing Antelope reminded them. "Why don't you ask your questions, Rafferty?"

"Okay. Got anything I can take notes on?" He looked around the circle of men. "I'm willing to listen to your views and give them adequate mention in the feasibility report I'm writing for the government committee. But first, shouldn't we do something about that ransom note you sent Levi Tate?"

"Shoot, there was no ransom note," Wolf admitted. "We were just bluffing."

"Well, is there some way you could let him know where we are? I don't want him to worry about LaRue."

"I'll send someone with a message," offered Loping Wolf. "And since we don't know how long this is going to take, why don't you stay the night? We're having a powwow of sorts this evening."

"You know, that gives me an idea," Singing Antelope said. "While they're here, maybe LaRue will help us out with that ceremony."

"Hey, good thinking," exclaimed Wolf. "If someone will go get LaRue, we'll ask her."

When LaRue appeared in the doorway of the tepee, her eyes immediately sought Rafferty. He grinned broadly. "They haven't scalped me yet," he said.

"That must mean you've been letting them air their views on the prairie park."

"Rafferty has agreed to confer with us about that," Wolf said. "But before we start, we want to ask a favor of you."

"What kind of favor?"

"Next month, the public-television channel is going to be filming a documentary abut the Wah-Shun-Gah Days Festival at Council Grove," he began.

Seeing Rafferty's questioning look, LaRue explained, "It's a three-day celebration of local history. Go on, Wolf."

"Well, the area Indians have been asked to participate—doing tribal dances and that kind of thing. We signed up to do a wedding ceremony. It was appropriate at the time because Virile Warrior was engaged to be married, and he and his fiancée had written their own vows. We thought we could add some drums, a little buckskin, a feather here and there. But...."

He paused a moment to give Virile Warrior an apologetic look. "The young lady in question has had second thoughts and cancelled out."

Rafferty coughed, quickly putting up his hand to hide the smile twitching at the corners of his mouth. So, the great Bison Biceps had been dumped. Who'd have believed it?

"The bride's dress doesn't fit any of our other women," Loping Wolf went on, "but you're about the right size. Since we have often performed for the entertainment of your grandfather's wagon trips, we thought maybe you would help us out by being in the ceremony...at least this evening, so we can practice. We need to work out the kinks."

Good choice of words, Rafferty thought, *since Virile Warrior helped write the thing. Any guy who wears a fringed diaper must be pretty kinky.*

"Well, sure," LaRue said, shrugging. "What would I have to do?"

"Wear the ceremonial dress and read the part of the bride," answered Loping Wolf. "And maybe give the groom a small kiss at the end." He winked mischievously.

"Now wait just a damned minute."

Everyone in the tepee was surprised by the sudden, harsh words, but no one more so than Rafferty himself. He hadn't known he was going to feel such a rush of unreasoning anger.

"I don't think we have time to hang around here until evening," he rapidly improvised. "The others will worry about us."

"Wolf can send word to Grandpa," LaRue said calmly.

"I've already agreed to do that. And I can tell him that if we get the thing perfected, we'll perform it for his overland guests. He'd like that, wouldn't he, LaRue?"

"Sure. You could do it at the rodeo he's having next week."

"And he wouldn't even have to pay us," Old Dog interjected. "He usually gives us a side of beef for our camp outs when we entertain for his covered-wagon trips."

"I just don't think it's a good idea," Rafferty said, getting to his feet. "We need to get back."

"Oh, hogwash!" LaRue's chin went up stubbornly. "These people are my friends and I don't mind helping them out. I want to do it." She put her hand on Virile Warrior's arm and smiled up at him. "I'm sorry your fiancée backed out, but I'm willing to try and take her place. When do we start?"

Rafferty struggled for control. "You don't. At least not with him."

"What is wrong with you?" she gasped.

"If you insist on going through with this ridiculous notion, it will be with me as the groom."

Oh, God—had he really said that? From the looks on the various faces around him, he must have.

"You?" she laughed. "Now *that* would be a ridiculous notion!"

"Why?" he asked ominously.

LaRue looked embarrassed. "Can't we argue this out later?"

"No."

She, too, glanced at the circle of avidly interested men. "All right," she said through gritted teeth, "it's ridiculous because you aren't an Indian...."

"Neither are you."

"At least I know a little bit about their customs...."

"This will be a wonderful opportunity for me to learn."

"Rafferty, you—you'd..." She broke off, intrigued by the thought that had stolen into her mind.

"What?" he snapped.

"Well, you'd feel pretty silly in a loincloth, wouldn't you?"

His black eyebrows drew together. "What makes you think that?"

She shook her head, overcome by the inane urge to smile. She couldn't seem to help herself. The image of Rafferty in a leather breechclout had taken hold in her mind and she was unable to rout it out.

"Now you listen to me, Miss LaRue Tate," he stormed. "If you go through with this stupid ceremony, it's going to be with me as your partner. That's final."

"I'd like to know your reasoning," she challenged.

Virile Warrior stepped between them, speaking for the first time. "Please, LaRue, it makes no difference to me. I think your man is insecure about your affection for him and doesn't want to see you even pretending to marry someone else." He turned to Rafferty. "Give it to us straight. That's right, isn't it?"

Rafferty would have loved giving it to him straight...straight on the chin. And the only right he could think about came equipped with knuckles.

He opened his mouth to deny every demeaning word, then snapped it shut. In the Westerns he'd read, when there was a poker game at the old saloon, sooner or later someone always got his bluff called. That was exactly what Virile Warrior had just done to him, and he might as well be man enough to admit it.

"Okay," he conceded, "you're right. If it makes you feel any better, I'm jealous. And probably insecure. And definitely insane. I'd have to be to even consider putting on one of those things." He indicated the square of leather hanging loosely from Warrior's sinewy hips. Then, wincing at his mental picture of those hips standing next to LaRue...even in a mock wedding...he gave her a slow, lopsided smile. "How about it?" he asked. "Will you marry me instead?"

LaRue's heart chose that moment to skitter like a frightened rabbit, but she managed a weak smile and nodded. "Whatever you say."

Rafferty suddenly felt as young and exultant as a sixteen-year-old who'd just stolen the homecoming queen from the star of the varsity football team.

He laid an arm along her shoulders and spoke to the grinning assembly. "I'll walk LaRue back to the women's tepee, and then we can get started on that Tallgrass Park discussion."

"Rafferty," Loping Wolf spoke up, "I think you should know, the ceremony doesn't include the offer of a honeymoon."

Rafferty looked insulted. "I didn't expect it would," he said. "But I want the job anyway."

Outside in the sunlight, Rafferty and LaRue faced each other. After a few seconds, she tilted her head and grinned up at him.

"I had no idea you could be so forceful," she said demurely.

"You'd be surprised how I can react when someone invades my territory."

"Your...territory?"

He put his hands on her shoulders, then bent to touch his mouth to hers. "Yes, mine." He pulled her to him, letting his lips coax her into acceptance of his blatantly macho declaration. If the way she arched upward against him was any indication, she hadn't minded.

"Rafferty," she whispered after a moment, "I know you're going to look terrific in a loincloth."

He growled in pleasure, then leaned back to gaze into her face.

"Sugar, I think I'm going to like getting married to you."

She traced the curve of his bottom lip with her forefinger before confessing, "And I think I'm going to be glad I agreed to this crazy plan."

"Good," he teased, playfully nipping at her finger, "because you really had no choice at all in the matter."

"You're a hard man, Rafferty."

He sighed. "You can say that again."

Chapter Fourteen

"As soon as the brass collection plates I ordered have arrived, I'm going to set up a proper church. It's about time some decent folk showed those savage Red Men with their pagan rites what religion is all about."
—Rev. Jack Gamble,
Hymer, Kansas, 1884

Preparations for the evening's powwow were relatively simple. Arrangements had been made for a schoolbus to deliver the tribal children directly to the camp site, and when they arrived in late afternoon, they were sent out to gather flowers to decorate the card tables the Indian women had set up for the feast. Loping Wolf assured everyone that a hunting party had been dispatched and would soon return with the food.

While they waited, the ladies decided they would prepare the make-believe bride for the wedding ceremony. LaRue, having agreed to the whole thing, went along without too many doubts, especially after it was explained that the television crew would be interested in a few preceremonial shots and the women wished to brush up on the technicalities.

A deep, clear stream ran along the back of the camp, and here the women orchestrated an elaborate bath.

"Osage women were known for their fastidious ways and, even in the old days, bathed daily," explained a plump but pretty young woman called Leaping Shadow. "Since many of us are Osage, we are making this primarily an Osage ritual, you see."

Taking note of this fact, the ladies inevitably decided to join LaRue in her ablutions. And, hearing their shrieks of laughter, the children were quickly on the scene, casting off their jeans and T-shirts to splash and shout in the crowded stream.

Standing on the high bank, trusted to keep his broad back turned, was Virile Warrior, a stoic sentry whose duty it was to turn away any inquisitive male who might happen on to the bathing place. Rafferty watched him from afar, unashamedly unconvinced of the man's honor. As far as he was concerned, appointing Virile Warrior as harem guard was like putting the Cheshire Cat in charge of the guppy bowl.

After the women had vacated the stream, Rafferty caught the merest glimpse of LaRue, wrapped in a bath sheet, wet hair streaming down her back, being led into a distant tepee. She was surrounded by a gaggle of women, a sure sign he would not see her again until the festivities began.

Thinking of the evening ahead, he inevitably found himself mulling over a series of stimulating memories from the night before. All in all, it was just as well when the men of the tribe decided they, too, would go down to the stream for a cool bath. Not surprisingly, Rafferty was the first one in.

The women's tepee was in a flurry of activity. While some of its occupants debated about the clothing LaRue should wear for the celebration, others were setting out makeup and jewelry for her to choose from. She was treated to a manicure, ending with fingernails and toenails being painted a soft coral color. Then she was given a brisk rubdown with a fragrant oil, which one of the women, Mottled Doe, Loping Wolf's wife, explained was distilled from columbines, an old Osage tradition.

"After bathing, the women anointed themselves with a perfume made of calamus root, horsemint and columbine seed," she said, sprinkling the liquid liberally over LaRue's bare back. "We're lucky that Quivering Aspen learned the recipe from her grandmother."

And indeed, it did smell wonderful. LaRue smiled to herself as she imagined Rafferty's reaction to it.

"It's supposed to be an aphrodisiac," one of the others stated.

"Who needs it?" laughed Quivering Aspen. "With a magnificent specimen like Rafferty, I mean."

"Ah, yes…Rafferty. Finally someone who's a real threat to Virile Warrior," giggled Gossiping Otter. "Not that I don't feel sorry for him—the way that little witch treated him."

Amid comments on the broken engagement, LaRue was pushed onto a camp stool in front of a mirror, and two of the women began brushing and braiding her hair. She sighed, amazed that she was allowing all this pampering. For the first time in her life, she really understood the enjoyment there was in being feminine. She suspected the reason was the very masculine influence of J. B. Rafferty.

The hunting party arrived only minutes before sundown. Proudly displaying the trophies of the hunt, the braves beamed from ear to ear.

"The spirits were with us," their spokesman, Slithering Lizard, loudly proclaimed. *Watash pemmican*—Colonel Sanders!"

They began loading down the dinner tables with cardboard buckets of fried chicken, containers of coleslaw and potato salad and boxes of hot biscuits. Three coolers of iced beer and soda pop, paper plates and plastic silverware completed the preparations.

"Watermelon for dessert," announced Old Dog, causing the excited children to cheer in delight.

"Bring forth the bride and groom," cried out Loping Wolf, "so that we might commence with the meal and the ceremony."

Led by a group of braves from Wolf's tepee to the fire, Rafferty had never felt like such a fool in his life. When he had agreed to this wedding ritual scheme, he'd had no idea the Indians would take it so seriously. The scrap of buckskin and scattering of feathers he'd been given to wear was all but indecent. True, it was the same garb worn by all the younger men present, but then, an emissary from Uncle Sam had a certain dignity to maintain.

He forgot all about his dignity the moment he saw LaRue emerge from the women's tepee. A group of women brought her to him, then indicated that she, too, should sit on the woven blanket.

There were many facets to LaRue, but Rafferty suspected the image she now presented was as close to her real personality as it was possible to get. Dressed in beads and buckskin, eyes shyly downcast, she presented a lovely picture . . . one not conveyed by her everyday blue jeans and cowboy hat.

She looked young and freshly beautiful, an earthy innocent. But—perhaps it was the Indian adornment—she seemed in touch with the basic, primitive aspects of man's own nature. There was a nobility about her, an inner peace, a knowledge of mystic concepts.

Rafferty reflected that the cold beer he was drinking must have gone directly from his empty stomach to his head. But then, it had been a week for wild flights of fancy. . . .

LaRue was wearing a straight buckskin dress with fringed sleeves and a fringed hem that nearly reached the ground. As she settled herself by the fire, curling her legs beneath her, Rafferty caught a glimpse of slim calves and bare, dusty toes.

Makeup had enhanced the smooth prettiness of her face, emphasizing the hollows of her cheeks and the wide, almond-shaped eyes. Rafferty couldn't help but wonder if she did actually have an Indian or two in her ancestry.

When she saw him staring at her, LaRue turned her full gaze on him for the first time and the look in her eyes seemed to ask, What in the world have we gotten ourselves into now?

Her smile revealed the hint of straight, white teeth behind pale coral lips, and Rafferty didn't really care anymore. He was ready for whatever lay in store.

He continued his assessment, as if needing to lock her image into his mind. He admired her hair, which had been plaited into two long braids, with beads and tiny silver bells woven into the strands. The ends of her braids brushed the low, laced neckline of the dress, emphasizing the rows of wooden and silver disks that decorated her breasts, dancing with each breath she drew. The dress was a little snug across the bust, and when LaRue became aware of his intense study, she blushed faintly and raised one hand, as if to shield herself from his marauding gaze.

Virile Warrior stepped up to Rafferty and extended a bucket of chicken. With a grin, he said, "Leg, man?"

Rafferty cast a wicked leer in LaRue's direction. "No thanks, I'm a breast man, myself."

He reached into the container and withdrew a piece of white meat, chuckling softly at her embarrassed confusion. Virile Warrior's grin stretched wider. In an attempt to regain her composure, LaRue reached into the bucket and took the first piece of chicken her fingers encountered.

"Oh, good," she breathed, "a thigh. I love thighs."

Both Rafferty and Virile Warrior laughed aloud as a wave of scarlet swept over her face. She started to rise, but Rafferty's warm fingers closed over her wrist.

"Come on, honey, stay here. If you run away, you'll spoil the rehearsal." His eyes caught her golden-brown ones and held them intimately. "And you'll spoil my plans, too. I've been looking forward to this. Haven't you?"

She had to smile. "Yes, I guess I have." She grimaced. "I just feel so strange in this . . . getup."

He leaned closer, putting his lips to her ear. "You look so beautiful I can barely stand it. Please, say you'll stay and go through with this."

"I'll stay."

The wedding ceremony came sometime after the chicken and before the watermelon. Night had long-since fallen when Loping Wolf rose and called for the ritual to begin.

The generator roared to life, and Old Dog brought out the ceremonial cassette player. Soon the low, rhythmic throbbing of tom-toms filled the air.

"We haven't found anyone who has time for drum lessons yet," he said apologetically.

The ceremony was destined to be an odd mixture of cultural customs, although Loping Wolf assured them that the makers of the television program had already been warned of that fact.

Rafferty and LaRue were led to the tribal priest by children scattering the petals of wildflowers. At that point, LaRue stole a swift glance at Rafferty, but he didn't seem the least perturbed by the effect on the earth's ecosystem.

Singing Antelope, dressed in a buffalo cape with scarlet plumes waving from his unique hairdo, began the ceremony much as he had begun the one earlier in the day. When all the appropriate spirits had been summoned, he commanded the bride and groom to render their pledges to each other.

"Here are your cheat sheets," he whispered, handing them slips of paper. "It'll be okay to read the responses."

Rafferty almost balked. He'd dreaded doing this sort of thing at a real wedding. How could he justify doing it for this farce?

He took another look at LaRue, and suddenly it didn't seem such a farce. He scanned the paper, then began his recitation, looking down at her.

"My love for this maiden is like the red-tailed hawk, soaring through the heavens without restraint. By my oath, I will never allow it to falter or plummet to the earth."

LaRue smiled up at him. "My love for this brave is like the golden doe. It dwells, free and strong, in hidden places. It is my oath that I will keep it forever safe in the deepest forests of my heart." Her gaze skimmed over Rafferty's face, tenderly.

Rafferty held out his hand, and LaRue laid hers within it.

"I, Rafferty," he read, "pledge myself to you." His eyes, intensely dark, captured hers. "I offer you my tepee, my sleeping mat, my worldly trophies. Until the Thunder Spirit comes to mark the Last Storm. Unto eternity."

Reassured by his firm grip, LaRue squeezed his fingers and made her reply.

"I, LaRue, pledge myself to you. I will share your tepee, your sleeping mat, your worldly trophies. Until the Rainbow Spirit comes to mark the start of a New World. Unto eternity."

An awed silence had fallen over the crowd, and Singing Antelope had to clear his throat before speaking the incongruous end to the ceremony. "I commend this man and this woman to you, O Great Spirit. Make your face to shine upon them."

He waved a plumed prayer stick above their heads. "I pronounce you man and wife—uh, warrior and... You can kiss your bride, Mr. Rafferty...and may your happinesses number as many as the blades of grass upon the prairie."

Rafferty reflected that he should feel like an absolute imbecile standing there in front of so many people, half-dressed and mouthing words from a patch-work ritual. Instead, he felt moved, humbled. His fingers trembled slightly as he brushed them along the side of LaRue's upturned face, cupping her chin and drawing her mouth to his. Their kiss was soft and full of promise, as though their souls knew something they themselves had only begun to suspect.

The moment was broken by a round of enthusiastic applause, and they drew apart, looking somewhat dazed.

"Good ceremony," approved Loping Wolf. "I think it's going to be just fine."

The rest of the evening was a blur to Rafferty and, he suspected, LaRue. They declined slices of watermelon, preferring to sit on the blanket and watch the others. Their hands intertwined so naturally that he was barely aware of the fact.

Even when more modern music was being played for dancing, they remained in the shadowy firelight, not really speaking...but communicating nevertheless in some comfortable, unspoken way.

LaRue's eyes were constantly drawn to the coppery highlights the leaping flames threw upon Rafferty's wide shoulders and chest. The buckskin loincloth tied around his narrow hips was tantalizing in its briefness, and her cheeks burned each time she realized she was staring. Quickly moving her gaze to the display of long, hair-hazed legs didn't help her equilibrium much, either. She was, she knew, totally enamored of the man. The emotions she was feeling at that moment were the very ones she had expected to feel only on the occasion of a real marriage. But she was grateful she had been allowed to experience them with Rafferty. Even if it was only in fun, she found that it meant a great deal to her. No one else need ever know how she would cherish the memories of this night.

Not long before midnight, LaRue forced herself to broach the subject of returning to the wagon train.

"No need to leave just yet," exclaimed Loping Wolf. "In fact, in the note I sent your grandfather, I told him you might spend the night. He knows how these powwows are."

LaRue's gaze sought Rafferty's, and he smiled. "Why don't we stay?" he asked. "We can leave early enough in the morning to catch up with the wagons."

"All right . . . but only if you'll dance with me."

"It will be my pleasure . . . Mrs. Rafferty." He rose and held out his arms.

LaRue knew they wouldn't be able to get any closer than this for the rest of the night, so she tried to content herself with the feel of Rafferty's strong body against her, his warm breath on her cheek. At least the fantasy of being lovers could be continued one more night before they had to return to the real world—the world of wagon trains, prairie parks and problems with no solutions.

The tom-toms had started again, thudding out a slow, rhythmically sensuous beat. Rafferty was alone in the tepee, lying on a sleeping mat, arms behind his head. Only a short time earlier, Twisted Serpent had received a call on his pager and had driven back to town to deal with a medical emergency. Rafferty, knowing the other man wouldn't return until morning, fought a losing battle with frustration. Why couldn't LaRue be there with him instead of halfway across the camp, sharing a tepee with two other young women?

It had seemed such a waste to end the evening saying goodnight to her in front of the others and being led away to a tepee at the far end of the campground. A fierce longing seized him, and he stirred restlessly, impatiently. Damn it! Only last night they had lain in each other's arms, sharing an experience quite unlike anything Rafferty had ever known. It scared him to think they might never have that again. And time was so short. . . .

With a muffled curse, he leaped off the mat. He needed to get outside, to pace...or swim. Anything to clear his mind of thoughts of LaRue as she had looked tonight. Anything to purge his body of the unrelenting desire that raged through it, demanding release.

He threw back the skins covering the doorway and stepped out into the night. A round white moon had risen, spilling pale light across the landscape. Rafferty heard the murmur of the stream and headed that way, grateful for the breezes that cooled his feverish body.

LaRue stopped in the shadows to watch him. She needed a moment to get her rampaging emotions in check again. She couldn't help it—she felt like a bride! She had discovered that, as far as her heart and mind were concerned, tonight's ceremony had been for real. And the truth of it was, she was just as tense and nervous as if it really were her wedding night. As if she actually were going to her new bridegroom.

Rafferty had never looked more like the athletic brave in her grandfather's painting than he did at that moment. LaRue let her eyes range over his tall, beautiful physique. She thought him darkly handsome, with his unruly black hair falling across his forehead, shadowing the sharp angles of his face. She didn't know how it had happened, but the easygoing government man had become a Native American.

"Rafferty," she called softly.

"LaRue? What are you doing out here?" He turned and came to her, drawing her into his arms at once.

"Quivering Aspen told me she saw Twisted Serpent leave." She smiled. "She also told me I was crazy if I didn't come find you."

"Aren't you worried the others will know?" he questioned, studying her upturned face.

She shook her head. "I trust Aspen not to say anything."

Entranced by the play of moonlight in her hair, now brushed and hanging loose about her shoulders, he put out a hand to lift a strand, rubbing it gently between his fingers.

His warm knuckles brushed her cheek and she caught her breath. "Aren't you going to invite me in?" she asked shyly.

As they entered, Rafferty was again struck by LaRue's beauty as it was revealed by the light of the small fire in the center of the tepee.

LaRue dropped gracefully to the sleeping mat, and Rafferty knelt beside her. "A few minutes ago, I was lying here wishing I could hold you," he said, his voice growing husky. "I can't believe you actually came to me."

He put his arms around her waist, drawing her up to rest, thigh to thigh, against him.

"But I did," she declared quietly. "I wanted to see and...touch you, too."

Rafferty lowered his head to claim her mouth in a sweetly demanding kiss. Then, as his lips moved ardently against hers again, she put her arms around his neck and pressed herself tightly into the hard curve of his body.

"I couldn't stop thinking about you," he muttered. "Or about that damned wedding ceremony...."

"I know. I couldn't sleep, either."

Slowly, she stroked the hard planes of his chest. "Rafferty," she whispered.

He covered her hand with his, loving the feel of her fingers upon him.

"Hmm?"

"I've never had a wedding night before."

His reaction was immediate and intense. His mouth captured hers in a possessive kiss that liquefied her bones and sent tongues of flame curling throughout her body. His strong, sure hands made short work of the lacings at the neck of her dress, and then he was pulling it off, over her head. He groaned in surprised pleasure when he saw she wore nothing beneath it, and before she realized his intention, LaRue found herself tumbled among the cushions on the sleeping mat, her make-believe husband lying beside her.

It was a delight to discover that the Indian women had modernized the bed enough to make it extremely comfortable. Beneath the sleeping mat was a cushiony double-width air mattress, and on top were a number of soft feather pillows. "You'd almost think they had something like this in mind, bless them!" Rafferty laughed and began placing fervent kisses along her collarbone. LaRue shivered with pleasure. "My God, but you smell wonderful, sweetheart," Rafferty murmured. "Like you've been lying in a field of sun-warmed flowers...."

He worked his way back to her lips, savoring her heated responses—the way her mouth softened and parted under his loving assault, the way her hands clutched his naked back, drawing him even closer. There was an intensity about LaRue tonight that touched him...as well as inflamed him.

He drew back, resting his weight on his forearms. With eyes as dark as a starless night, he gazed at her breasts, adorned only by the delicate strands of beads. Impatiently, she stirred beneath his scrutiny and he lowered his head, his hungry mouth seeking the sweetness of her body, teasing her nipples into tender rigidity.

LaRue groaned and laced her fingers through his thick black hair, forcing his mouth back to hers. A merciless passion pulsed within her, keeping time to the relentless beat of the tom-toms. She writhed against him, and her breath came in short, sharp gasps.

"Rafferty, aren't you ever going to get undressed?" she murmured into his ear. Against her chest she could feel the erratic beat of his heart before he pulled away and began untying the leather loincloth. With eager movements, he peeled the garment away, his breath catching in his throat as LaRue's hands began roving freely over his heated flesh.

His breathing grew more ragged and strained as she bent to place kisses along his bare hip. The intensity of the moment was almost painful.

He caught her by the shoulders, easing her down and his own body upward, over hers.

She shifted slightly, welcoming the union. Accommodated by her obliging warmth, Rafferty found himself too impatient to go slowly. Sensing her matching ardor, he began moving with an urgency that carried them both to a fever pitch. LaRue's hips rose to meet each powerful thrust and her hands stroked and massaged his back.

From outside came the muted sound of Indian music, and once again, they were caught up in the sensual beat of the drums. Lost in each other, they let the rhythms carry them to a shattering crescendo.

Shaken by the thrilling strength of her release, LaRue cried out, and Rafferty smothered her cries with his mouth as he murmured mindless endearments.

In the intensity of the moment, it was difficult for Rafferty to keep from baring his soul. He finally resorted to humor. "Kowabunga," he quipped. At her startled look, he had to laugh. "Loping Wolf has been teaching me his language," he explained.

"What does it mean?" she asked.

"Remind me to tell you after I've rested awhile."

He changed his position to enfold her within the protective circle of his arms. They lay together in replete and restful silence, watching the shadows dance on the tepee walls.

Gradually, as an understanding of her own heart and mind came to her, LaRue felt a tremendous need to speak. She turned to Rafferty and reaching out to gently caress his face, whispered, "Rafferty, I love you."

Just as she spoke, he bent his dark head to look into her smoky topaz eyes, and his words rushed out to meet hers headlong. "I love you, LaRue."

For an instant, he looked startled, and then they laughed together.

LaRue neither knew nor cared if it was meant to be make believe. On this magical night-out-of-time, all things were possible, all things uncomplicated and real.

Wrapped in each other's arms, they lay back among the pillows, and Rafferty drew the sheet over them. From out of the dark came the throbbing, haunting boom of the drums, matching the rhythm of their combined heartbeats, steadily lulling them to sleep.

When Rafferty awoke at daybreak, LaRue had gone, slipping back to her own tepee. Lying on the pillow beside him was a strand of the wooden beads she had worn the night before. He thought she must have left it there deliberately.

He picked the beads up, charmed by their primitive beauty. A smile played over his firm mouth as he curled his fingers around them and lay back, recalling every detail of the night just past.

Even after he'd fallen asleep again, the smile didn't fade.

Chapter Fifteen

"I'd just as soon take a whip to an ornery man as a good animal. It's always been my experience that two-legged jackasses cause more trouble than four-legged ones ever did."

—Verner Schmidtt, muleskinner,
Dunlap, Kansas, 1879

The next morning, LaRue was back in jeans and a plaid shirt, her hair in a ponytail. As soon as he saw her, Rafferty was filled with the need to touch her. He wasn't surprised that his mood had outlasted the moonlight, for it was becoming more and more obvious that LaRue Tate was not an issue to be dealt with and forgotten. Rafferty was beginning to accept the fact that, for the rest of his life to have any meaning at all, she was going to have to be a part of it. It scared him to think how a solution to the prairie-park controversy had suddenly taken on a whole new importance.

They left the Indian encampment shortly after breakfast. As they saddled their horses, Loping Wolf imparted a bit of interesting information.

"Rocky... er, Virile Warrior went back to town this morning. The wedding ceremony last night inspired him to try to patch things up with Marta, his fiancée."

"So you may not need me to fill in, after all?" LaRue observed.

"Perhaps not. We should know by the time we get to your grandfather's rodeo Saturday."

"I hope it works out for him," Rafferty said, swinging up onto Mert's back. "Besides, it's only right that someone like him be taken out of the running... for the sake of mankind everywhere."

Loping Wolf chuckled. "I believe his... popularity with the opposite sex was the problem behind the broken engagement. Marta was jealous of all the women he meets at the gym where he works, and she wanted him to find another line of work."

"Think he will?" LaRue asked.

"Yes, I think he might. Rocky told me that, after seeing the two of you together, he began to understand what it means to make a commitment to just one person."

Rafferty and LaRue shared a surprised glance, while the older man looked on with a benign expression.

"Well," LaRue said briskly, "we'd better get going. We've been gone from the wagon train so long that Grandpa is going to skin me alive."

"Come back and visit us any time you want."

"Thanks, Loping Wolf," Rafferty said. "We enjoyed your hospitality—once we figured out what was going on."

"I'm sorry about the deception, but you have to admit, it did work. Oh, there's one more thing, Rafferty," Wolf said with a sheepish grin. "About that silly gibberish we used... we were only pulling your leg. We didn't really make up a language."

"It's just as well," Rafferty commented dryly, "because when I get back to Washington, I'm planning on having the Bureau of Indian Affairs mail you some cassette tapes that will teach you to speak Sioux. It'll be easier if you don't have another language cluttering up your minds."

"You know, I'm going to approach the elders about making you a blood brother. You'd be a good man to have on our side."

"I'd be honored," Rafferty said sincerely.

"Then, till we meet again," Wolf said, extending his hand. "Goodbye. And *neodesha potawatomie*." He winked broadly before turning back toward the cluster of tepees.

Rafferty and LaRue rode silently for the most part, reluctant to talk about their return to the real world. They paused once or twice to admire a sweeping view of a distant hill or valley, and once LaRue stopped to point out one of the now-rare jackrabbits that inhabited the area. They heard the strange muffled drumming of the prairie chicken's mating call . . *thump-thump rup-rup r-r-r-r*. Rafferty pretended ignorance and LaRue carefully explained the entire process. Then, catching sight of the twinkle dancing in his hazel eyes, she cried, "Oh, you! I forgot that you know all about . . . biology."

"I thought I did," he said with a straight face, "but even working for a college degree didn't teach me as much as one night with you in a tepee beneath the prairie stars."

LaRue's cheeks turned a becoming shade of scarlet. "Stop teasing me," she muttered, her lips curving softly despite her embarrassment.

"Only if you're offering another lesson," he bargained.

"Sorry, school's out," she said with a laugh, and urged her horse into a run.

"Damn," he shouted, "and I was looking forward to earning a little extra credit."

He rode after her, forcing the onset of a genuine race. Soon as they galloped over the crest of a hill, they saw the circle of covered wagons below. Fanned out alongside a large, water shed pond, they looked like a scene from the past.

"Last one to the wagons has to have private lessons," challenged Rafferty as Mert bypassed Wind-dancer, LaRue's pony.

"In what?" she shouted.

"Teacher's choice," he said, leering at her over his shoulder.

"You're on," said LaRue, and with a murmured command in her horse's ear, she and Wind-dancer shot past Rafferty and Mert, barreling down the side of the hill. Mert, with an impatient shake of her head, closed the gap again.

Just as they reached level ground and Rafferty thought the race was lost, Mert tossed her head and sniffed the air. Then, like an old steamboat whose furnaces have just been filled with a load of coal, she gave a massive shudder and surged forward, gaining on LaRue's horse and passing it by. Rafferty turned to give her a triumphant wave, but his glee was short-lived. As he turned back, bending low over Mert's corded neck, his eyes caught sight of the huge expanse of water ahead. It glittered ominously in the morning sunshine.

Damn! In his preoccupation with LaRue, he'd forgotten all about Mert's little problem. He snatched the hat from his head and clapped it over her eyes, but it was too late. Having already focused on the pond, Mert ran headlong toward it, and it became quite obvious to Rafferty that nothing was going to deter her. He swiftly calculated his options and decided that it would be less risky to remain in the saddle and go out in a blaze of glory than to bail out at that speed.

They hit the water with a jarring impact, and Rafferty concentrated all his efforts on keeping his feet free of the stirrups so that the force of Mert's dive whisked him backward, out of the saddle and into the water at a safe distance from her flailing hoofs. He went under once and came up spluttering, to watch the horse roll and turn, snorting and blowing water. As he waded back toward shore, he found himself thinking she might benefit from a session or two with an animal psychologist.

LaRue had dismounted and was standing at the edge of the pond, doubled over with laughter.

"Oh, Rafferty," she moaned, hand over her mouth, "I'm sorry—but you looked so funny!"

"Oh, yeah?" He stopped, clothes streaming water, and put his hands on his hips. "That's all you thought of? How funny I looked? Not whether I would be killed or not?"

"Come on," she choked, eyes crinkled with merriment. "Pond water isn't that dangerous."

"Then I guess you wouldn't mind going in for a little dip?" he said, suddenly striding toward her.

LaRue uttered a small scream and started to run, but Rafferty caught her around the waist and scooped her into his arms.

"Rafferty," she cried, thrilled and terrified by the unexpected contact with his hard, clammy chest and the steel-edged grip of his arms. "I'm sorry... really! I apologize for laughing.... Oh! Rafferty!"

He walked straight into knee-deep water and, with a wicked grin, gave her a toss that sent her flying through the air to land with a spectacular splash. She came up gasping for air, her hair plastered over her face.

"I'll get you for this," she threatened, using the heels of her hands to wipe the water from her eyes.

"Get me? You can't deny it was your fault that I had to ride such a demented animal," he stated indignantly. "I'm the one who's supposed to be mad."

"Well, you're not the only one," she yelled. "You make me furious!"

He began to laugh, further infuriating her, and she moved through the water toward him, teeth clenched and hands balled into fists.

Just as she got within striking range, Rafferty seized her and, with his hands at either side of her waist, lifted her high, holding her tightly against the length of his body. Despite the barriers of wet clothing, heat sizzled between them. LaRue's hand raised to his shoulders and her hips wriggled into closer contact with his. Rafferty's hands slid around her, one pressing the small of her back, the other cupping her buttocks.

"God, LaRue, I..."

Whatever he had been about to say was lost as his mouth seared hers, burning away anything but the sensations that tore through them. They clung together, enmeshed in the fierce kiss, Rafferty only vaguely aware of the small crowd gathering on the shore. It was only when he was aching with compelling needs—not the least of which was the necessity for breath—that they broke the embrace and became increasingly aware of their surroundings. A spattering of applause and a few bold remarks from the various drivers greeted them. Rafferty felt his face redden, and LaRue hid hers against his soaked shoulder. He could feel her moan inwardly, and he regretted having placed her in this embarrassing situation.

"All right, everyone," Levi Tate said, "the show's over. Let's get the wagons moving."

As the others reluctantly headed back toward the wagon train, LaRue pushed weakly against Rafferty's chest and he set her down, keeping an arm at her waist to steady her. She gave her grandfather a guilty glance.

"I'm sorry it took us so long to get here..." Her words faded, but the color in her cheeks didn't.

Levi studied them intently for a few, long moments. "No harm done, sister. As long as you're okay."

Their eyes met and held, and Rafferty began to feel like a rooster who suspects he's about to become Sunday dinner.

"I'm fine, Grandpa," she assured the older man. "Just fine." She started wading toward him. "Never better."

No one could fail to detect the meaning loosely disguised by her words. Rafferty knew she was defending him, letting Levi know that he had better not create a scene.

"Look, this was all my fault," Rafferty said, unwilling to hide behind LaRue's drenched skirts, figuratively speaking. "I apologize for any delay we've caused you."

"No problem," Levi said without rancor. "And I never was concerned about...delay."

"Then what?" asked LaRue. "I'm fine. Rafferty's fine. All our business has been taken care of." She grimaced at her own choice of words.

"And we're all set to get moving," Rafferty quickly added. "We could use some excitement for a change."

Levi reached into his pocket for a sack of tobacco, his expression guarded. He tucked a wad into his cheek and presently said, "Lord, but you two must think I'm a dumb old geezer."

With that, he rolled up the foil pouch, stuck it back into his pocket, turned and walked away.

"He knows," LaRue said in a flat voice.

"We weren't doing much to hide our feelings," Rafferty pointed out.

"Maybe not . . . but I'm a grown woman, and there's nothing he can say. So he'd better not try to lecture me."

"Sugar, it's only natural that he'd be worried about you," Rafferty said, gently.

"Oh, you're right, of course," she said with a sigh.

"After all, you really don't know much about me. He's only concerned that you might get in over your head." He smiled. "And not just in the pond."

"Poor Grandpa. He's probably imagining all sorts of things—"

"Like shotgun weddings?" Rafferty interjected with a laugh.

"Sure," she said, starting toward the wagons. "I mean, how could he know that we're two sensible people who realize the truth . . . that while this has been fun, in a few days you'll go back to Washington, and I'll stay here to take up where I left off."

Filled with despair at her casual words, Rafferty watched her retreating back.

Now how in the hell does she figure that? he thought. *I haven't said one damned word about going home. She'd better not be thinking she'll get rid of me that easily.*

For a few seconds he considered going after her to explain that he was no longer so anxious to return to Washington, but he decided the timing might not be right. After the scene she'd just been through, perhaps he'd better wait for a more propitious moment.

LaRue felt her feet dragging. She should have known better than to expect Rafferty to come after her to refute her assumption that he would soon be gone, leaving her behind. His silence effectively dashed the scant hope she'd allowed herself.

That afternoon they traveled through a privately-owned game preserve, and the sight of grazing buffalo only added to the feeling of being in another time. Hollister snapped pictures wildly, exclaiming with pleasure over every shaggy bull or awkward calf trailing its mother. He experimented by taking several close shots of buffalo, with the covered wagons in the background, hoping for a cover photo to accompany the article he was putting together.

In the evening, they made camp just beyond the preserve, at the foot of a hill so steep the ascent would have to be made on foot, with the wagons empty. The weather had grown noticeably warmer in the last few days, so most of the passengers drifted away from the cooking fire to eat their supper of ham steaks, roasted sweet potatoes and fried apples. After the meal, while LaRue helped Ragweed and Gertie with the cleanup, Rafferty went in search of Quincy.

"Have any saddlesoap?" he asked the foreman. "My saddle got a little wet this morning...."

Quincy grinned. "Yeah, I noticed that. I also noticed that you and the boss lady have gotten pretty friendly."

There was no malice in the statement, so Rafferty just nodded. Ever since his encounter with Quincy the night Rafferty had first kissed LaRue, a more comfortable relationship had grown between them. Quincy treated Rafferty with new respect, and Rafferty, now that he knew LaRue had no interest in the lanky cowboy, had relaxed his guard.

"I'm a damned fool for getting carried away and embarrassing her in front of everyone like that," Rafferty said flatly. "I don't think Levi liked it much."

Quincy's eyes sparkled. "But I reckon 'Rue did, and that's all that matters." He gave Rafferty a shrewd look. "You know, I admire you fer takin' the blame, but durned if I can help thinkin' it must've suited LaRue jist fine. She didn't throw a single punch."

The two men laughed companionably. "Thank God for that," Rafferty muttered.

"I'm real glad about it, too, cuz she's needed someone like you fer a long time. It gits pretty lonely for her, sometimes."

"I only hope she isn't too stubborn to see that."

Quincy shrugged. "She didn't look to be resistin' too much this morning. Come on, I'll git you that saddlesoap. Know how to use it?"

Rafferty listened while Quincy gave him a crash course in saddlesoaping leather, then set to work. They had been chatting amiably for several minutes when Quincy suddenly fell silent. Rafferty looked up to see Levi standing over him.

"I want to talk to you, Rafferty."

Knowing it had only been a matter of time, Rafferty said, "Sure. What's on your mind?"

"LaRue."

"I thought so. What do you want to know?"

"Quincy," snapped Levi, "git outa here and give us some privacy."

With a wink and a nod at Rafferty, Quincy ambled out of earshot to lean against a wagon wheel and light up a cigarette. Rafferty wondered if the man thought he'd better stick close, just in case something happened. Levi had always been so mild-mannered, it was difficult to imagine him losing control.

"I don't need to ask no questions to know what's goin' on between the two of you," Levi stated. "And it really ain't none of my business, cuz 'Rue's a grown woman."

Rafferty was frankly surprised that the other man was modern enough to realize LaRue didn't need his permission to live her own life. He seemed like such a throwback to the Old West that Rafferty had almost expected outraged indignation and the challenge to a duel. As it turned out, Tate was going to be reasonable, filling Rafferty with the urge to reassure him.

"I know you're concerned about your granddaughter, Levi, and I don't blame you. I would be, too, if I were in your position. But, let me assure you, I'll do everything in my power to keep from hurting LaRue. God knows, that's the last thing I want to have happen."

"You sayin' you got honorable intentions?"

Rafferty had to smile. "Yeah, I think I do." His smile faltered a bit. "Of course, there's a lot that needs to be worked out, and I'm not at all sure how or when to approach her. But, Levi, I'm in love with LaRue. I want some kind of future with her."

"Well, it's been a mite sudden . . . but I approve." The white moustache twitched slightly.

With a sigh of relief, Rafferty said, "I'm glad. I wasn't really certain how you'd take the news."

"I'm takin' it real fine, now that I know I ain't gonna have to horsewhip you."

For the first time, Rafferty caught sight of the coiled whip Levi held against one leg.

Rafferty's eyes widened and his mouth thinned into a straight line. "Damn it, Levi—I hope you're joking about using that thing."

Levi chuckled. "Hell, I ain't used this whip in years. Probably wouldn't even remember how."

Rafferty relaxed. "Good."

"Well, now that we understand each other, I'll let you git back to yer soapin'. 'Night, Rafferty."

"Good night."

Rafferty watched the old man walk away on scrawny, bowed legs, silently admiring his audacity in approaching a man more than thirty years younger and sixty pounds heavier, armed with nothing but bluff courage and an ineffectual bullwhip. That had to be where LaRue had gotten her grit.

As he spied the red ash on Quincy's cigarette, Levi stopped short.

"How many times do I have to tell you it's too dry to be smokin' out here on the range?"

With that, he uncoiled the whip he carried, easily flicking it through the air to sever the cigarette in Quincy's mouth neatly in half. He strode away without a look back.

"Dad-damned old fool," stormed Quincy, busily stomping out the cigarette lying on the ground at his feet.

Rafferty stood with his mouth agape, unable to say a single word.

A short time later Rafferty went in search of LaRue and found her in one of the covered wagons, reading.

"Hi," he said softly. "You trying to avoid me?"

Startled, LaRue jumped and nearly overturned the lantern she was using.

"Careful," warned Rafferty, starting to climb up into the wagon.

"No, don't get in here," she admonished, steadying the lantern.

"Why not?"

"Well . . ."

"You're worried about what people will say, aren't you?"

She nodded. "We've already given them plenty to talk about."

He frowned. "That was my fault, and I'm sorry."

"Quincy told me that . . . Grandpa had a talk with you," she said, hesitantly. "Was he mad?"

"No, he was very reasonable. Probably more than most men would have been in the same situation."

"I suppose you've never been lectured by the menfolk of any of your Washington women, have you?" She gave him a forlorn smile, making a feeble try at humor.

"I can't say that I have," he replied, his features lighted by an answering smile. "Guess that just goes to show how serious things have gotten between you and me."

She chose to ignore that remark. "I'm sorry about Grandpa," she said. "I hope he didn't say anything too awful."

"As a matter of fact, I was impressed with his liberal attitude, all things considered. I sure was glad I'd given him all the right answers, though, once I saw that bullwhip."

"Bullwhip? My God, Quincy never mentioned that. Oh, Rafferty, I'm sorry."

"Prove it, then," he teasingly challenged. "Either let me get in this wagon or go for a walk with me."

"But—"

"Look, I promise to behave. The moon's almost full, so I can't get you off in the darkness somewhere. People won't see anything but us strolling along the edge of the pond. What do you say?"

"All right." She sighed heavily. "There are some things we need to talk about, I guess."

She turned out the lantern and stepped to the back of the wagon. Rafferty put up his arms to lift her down, but once her feet were on the ground, he released her.

"See how honorable I intend to be?" he asked. "Though it isn't easy, I assure you. That kiss this morning left me . . . very unsatisfied."

LaRue looked miserable. "I know."

"Still, we knew this would happen—that once we got back to the train, we couldn't just do as we pleased. We should have been prepared."

"I know that, too. But it doesn't help."

He put out a tentative hand, wanting to stroke her cheek, then let it drop. "We'd better start walking, sugar, or all our good intentions are going to be forgotten."

They had gone only a few yards before Rafferty's hand closed over hers. Even that simple gesture would draw notice, she knew, but the warm security of his grip was so pleasant that LaRue decided not to argue the point.

"Look, there's a ring around the moon," she said as they approached the edge of the water. "Sign of unsettled weather."

Hung crookedly in the night sky, the moon looked like a tarnished silver coin tossed carelessly against dark, billowy cushions of cloud. It was surrounded by a pale golden circle of haze.

"Probably a storm to come," agreed Rafferty. "There are a couple of stars in the ring, so supposedly it'll rain for two days."

"You believe in that sort of thing?" she asked, surprised.

"I once had a class in meteorology where the professor lectured for an entire week on old sayings and weather superstitions."

"You mean sayings like: the first killing frost comes three months after the katydids start singing? Or, it'll rain within a few days if the horns of a crescent moon point downward?" she queried.

"Exactly. My professor believed in folklore—said it wouldn't still be around if farmers hadn't found some merit in it."

They paused at the rim of the pond, watching the moon's light gleam on the choppy, restless water.

"Grandpa always says the twelve days following Christmas will tell you what the next twelve months will be like," LaRue said, absently wiggling her fingers just so Rafferty would tighten his grip. His broad palm rubbing against hers made a pleasurable sensation spiral upward along her arm.

"And I'll bet he plants potatoes in the dark of the moon," Rafferty chuckled, looking down at her. "And harvests them when the moon is old."

"Yeah, and we always eat black-eyed peas on New Year's Day for good luck."

"So do I," he said. "And I hate black-eyed peas."

They laughed together, but as their eyes met, the laughter slowly faded. Rafferty's hand slid up to encircle her wrist, and LaRue's mouth went dry at the look in his eyes.

"Did you know that if a woman carries an acorn in her pocket, she'll never grow old?" she said faintly.

He shook his head. "Uh-uh."

"Or that sleeping in the moonlight makes you insane?"

"I'm finding out that *standing* in it does. God, LaRue, you don't know what's going through my mind."

"Oh, yes, I do," she murmured. "What do you think is going through mine?"

His gaze swept over her oval face, from the dark fire in her glowing eyes to the inviting glimmer of her soft mouth.

"Are we in trouble here or what?" he joked.

"It's entirely possible."

"Lord, I can't think of anything but how much I want to kiss you," he said, his voice harsh.

"I want it, too. But the rest of the passengers are right over there, looking on. I have to think of Grandpa. I don't want my actions to shame him."

"You're right. We have more than just ourselves to worry about. If that were all there was..."

She nodded in agreement with the unspoken thought.

"Look, LaRue, there's something I've got to tell you."

"All right. And then there's something I need to tell you."

"The night at the ranch, when I said I loved you? Well, I know you thought I was pretending, but I wasn't. That night never seemed like a game to me, LaRue. It was the single most memorable event of my life."

"Yes, I know."

"You believe me?"

She nodded affirmatively. "I have to, because I felt the same way."

"What way?" He asked the unnecessary question simply for the pleasure of hearing her answer it.

"I love you, Rafferty... *really* love you."

Rafferty shifted his weight from foot to foot, wanting to throw his arms around her, but struggling for control.

"Damn," he muttered, "why does the most important discussion of our relationship have to take place within view of a dozen curious people?"

"Maybe so we won't cloud the issue with kisses or lovemaking?" she suggested.

"Well, that sort of thing does tend to take the importance out of mere words." He grinned. "I can't believe I fell in love with a cowgirl. I'd never even seen a real one until I came out here."

"I know—and that's a problem. Rafferty, I'm not the type of person who can fall in love, have a fling and then forget it."

"I'm glad. I'm not that way, either."

"I thought you were anxious to go back to Washington."

"No. Does that disappoint you?"

"It scares me. What are we going to do about it?"

"I don't know," he admitted. "But I'll work on it."

"There are so many things we can't just overlook."

"Yes, and I'm well aware of what they are—"

At that moment an errant cloud dared to drift in front of the moon, temporarily obscuring its light. Swiftly, Rafferty tugged on LaRue's wrist, spinning her into hard contact with his chest. His mouth wasted no time seeking hers, and after her initial surprise, she responded eagerly. The kiss had to contain a night's worth of love and passion, for both knew it was all they could allow themselves.

Rafferty groaned with frustrated delight as he felt her lips part, her tongue tentatively searching the contours of his mouth. He knew he would feel the press of her body against his for many long, sleepless hours.

And then the moon reappeared and they drew apart, becoming just two ordinary people out for an evening walk.

Chapter Sixteen

"Weather on the prairie is like a contrary woman...either it'll ignore you, or it'll fuss and fume, and try to rip your head off."
—Dr. Willoby Coles,
Emporia, Kansas, 1885

By the next afternoon the walk in the cool moonlight seemed only a dream. It had been a long day, the most grueling of the entire overland trip.

It had started out with all the passengers walking so the teams could haul the covered wagons up the steep hillside more easily. As the morning progressed, it became sultry, with the hot air still and unmoving. The oppressive humidity filled the atmosphere with moisture, blurring what would otherwise have been a magnificent vista from the crown of the hill.

Lunch had been a rather silent event, with the unusual heat enervating even the most lively members of the train.

Around four o'clock, a cool breeze sprang up, bringing a false sense of relief.

"Thank God for a little cool air," Hollister Ames exclaimed, his bare feet sticking out the end of one of the wagons. "One more hour of this blessed heat and I was going to go mad and strangle you, J.B."

Rafferty, who was riding close by, wiped his brow and cast a sympathetic glance at Hollister. The other man was wearing a white shirt and dress slacks, and looked thoroughly miserable.

"Don't get into a benevolent mood too soon," he warned. "If we get the storm I'm expecting, you still may want to do me in."

"Storm?" Holly raised his eyes to the sky overhead. "It doesn't look stormy to me."

The sky was a flat, pale sweep of steely blue, with only a few wisps of cloud in sight.

"I hope I'm wrong...but I'm not counting on it."

Thirty minutes later, the breezes were even cooler and off in the southwest a wall of blue-black clouds was building. An occasional flicker of lightning flashed along the horizon, followed by the low, rumbling boom of distant thunder.

Levi reined in, signaling the wagons to stop. "Looks like a pretty bad storm comin'," he shouted, his leathery face set into deep lines. "We ain't gonna be able to outrun it, I'm afraid. Reckon we'd better find what cover we can."

"Wanna head toward the old Wilson place?" Quincy spoke up. "It's low ground and there's a shelter of sorts."

"'Spect that's about all we can do," Levi responded. "And if we don't get a move on, we ain't even gonna make it there."

The drivers turned off the worn wagon trail and followed Quincy's lead with little regard for their passengers' comfort. There wasn't one of them who didn't realize the danger of being caught out in the open during a bad storm. Their faces were grim as they clutched the wooden sideboards and strained their eyes for any sign of shelter.

Just as Levi shouted and pointed toward a circle of trees and the crumbling rooftop of an old farmstead, a wicked streak of lightning sliced through the layer of black clouds rapidly cloaking the sky. Immediately afterward a deafening crash of thunder startled men and horses alike.

Rafferty didn't have to urge Mert to hurry; she dogged the heels of LaRue's pony like an old hound. Still, it seemed an eternity before they followed the wagons through a wide gate and into an overgrown yard. A house, windows broken and roof sagging, was the only cover of any sort. The barn had long since collapsed into a pile of rough lumber, and the storm cellar had caved in, filling up with dirt and rocks.

The wind began to gust, feeling as if it was blowing directly off arctic ice floes; its howl was eerie. The clouds overhead were boiling angrily, churning across the sun, making the afternoon dark and ominous.

"Get out of those wagons," Levi yelled, leaping off his horse. "No need to try and circle 'em—jist git out now!"

The drivers struggled to unhitch the teams of animals, while the senator and environmentalists ran for shelter.

"Don't go inside the house," LaRue shouted. "That roof might not survive a storm. Get underneath."

She flung herself off her horse and began herding the men toward the crawl space beneath the swaybacked front porch.

"Good thinkin', sister," Levi said in approval. "Not so much to come down on top of 'em there." He glanced up at the bruised sky. "This is real twister weather, ain't it?"

"Yes, it looks bad," Rafferty affirmed.

Levi turned to check the release of the final team of horses. With a slap on their rumps, he shooed the animals from the traces and made a dash for the house.

Rafferty slid off his horse and anchored his cowboy hat more firmly on his head. The wind was whipping about him with almost maniacal force, and bits of grass and twigs whirled past. He grabbed for Mert's reins and those of Wind-dancer, tying the horses securely to the back wheel of one of the wagons. Then, with a last appraising look at the oncoming storm, he ran across the yard and slipped beneath the splintered front steps into the musty space under the porch.

"Damn," Levi was saying, "I sure hope Ragweed and Gertie didn't git caught out in this."

"They probably saw the storm coming," LaRue said. "I'll bet they're sitting in town somewhere drinking coffee."

"Good Lord, look at that," gasped Holly, his face pressed to the unpainted lattice board that fronted the crawl space.

The others crouched low, peering upward. All along the sharp black edge of the storm were little tails of cloud, being spun out by the fierce wind.

"Any one of 'em could turn into a funnel," observed Levi, frowning.

Rafferty draped an arm across LaRue's shoulders, thankful they had made it to shelter in time. The open prairie was no place to be in weather like this.

"Jesus Christ!" breathed Ned Jackson. "Would you look at that?"

One of the tag ends of the cloud had dropped even lower and was now working itself into a frenzied whirl. As it dipped closer to the ground, the wind it contained formed a vacuum, suctioning dirt, leaves and grass upward, swallowing and then spitting them out again with malevolent force.

LaRue sidled closer to Rafferty, her breath caught in her throat as she watched. There could be no doubt about the tornado's capacity for destruction, just as there was no question of man's inability to prevent it. Feeling small and helplessly human, the members of the wagon train could only stare in horror at nature gone berserk.

The deadly-looking funnel covered the ground swiftly, looming against the darkened sky. Accompanying it was a dull roar that grew increasingly louder, like the rumble of an oncoming freight train.

"My God, it's on the ground," Holly half whispered.

The lashing tail of the funnel caught a row of hedge trees, sweeping through them quickly, leaving them bare-topped and grotesquely twisted. Then, angling in another direction, it began moving purposefully toward the old house. A collective moan of terror escaped the onlookers as the twister engulfed the collapsed barn, sucking up shingles, broken boards and moldy straw, to rain them down on the earth again with lethal intensity. The grasping tentacle of cloud reached for the first covered wagon, and to those watching, it looked as though the wagon simply exploded, sending splintered wood, jagged scraps of canvas and contorted pieces of iron flying. Falling debris struck the warped porch overhead, creating a deafening din. LaRue's hand clutched Rafferty's shoulder, her fingers digging painfully deep.

"The horses," she cried suddenly, surging to her knees. "Someone left the horses tied!"

Before anyone realized her intention, LaRue darted out from beneath the porch, determined to reach Mert and Wind-dancer before the funnel did. Rafferty's heart plunged and rolled over in his chest.

"LaRue!" he shouted, his words lost in the roar of the storm. He crawled from the shelter to go after her, trying not to think of her being struck down and killed for fear he would make it happen. He raced across the littered yard, chanting her name in soft, breathless desperation.

LaRue's hair whipped about her head, stinging her eyes and impeding her vision, but her hands were rapid and sure as she unknotted the reins and set the horses free with a smart slap on each rump. With terrified whinnies, both animals danced and reared, then galloped blindly in the opposite direction from the funnel.

Just as LaRue turned back toward the crumbling house, a flying board struck a glancing blow to her forehead and she stumbled and fell. She lay sprawled and unmoving, the wind tearing at her hair and clothing. Rafferty was at her side immediately, dropping his body over hers to shield her while trash continued to drop from the tornado whirling above them.

"Are you hurt?" he shouted, his searching fingers locating the pulse in her neck. She groaned and stirred, and he felt weak with relief.

"I'll be okay," she managed to say, though his protective weight made speaking almost impossible. "No thanks to the damned fool who tied up those horses...."

Rafferty felt her stiffen as if she had just realized who that damned fool had to be.

"Look," he muttered into her ear, "you can call me any names you want, but later, okay? For now, we'd better concentrate on staying alive."

She nodded, winced at the pain and lay still beneath him. Rafferty spread his legs to cover hers, then crossed his arms over their heads and began recalling every prayer he'd ever learned. A barrage of small boards and sticks struck his back and shoulders and the crazed wind plucked at his clothing.

He couldn't judge how long they lay there before the storm began to lose force. One moment he was trying to keep horrible thoughts of being snatched up by the funnel out of his mind, the next he was realizing the roar was abating. Slowly the noise of the storm faded and was gone. Only then did he dare raise his head and look about.

The others were pouring from beneath the porch, picking their way through the storm-strewn yard toward them.

"How bad's she hurt?" Levi rasped, dropping to one knee.

"I think she'll be all right." Rafferty moved aside, gently helping LaRue sit up.

"I'm fine, Grandpa," she muttered, fighting dizziness. "It's only a little bump on the head."

"Maybe it'll knock some sense into ya," he groused, though his relief was apparent. "You knew better than to run out in a storm like that."

"Of course I knew better—but I couldn't let those horses get killed."

"It was my fault," Rafferty admitted. "I wasn't thinking when I tied them up. Guess I was too engrossed in everything else that was going on."

"That's natural, son," Levi soothed. "This probably bein' yer first twister and all. The important thing is that neither of you got hurt. Though we oughta have a closer look at that bruise, 'Rue. It's pretty nasty."

"I can't believe it," Holly was saying as the others helped LaRue to her feet. "The big cloud just sucked that funnel right back up like it had never been." He tapped his ever-present camera. "I hope the pictures I took turn out okay. If they don't sell a magazine article, nothing will."

"Here comes the rain," shouted Quincy, pointing to a curtain of gray stretching across the pasture. "Better get into the wagons—looks like it's gonna last a while."

No sooner had Rafferty lifted LaRue into the back of one of the wagons than the rain began. Though the sky had lightened considerably, it was now tinged with the yellowish-green color that presages a hailstorm, and, indeed, the rainfall was liberally mixed with pea-sized balls of ice that twanged against the canvas covers. As Rafferty waited for Levi to climb into the wagon, hailstones rattled against his hat brim and stung his skin through his soaked shirt. Once inside, he huddled on one of the side benches, cold, wet and miserable.

He looked down at his hands, which had unexpectedly begun to shake. Damn! He deserved to be miserable after the stupid, greenhorn stunt he'd pulled. His forehead prickled with sweat as he remembered the sight of LaRue dashing out into the storm and being struck down. He knew how easily she could have been killed. It galled him to be the one who'd put her in danger. God knew it was the last thing on earth he'd wanted to do.

He stole a quick look at her. She was sitting patiently while her grandfather fussed over the darkening bruise on her temple. Rafferty thought she looked worried, but as soon as he caught her eyes, she smiled and he knew her concern was for him. His heart felt like a wrung-out dishcloth as he struggled with feelings of unworthiness. Lord, he'd been responsible for nearly getting her killed and she still looked at him as though he was the most important thing in her life. Rafferty shoved his guilt aside and moved across the wagon to sit next to her. He took her hand and her fingers curled trustingly within his.

"Sugar, I—I'm so sorry," he stammered. "I don't know how I could have been so damned ignorant."

"It's all right," she said gently. "Really."

"I thought I'd die when I saw you run out into the storm. And when you got hurt..." His voice dried up abruptly and he dropped his head, unable to express the horror he'd felt.

Levi clapped a hand on Rafferty's shoulder. "No need to dwell on it. You'll know better next time."

Rafferty's grin was sardonic. "Is it too much to hope there'll never be a next time?"

The hail didn't last long, but by the time the rain had slowed to a drizzle, it was growing dark. The men busied themselves rounding up the horses and moving the wagons out of the storm-ravaged hollow onto higher ground. Everyone felt a real sense of relief when they saw Ragweed and Gertie approaching, chuckwagon in tow.

"Hell, the storm missed us," Ragweed informed them, "but we figured you was gittin' it. Looks like it did some real damage."

"Yeah, but at least we only lost one wagon," replied Levi, "and none of the livestock was injured."

"Hey," interjected Quincy, "you got anythin' fer supper?"

"How about havin' a weiner roast?" asked Gertie. "You menfolk can put up a canopy so we'll have a dry spot to sit."

The excitement caused by the tornado lasted throughout the evening, despite the fact that the rain returned with a vengeance before midnight.

In the wagon he shared with Hollister, Rafferty tossed and turned in his bedroll, reliving the events of the afternoon. Over and over, one thing came to mind—he had come dangerously close to losing LaRue forever. It could happen so quickly, so easily! The knowledge forced him to make a decision on a matter he had been turning over in his mind for the last few days. No one could outwit the vagaries of fate, of course, but at least he could quit wasting valuable time and take steps to ensure that he and LaRue would be together for as long as possible.

Satisfied with his latest plan of action, Rafferty lay quietly, thinking of LaRue and listening to Holly's soft snores. Eventually, the monotonous drum of raindrops lulled him to sleep.

It was still raining the following morning, so Levi declared it a day of rest.

"Ain't no sense tryin' to travel in this weather," he said, reaching for his tobacco. "Might as well sit here and play cards as be out there, knee-deep in mud. It won't take us long to git back to Sin Creek anyway."

LaRue and Rafferty exchanged long, meaningful looks. Returning to the ranch meant they would have to face their differences, once and for all. It was a frightening thought for both of them.

Huddled together under the canvas canopy, the members of the wagon train ate homemade vegetable soup and cherry cobbler for supper, then sat back to listen to Smoky and Quincy regale them with stories of the Texas trail drives they had worked on before coming to Sin Creek. Eventually, just before the sun dropped behind the horizon, one of the cowboys took out a harmonica and began to play. Tilting his hat over his forehead, Quincy leaned back and took up the tune.

"Oh, Shenandoah, I long to hear you,
And see your rollin' river,
Oh, Shenandoah, I long to hear you . . ."

One or two of the others joined in.

"Away, I'm bound away,
'Cross the wide Missouri."

Rafferty bent to whisper into LaRue's ear. "Rain's almost gone. Come for a walk with me?"

She got to her feet, reaching for his hand. As they left the shelter of the canopy, they stepped into a sparklingly clean world. Despite a few scattered raindrops, the clouds had cleared away, leaving a blue sky washed in the pale colors of sunset.

The prairie grasses, bent low beneath the weight of heavy moisture, were a startling green, and a whole new crop of wildflowers seemed to carpet the pastures.

"Hard to remember there was such a storm yesterday, isn't it?" LaRue asked, picking her way carefully over the slippery grass.

"It wouldn't be if we were back down at the old farmstead. Those ruined trees will tell the story for a long, long time." Rafferty slipped an arm around her waist. "How's your head today?"

"It hasn't bothered me at all," she answered. "I wish you would quit worrying about it."

"*I* just wish I hadn't done such a stupid thing in the first place. No," he said, seeing her start to protest, "don't try to make me feel better." He stopped, placing his hands on her shoulders. "Listen, LaRue, this has made several things a lot clearer to me. We've got to talk."

"What about?"

"Us. The future."

She shifted uneasily. "Rafferty, I'm not sure what you have in mind, but...."

"Marriage is what I have in mind," he said softly. "*Our* marriage."

LaRue lowered her lashes, hiding the expression in her eyes.

"Sugar, let me see what you're thinking," he admonished, putting a finger beneath her chin and gently raising her face. "I need to know how you feel about this."

"I feel ... confused," she admitted.

"But why?"

"Well, do you mean—?"

"I mean you and me," he broke in, "standing before a minister. You and me together for the rest of our lives. Eating at the same table, sleeping in the same bed. Raising a bunch of young cowboys and cowgirls."

LaRue smiled mistily. "You do an impressive proposal, Rafferty, but your timing is way off."

"What do you mean?"

She cupped his elbows with her hands and stood on tiptoe to look up into his face. "We can't be making any plans for the future until ... until the prairie-park issue is settled."

"The two have nothing to do with each other," he stated flatly.

"But they do," she insisted. "Oh, I can't deny that it's tempting to just say yes and forget all the problems, but I can't do that. There's too much at stake for Grandpa and the others. For me." Her eyes begged him for understanding. "For us."

"Are you saying that your acceptance of my marriage proposal will be based on my verdict about the park?"

"It isn't as callous as it sounds, Rafferty." Her fingers tugged nervously at his shirt sleeves. "And I'm not trying to pressure you to make the decision I want. The last thing I intend to do is issue any sort of ultimatum. I hope you know that."

"I didn't think that was what you were trying to do," he murmured, smiling for the first time. "Honey, I realize how important this park thing is to you. Would it make any difference if I said I—''

''Shh,'' she cautioned, placing a silencing finger against his lips. ''Don't make any promises you may not be able to keep... please. I'd rather you waited until after we get back to the ranch before you decide what to do. Then, once the town meeting is over, if you still feel the same way, we'll have this conversation.''

''There's no need to wait,'' he argued, but again her finger pressed his lips.

''Don't, please. First things first, all right?''

''Oh, all right. Just promise me one thing.''

''What's that?''

''That you won't marry anyone else in the meantime.''

LaRue laughed. ''I promise.''

''Now, I'd like very much to kiss you. Do you suppose that would be acceptable?''

''Well, I don't think it would come as any great surprise to anyone. I have a feeling they've all figured out how matters stand.''

He bent his head, caressing the bruise on her temple before letting his mouth drift downward to hers. LaRue strained against him, thrilled to be in his arms again, but relieved that he was reasonable enough to honor her request for time. God, she hoped that things could work out for them. She wasn't at all positive she could survive without him now.

''Look,'' Rafferty whispered when he finally tore his mouth from hers. ''There's a rainbow.''

She turned within his embrace so that her back rested against his chest, his arms folded tightly around her waist. She caught her breath when she saw the rainbow. It was a brilliant arch of color across the evening sky.

''That's a lucky sign, isn't it?'' she asked, her voice husky.

He buried his face in her sweetly scented hair. ''I hope so, sugar. I sure as hell hope so.''

From the campfire came a low drift of song.

''Wagon wheels, wagon wheels....

Keep on a-turnin', you wagon wheels.

Roll along, sing your song—wagon wheels, carry me home.''

Chapter Seventeen

"In the rodeo of life, we don't bust many broncs.
'Bout the best we can hope for is to end up safe in the
barrel with the clown...."
— Shorty McClenahan, bulldogger,
Saffordville, Kansas, 1888

To Rafferty, returning to Sin Creek felt like coming home,
and he decided that was another good omen. It seemed to ver-
ify that he was ready to move out of his old life and into a new
one with LaRue.

The first night back at the ranch found him waxing nostal-
gic. After supper, while LaRue helped Mrs. Mendoza prepare
bedrooms for all the guests, Rafferty sat on the screened porch
with Levi and several of the environmentalists. Down at the
corrals, the hired hands were rounding up livestock for the
amateur rodeo the Tates were hosting the following evening.
The lusty bawling of the calves mingled with the shouts of the
men, taking Rafferty back to his boyhood. How he'd loved the
excitement of rodeo time at his uncle's dude ranch! The heat of

the sun, the taste of the dust, the bold laughter of swaggering cowboys—it had been a dream come true for a boy from the city.

Well, look at that boy now, he thought, his face stretching in a wide grin. His fingers curled involuntarily, as if aching for the feel of worn leather or the burn of a rope. When Levi suggested they take a walk down to the corral, Rafferty eagerly agreed. He was determined to be a part of this rodeo, as he had never been allowed to be as a child. He wanted to prove to LaRue and the others that he had a place here. But more than that, he wanted to prove it to himself.

It was after eleven o'clock when he returned to the house. Slipping quietly down the hallway, he paused outside LaRue's room. Seeing a crack of light along the bottom of her door, he tapped softly and turned the knob.

LaRue had fallen asleep reading. Her face looked pale in the lamplight, the bruise purplish-dark by contrast to her smooth ivory skin.

Rafferty silently crossed the room to stand looking down at her. He thought she looked exhausted. Carefully, he removed the book from her limp hands, closed it and laid it on the bedside table. As much as he wanted to tell her about his plans for the rodeo, he knew she needed her sleep. He'd tell her later...or maybe even save it as a surprise.

Unwilling to wake her, he controlled an urge to kiss her goodnight, switched off the lamp and tiptoed out of the room.

Amateur rodeo or not, it seemed a big portion of the populations of Cottonwood Falls and Strong City had turned out for it. The temporary bleachers set up at either end of the largest corral were full, and cars and trucks lined the driveway and both sides of the road for a half mile in each direction.

Rafferty moved through the crowd with an ever-increasing sense of pride. Pride in the traditions being kept alive at Sin Creek, and pride in the old man and his gritty granddaughter who struggled to keep those traditions alive. He couldn't think of anything he wanted more than to become a part of it all himself.

Mistaking him for one of the ranch hands, a woman with two small children in tow stopped to ask him directions to the concession stand the Harrises were running. He thought he remembered her from the town meeting, but it was obvious she didn't recognize him as the government biologist. Pleased to be taken for an ordinary cowboy, Rafferty grinned and pointed her in the right direction. Then, settling the Stetson he wore a little lower over his forehead, he started for the corral, a slight but unmistakable swagger to his walk.

He was pleased to encounter Loping Wolf and some of the other Indians. With a wink, the chief informed him that Rocky Armstrong had won his ladylove back and that the couple would be performing the wedding ceremony right before the evening's dance. Rafferty offered his congratulations and assured the Indians he'd be in the audience.

As he rounded the barn, he was greeted by the sight of a half-dozen colorfully dressed cowgirls waiting their turn in the arena for the barrel racing. His eyes moved past the bright satins to the no-nonsense figure dressed in denim and blue chambray. LaRue had come dressed to compete, not merely look pretty. But Rafferty, oblivious to the feminine charms of the other contestants, thought she was the most beautiful thing he had ever seen. There was a lithe grace in the way she swung herself into the saddle, an appealing vulnerability about the nervous adjustment of her hat. She waved a gloved hand as she urged Wind-dancer into the corral, and Rafferty gave her a thumbs-up gesture of encouragement.

Rafferty sauntered over to the fence to watch, and immediately found his heart in his throat. Where had he ever gotten the impression that barrel racing was a sissy competition—something relatively safe that a woman could do and still look pretty while doing it? LaRue rode her horse like a hell-bound demon, wheeling sharply, skirting the barrels neatly, stopping on a dime. At times it appeared that her body, completely melded to Wind-dancer's, was parallel to the ground below. At those times, when it seemed impossible for horse and rider to regain their balance, Rafferty closed his eyes and swallowed deeply. This rodeo business wasn't so damned enjoyable all of a sudden.

When it was over and LaRue had won, as he'd had no doubt she would, Rafferty allowed himself a gigantic sigh of relief. He struggled against the desire to reprimand her for taking such chances and got out words of congratulations instead. When she announced that she had to find Quincy and get ready for the team roping, he bit his lip and shoved his hands deep into his pockets to keep from pulling her into his arms and forbidding her to take any more risks. Over and over he reminded himself that she had been doing this sort of thing all her life—and that it would make her furious to know he was worried about her safety. But he did think it might be best if he sat down for this contest.

Common sense told Rafferty that this event was not a particularly dangerous one, but as soon as he saw the longhorned steer released from the chute, common sense played very little part in his thinking. As the "header," LaRue rode toward the steer, her face a mask of concentration. She took a few practice swings with the lasso she held, then, rising slightly in the saddle, she flung the lariat and it settled unerringly over the animal's horns.

As the crowd breathed in audible admiration, LaRue swiftly dallied the rope, wrapping it around the saddlehorn. Then, riding to the left, she pulled the steer around in an angle that removed all slack from the tether.

Quincy, his arrogant grin exuding confidence, made his approach, taking a couple of practice swings with his lasso. As the "heeler," it was his job to secure the animal's hind legs. This he did with unbelievable speed and accuracy. One second the rope was floating lazily in the air above his head, the next it snaked out, looking very much as if he had bounced it off the ground, and tightened around the steer's legs. The two riders, facing each other, backed their horses until the ropes were taut, the steer lying on his side, quickly and easily subdued for branding or castrating, the original purpose of such roping. This steer fared better than that, for he was released and shooed out of the arena to the approving shouts and applause of the audience.

Rafferty quit holding his breath once LaRue had ridden away, talking and laughing with Quincy. But now that his fear for her had abated, he was experiencing a whole new emotion. Complete and total inadequacy.

Watching LaRue's expertise had left him feeling more like an ignorant tenderfoot than ever. He might as well be a nine-year-old kid again, standing on the sidelines wishing. How could he even begin to consider living out here unless he found some way to fit in?

He pulled the printed program from his shirt pocket and unfolded it. The bronc-busting event was coming up. Could he go through with his plan to enter it? Until just hours ago, he'd planned to ask Quincy for a few pointers and then surprise them all by riding. Naturally, it would be a gold-plated miracle if he managed to stay on for even half the eight seconds required, but the fact that he was willing to try ought to prove something.

Yeah, that I'm an idiot, he thought wryly, hauling his lanky frame off the hard wooden bench.

Still, he had read an awful lot about rodeos—had watched the national finals on TV every year. Maybe he knew more than he thought.

"How hard can it be?" he muttered, stalking off toward the stables. "Keep your head up and your butt in the saddle. How damned difficult can that be?"

He'd survived the overland trip, hadn't he? If he had gotten through that by pretending to be John Wayne, why couldn't he do it again?

And, Rafferty old man, he reminded himself, *it's a chance to make a dream come true.* For his own sake, for the sake of his relationship with LaRue, he'd do it. Sitting and observing, he'd look like a wimp. But getting in there and getting some dirt on his pants would let LaRue know he was at least man enough to try.

Keeping John Wayne firmly in mind, he went looking for Quincy. He had a lot of questions to ask and not much time to ask them.

It wasn't until Rafferty had eased himself into the small bronc-busting saddle, his legs brushing either side of the wooden chute, that he had one last, harrowing thought. With all the movies he'd seen, he suddenly couldn't remember a single one where Duke had ridden a bucking bronc. Not a single one....

All hell broke loose as soon as the gate swung open. Rafferty was aware of little but a roaring in his ears, as if he were below a hundred feet of water, and the unmerciful pounding of his rump on the hard leather saddle. He could almost imagine he was trying to ride the tornado that had ripped across the prairie two days ago. The laugh that pushed upward from his chest was lost in his effort to keep from biting his tongue, and then it was all over anyway. He was sailing backward through the air like a clumsily launched missile, making a three-point landing on one knee, one shoulder and the heel of his hand. He flopped over on his back, realizing what a sickening sound the cracking of bone really was.

"Je-sus Christ!" yelled Quincy, vaulting over the corral fence and racing toward Rafferty. "I told you you were crazy as hell to try this! Why in tarnation couldn't you jist listen to me?"

Levi and a dozen others were right behind Quincy, and Rafferty thought they might suffocate him with their frantic attention.

"I'm okay," he insisted, through clenched teeth. "Except for my arm. Something seems to be wrong with it."

Quincy let loose with another string of swear words, all the time getting a grip on Rafferty's good arm and helping him to his feet. Relieved applause accompanied his limping departure from the arena.

"Get the truck over here," commanded Levi, clearing a way through the gathering cowboys. "We'd better drive him to Emporia to see a doctor."

LaRue had never been so scared. She shoved her way through the crowd, too distraught to apologize. As she got close to the pickup, she could see Rafferty's tall frame just ducking inside. Quincy came around the back of the truck, headed for the driver's side.

"Quincy," she cried, clutching his arm, "how's Rafferty? Is he hurt bad?"

Quincy gave her a cold look. "Why should you care?" he demanded.

"What? What are you talking about?"

"If you cared so damned much for him, why'd you talk him into ridin'?"

LaRue's mouth dropped open in astonishment. "But I—I didn't know anything—Oh, Lord, we don't have time to hash this out now! I'm going to the hospital with you."

"Oh, no, you're not," Quincy snapped, pulling his arm away. "We don't have room."

"I want to go," she insisted. "There might be something I can do."

"I think you've done enough, sister," Levi said quietly. "For once in yer life, jist do as yer told and keep outa the way." He climbed into the passenger side of the truck and slammed the door.

LaRue dashed angry tears from her eyes and watched the rickety pickup roar away. She couldn't believe it. They were mad at *her*! They obviously believed she had put Rafferty up to riding that horse. Of all the ludicrous ideas. How could they think she'd do something as stupid as that?

She considered following them in the car, but decided against it when she realized Rafferty hadn't asked for her, hadn't requested that she go with him. Was he mad at her, too? *Had* she done something to provoke his rash behavior? Could the whole incident in some way really be her fault?

She straightened her shoulders. No, blast it all, she wasn't going to take the responsibility for this. If J. B. Rafferty was fool enough to risk his silly greenhorn neck riding a killer horse, it had nothing to do with her. For all she cared, he could come home with his entire body in a sling!

LaRue didn't go back to the rodeo; instead, she went up to the house and, in a matter of minutes, was talking to one of the supervising nurses at the hospital. The woman, whose husband had purchased horses from the Tates, remembered LaRue. She promised to be on the lookout for Rafferty's arrival and call the moment she knew anything about his condition.

The next hour and a half crept by while LaRue paced the floor and worried. At last the nurse called to say Rafferty had been treated and released, and that his injuries were not serious.

"He may not be able to say that when I get through with him," LaRue muttered after replacing the receiver. "I ought to strangle him!"

Whatever had possessed the man to do such a dumb thing?

Suddenly LaRue smiled. She thought she had just figured it out. It couldn't have been anything but his ego—that small part of the male animal not attached to the brain.

"What the hell you lookin' so down in the mouth about?" Quincy asked, turning off the main road for Sin Creek. "Doc said you was lucky to break yer arm instead of yer fool neck."

"I know," Rafferty mumbled. "And he's right. But that's not what's bothering me."

"What is, then?"

"LaRue."

"Yeah, she's done gone too fer this time," Levi grumbled. "I couldn't believe it."

"Believe what?" Rafferty cocked one black eyebrow in the older man's direction.

"That she'd egg you on till ya rode that danged buckin' bronc. Lord, what was she thinkin' of?"

"Let's face it, Levi," Quincy spoke up. "She's always been a wild little cuss—half sister to the devil, her grandma usta call her."

"Wait a minute," interrupted Rafferty. "Just what is it you two think LaRue has done?"

Levi stroked his bushy moustache. "She suggested you ride that horse, didn't she?"

"No, she didn't. What the—Are you saying that you thought she was the reason I tried riding?"

"Yep, that's what we're sayin'."

"Well, you're wrong. Oh, I guess she is the reason I gave it a try, but she didn't know anything about it. It was my own idea."

"You tellin' us the truth?" Levi demanded.

Rafferty nodded, and Levi and Quincy exchanged chagrined looks.

"Guess we're in pretty deep sheep dip," observed Quincy, with a wide grin. "'Rue'll be after our hides."

"Why?" Rafferty decided the pain killer the doctor had given him was too strong—this conversation wasn't making any sense at all.

"Might as well confess," Levi grumbled. "After the stunts she pulled on the wagon trip, we figgered it was LaRue's fault that you entered the bronc bustin'. We...well, we kinda snapped and growled at her."

"And," finished Quincy, "we wouldn't let her come to the hospital with us."

Rafferty's puzzled expression cleared. "You mean she wanted to?"

"Champin' at the bit," Levi affirmed. "Reckon I mighta been a bit hard on her."

"God, she'll be hoppin' mad when we get back." Quincy shook his head. "Think I'll jist slip on out to the bunkhouse and lay low."

Rafferty chuckled. "Leave it to me, boys. I'll explain everything."

"You never learn, do ya?" Levi almost looked admiring. "Ya got one busted arm. Why would you wanna risk another one?"

"Would you believe that I was depressed because I thought LaRue didn't even care enough to go with me to see the doctor? As soon as we get home, I'll straighten things out."

"Jist hope it ain't yer neck that gits straightened," Levi said, half under his breath.

Rafferty went up the stairs two at a time, groaning as the stiff muscles in his thighs pulled and stretched. As he reached the top step, LaRue opened her door and walked out of her bedroom. She stopped short, staring at Rafferty. After a long moment, they both started to speak at once.

"LaRue, I—"

"Raff—"

They broke off, and Rafferty was sure LaRue's tentative smile matched his own.

"Are you—" LaRue began.

"I wanted—" Rafferty started. "Ah, hell, you go first," he said.

"No, you go ahead."

LaRue's smile broadened.

"I guess you know that I—" Rafferty gave a rueful grin. "I got dusted."

LaRue had to laugh at his use of the rodeo term that meant he'd been thrown by a horse.

"Yeah, I know. Are you hurt?"

He indicated the cast on his left arm. "Cracked radius, a couple of bruises. That's all."

"That's *all*?" Her brown eyes filled with dismay. "Oh, Rafferty, you idiot, you could have been killed! What were you thinking?"

They moved toward each other and he encircled her with his good arm. She pressed her face into his chest.

"I was thinking how much I hated being a tenderfoot," he admitted. "And how much I'd like to make you proud of me."

She looked up at him, tears of frustration springing into her eyes. "Damn it, Rafferty, why would you think that breaking every bone in your body would make me any prouder of you than I already am? I didn't ask you to ride that bronc!"

"I know. *I* asked me."

"Well, please don't do it again."

"I wasn't that bad, was I?"

"You were wonderful," she said softly, reaching up to draw his face down to hers. Her kiss was much more effective than the pain killer. It relaxed him all the way down to his toes.

She shifted closer and opened her mouth, letting her fingers drift upward into his thick hair, tumbling his Western hat onto the hallway carpet. She arched her body, fitting it to his.

After a while, Rafferty realized the relaxation was gone and that certain areas of his anatomy were suddenly wide awake and demanding attention.

"Come on," LaRue whispered. "I think you need a nap. Let me put you to bed."

"I don't mind being put to bed—" he chuckled "—but right now a nap is the last thing I need."

Once the bedroom door had closed behind them, LaRue le
him to the bed and gently pushed him down on the edge of i
She knelt before him and began pulling off his dusty boots.

"Sugar, you're all cleaned up," he protested, "and I've bee
rolling in the dust. Why don't I take a quick shower?"

"All right," she agreed. "You can use mine. But don't ge
your cast wet."

"Damn, I hate feeling so helpless," he groused. LaRue pa
ted his knee in sympathy before pulling off his socks. Next sh
helped him unbutton his shirt and slip it off without disturb
ing his injured arm. After unbuckling his belt, she tugged
from the loops.

Rafferty stood up and unsnapped his jeans. "Maybe bein
helpless isn't so bad, after all," he quipped. "This broken-bon
business may have its advantages."

"Go on," she scolded, watching him walk into the bath
room. "Just don't be too long, will you?"

He stuck his head around the door frame. "Sorry—you'
have to take me as I am. But I've never had any com
plaints...."

Then, with a wink and a wicked grin, he disappeared fror
view and in a few seconds she could hear the shower running.

Ten minutes later, Rafferty stepped back into the bedroon
wearing only the cast and a sexy smile. A smile that deepene
immediately when he saw LaRue had thrown back the bedcov
ers and now reclined against the pillows, draped only in a pal
mauve sheet. When she held out her arms to him, he wasted nc
time joining her in the bed.

LaRue snuggled close, careful not to jostle his broken arm
She stroked the shower-dampened hair on his chest, breathin,
in the clean, soapy scent of him. Her lips moved softly agains
his shoulder, then down his arm to the edge of the cast.

"Promise me you won't ever do such a thing again."

"All right," he easily agreed. "Next time I'm going to tr
bull-dogging."

"Over my dead body...and yours!"

He laughed quietly. "Come on, LaRue. Quincy said I hac
natural ability. Surely you wouldn't deny me the chance to de
velop it?"

She rolled her eyes heavenward. "Men! I don't know who ever invented the word. Not when *boy* would suit most of you until the day you die!"

"Ouch," he responded. "I hope you don't think I can let you get away with defaming the entire male sex?"

"What do you intend to do about it?" she challenged.

"Why, I'll have to think of some way to redeem my gender and restore your faith in mankind."

"Got any ideas?" she murmured.

"Lady, I sure do."

He pushed the sheet away and let his gaze move slowly over her body. Then, stretching out on his side, he slipped his right arm beneath her shoulder, letting his hand cup the back of her head. He leaned forward, catching her mouth with his, his lips softly coaxing hers open.

After a time he raised his head and glanced down at the breasts that sweetly stabbed at his chest. "This isn't easy with only one hand," he complained. "A fellow has to get awfully inventive."

He slid lower in the bed, resting his face in the hollow between her breasts, turning to kiss first one, then the other. His tongue made lazy circles that grew smaller and smaller until his lips closed over the hardened nipple. LaRue shivered with pleasure. She threaded her fingers through his hair again and moved down to fit her mouth over his once more.

Rafferty edged one leg beneath her hips and, using his undamaged hand, pulled her closer to him. He began a slow massage of her calf with his bare foot, inching higher, then finally laying his other leg across her hips, holding her in an intimate embrace. As he moved into her, LaRue sighed deeply and pressed her face against his neck where his pulse thundered.

"You're restoring my faith in mankind," she informed him between tiny, nibbling kisses.

"Glad to hear it," Rafferty said as he began to roll his hips in a disturbing and demanding fashion. LaRue groaned, slipping her arms around him. Her palms flattened on his back as her fingers smoothed and kneaded the warm flesh.

Awareness faded as they narrowed their concentration to each other and to the sensations that were burning through them. They were concerned with nothing but their own nearness, their wildly flaring passion and the eventual easing of emotions tangled by the events of the day. The restraint they practiced in deference to Rafferty's injuries only served to heighten the pleasure, leaving them panting and clinging to each other as pure delight rippled through them in the aftermath of their lovemaking. When Rafferty finally fell into a deep sleep, LaRue lay holding him, thinking how completely and satisfactorily he had redefined her opinion of the male gender.

Levi switched on the hall light as he and Quincy started up the stairs.

"I reckon I might as well make my apologies to LaRue right away," the older man was saying. "I ain't used to feelin' so all-fired guilty."

"I know what you mean," Quincy agreed. "When she didn't show up at the dance, I knew she was probably still madder than hell at us."

They reached the second floor landing. "Well," Levi drawled softly, "would you look at that?"

Lying on the carpet outside LaRue's door was Rafferty's dusty Stetson. Quincy's eyebrows rose as he turned to face Levi.

"That mean what I think it does?" he asked.

"Yep, I 'spect it does." Levi stooped to pick up the hat. "Guess that apology'll wait till mornin'."

With a grin, he hung the Stetson on the newel post and started back downstairs.

Chapter Eighteen

"Never mind sheep and cattle—more range wars were
started over pig-headedness than anything else."
—Clem Dickey, farmer,
Gladstone, Kansas, 1884

Rafferty was amazed to find himself still in LaRue's bed the
next morning.

"You should have awakened me," he said with a slow smile.
"Though, of course, I'm glad you didn't."

"You were so tired, I didn't have the heart to throw you
out," LaRue stated. "How do you feel today?"

"The arm throbs a bit—the doctor said I could expect that.
Otherwise, I think I'm okay."

"But hungry, right?"

"Right," he growled, reaching for her. With a laugh, LaRue
rolled to the far side of the bed.

"For bacon and eggs, I meant. If we don't show up for
breakfast soon, someone's sure to make a federal case of it."

"I suppose that's true. They're probably wondering where we disappeared to last night, anyway."

He sat up and reached for his clothes. Instead of offering to assist him, LaRue merely leaned back against the pillows and enjoyed the sight of him struggling into his jeans.

"I'll slip back to my own room to shower and shave," he commented. "Then I'll meet you downstairs."

"Rafferty?"

"Yeah?"

"Could I ask you something before you go?"

"Why not?"

She got off the bed, pulling the mauve sheet with her, and went to stand in front of him.

"You never did tell me what J.B. stands for."

He blinked in surprise.

"Oh, hell," he finally mumbled. "You would remember to ask."

"Come on, it can't be that bad."

"It can't?"

"Surely not."

"You haven't heard it yet," he stated.

"I know...and I'm waiting."

"You'd probably have to meet my mother to understand," he hedged. "She's somewhat flighty. I mean, before I was born she spent a lot of time reading novels about the Old South. I think it...well, it affected her judgment when it came to choosing a name for me."

"Oh? Sounds interesting. Let's hear it, Rafferty. Please."

He uttered a short, vehement swear word, and LaRue laughed again.

"Oh, all right," he said, "but if you tell one single, solitary soul, I won't rest until I've had my revenge."

"You don't have to threaten me. I won't tell anyone."

"Okay, here goes. It's...Julian Beauregard."

"Julian Beauregard?"

LaRue thought he looked adorable with his black hair tumbled across his tanned forehead and a tide of deep red rising rapidly along the strong, corded muscles of his neck.

"Damn, I hate that name!" he swore.

"It's not so bad," she lied, the corners of her mouth twitching only a little. "And, I promise, it'll be our secret. Now, go on and I'll see you downstairs."

Looking totally abashed, Rafferty snatched up his boots and disappeared through the bedroom door.

Still smiling, LaRue whispered the name aloud. "Julian Beauregard." It really wasn't so bad, was it?

Oh, my God, she thought, tossing the sheet aside and heading for the shower. *I must really be in love!*

LaRue and Rafferty were halfway through breakfast when reality settled around them again. Hollister and Quincy came bursting into the kitchen through the back door.

"Well, I've posted notices all over town about the meeting Wednesday night," Holly announced. "A lot of people seem interested."

"Yeah," agreed Quincy. "Why wouldn't they be? Have a look at this morning's paper."

He tossed the newspaper down on the table in front of Rafferty, who picked it up and unfolded it. The front page contained a bold headline: "Flint Hills Acreage To Be Sold for Industrial Development".

"What kind of industry?" LaRue asked with a sinking heart. This was exactly the sort of thing that fueled the arguments of prairie-park activists.

"Doesn't say," commented Rafferty, quickly scanning the article. "It just says a prominent rancher northeast of Cottonwood Falls has announced that a company made him a substantial offer for a few thousand acres of ground where they want to build a coal-powered factory of some kind."

"Coal?" murmured Holly. "Oh, dear."

"It's not the first coal-operated industry in the area," pointed out Quincy.

"No, but it's the first one right in the area designated as prime virgin prairie. And it's a sure sign of what's to come if someone doesn't take steps to prevent it," pointed out Rafferty. "You've already got some industrialization out here, including a nuclear plant on the east edge of the Flint Hills. Next year there'll be more, then more the year after that. That's what has happened in other states that used to have tallgrass prairies. If we can't stop things like this, it's all going to be gone before we know it.'' Rafferty flung the newspaper onto the table and glowered at his plate. "Damn it all, anyway. This is one complication we didn't need.''

At that moment LaRue realized that although he'd indicated he had already reached some hard-won decision about the park, that decision would have to be rethought in the face of this latest threat. She knew he hated the idea of factories destroying the prairie. She hated it, too. Really, what other choice was there but to depend on the government to take over the land? What good would it do to fight to save Sin Creek if it was going to be surrounded by factories on every side?

LaRue sighed and pushed away from the table. She gave Rafferty a wan smile, saying, "I'd better go find Grandpa and see what he has for me to do today.''

Rafferty watched her go. He knew what she was feeling. He ought to—he was trapped in the same dilemma. If he didn't advise the government committee to step in, valuable prairie would be lost to industry and its pollutants. If the government intervened, it would spell doom for Sin Creek Ranch...and any hope of a future for him and LaRue. He couldn't expect her to overlook the destruction of her beloved home because of his advice and counseling.

But then neither could she expect him to alter his opinion on the matter because of the love he felt for her. He owed it to the men who'd sent him out on this fact-finding mission—and to the American public, as well—to do the best job he could in evaluating the situation. He couldn't allow his personal feelings to interfere in any way. He had to put his love for LaRue Tate aside and make a final decision based on reason and logic. And on the cold, hard facts.

He hadn't worried much about it when he thought his decision was going to be a fairly simple one. But now, after this morning's headlines, he had to face reality. There wasn't going to be anything simple about it.

"Damn," he swore, bringing his fist down on the wooden table with an angry crash.

* * *

Coward, LaRue accused her reflection in the mirror. *You're nothing but a chicken-hearted coward.*

It was Wednesday evening and she was alone in the house. Alone because everyone else had gone to the town meeting. She had declined to go, unwilling to hear Rafferty's final decision in front of a roomful of people. Too proud to ask him beforehand what he was going to tell the townsfolk, she had announced that she would wait at the ranch and hear the news when everything was over.

Now, all by herself in the empty parlor, she was being driven nearly insane by the monotonous ticking of the grandfather clock in the corner. And by the wild imaginings of her nervous mind.

She glanced back at the antique mirror and saw herself sitting primly on the camelback sofa. She looked like a reasonable, poised adult—surely no one but she could detect the frightened child lurking just beneath the calm surface.

Well, she thought, *even if I feel like a child, I don't have to act like one. At least I can be mature enough to be there when Rafferty announces his recommendation. Anything would be better than skulking around here waiting.*

As it turned out, she was wrong.

It hadn't taken long for her to drive the old pickup to town; finding a place to park was the problem. Cars and trucks lined both sides of every street adjacent to the city hall. LaRue finally pulled into an alley and parked, figuring all the town's law-enforcement officers were at the meeting anyway. She left the keys in the truck and half ran the two blocks to the meeting place.

Rafferty was playing to a standing-room-only crowd. LaRue had to squeeze through the door, and then the only empty spot in the room was at the back behind a couple of bearded bikers. By standing on tiptoe, she could just manage to see over the shoulder of the shorter one. She knew Rafferty hadn't seen her.

He looked nothing like the cowboy she had grown used to during the overland trip. Dressed in a white shirt, burgundy tie and gray pin-striped trousers, he was the businesslike government man again. His hair was neatly combed, his dark eyes shielded by the horn-rimmed glasses. As she watched him pull a newspaper from the leather briefcase on the desk beside him, she suddenly began to focus on the words he was saying.

"I'm sure you all realize that the article printed in the newspaper a couple of days ago changed the entire complexion of the park situation.

"Until then I had convinced myself the citizens of this county were as capable of taking care of their prairie as they'd always claimed. But, folks, no one can deny the power of money to speak. And speak loudly. When a landowner is offered a huge sum for his property, he'd have to have some real impressive reason for turning it down. I've talked to the landowner in question—he's at retirement age and has no children to leave his land to. So there isn't any good reason for him not to sell. Frankly, in his position, the loss of valuable tallgrass prairie means little by comparison to financial security for the rest of his life."

The crowd shifted and muttered, and LaRue was aware of their acceptance of what Rafferty was telling them. It made a terrible, inevitable kind of sense.

"There aren't many ways to combat the dollars-and-cents clout of big business, I'm afraid. About the only element with any kind of corresponding strength is the government. And I can tell you, that fact weighed heavily on my mind as I made my final decision in this matter.

"Ladies and gentlemen, I have reached the conclusion that we need to take immediate and drastic action to preserve this last virgin prairie. We have to think of the generations to come. We can't allow ourselves to be swayed by sentiment, by personal loss . . . or personal gain. We have to band together to do what is best for the majority of the population. The time has come for the individual to lay his individuality aside and enter into a joint effort to save something that rightfully belongs to all of us."

Rafferty placed his fists on the wooden desk and leaned forward. "No matter what sacrifices it takes, *we've got to save the tallgrass prairie.*"

LaRue thought she was going to be sick. Despite her wish to be reasonable and mature, she still felt that Rafferty had betrayed her. That he was disregarding the past history of Sin Creek Ranch, tossing her, Levi...all of them...to the wolves. With one hand over her mouth, she made her way to the door and slipped out into the cool night air.

How could he? How could he hint all this time that he thought the people of the Flint Hills were doing a good job of caretaking, and then suddenly, at the last minute, change his mind and favor the national park, after all?

She leaned against the building for a long moment, breathing deeply to stave off the churning nausea she felt.

Finally, striving to be fair, she conceded that Rafferty's change of heart had come about after he'd read the newspaper article. On the overland trip, she knew he had come to understand the important relationship between the land and the men who owned it. But even though he might appreciate the fierce love of home and hearth these midwesterners felt, he had been sent here to do a job and, unfortunately, he seemed intent on doing it to the letter.

It's better, she thought, walking briskly toward the truck, *if I don't stay around and confront him. After all, this probably hasn't been exactly easy for him, either.*

But, damn, where did they go from here? That was something she was going to have to think about...a long, long time.

The ranch was dark when Rafferty and Levi returned from town. Their easy laughter faded as they walked into the kitchen and sensed the emptiness of the house. Rafferty knew without being told that LaRue wasn't there.

Levi made a hasty check of her bedroom, which revealed only that she had left in a hurry.

"Yer right, she's gone," he said, sauntering back down the stairs. "Guess I'll brew us up some coffee."

"Levi, for God's sake," Rafferty ground out. "Don't you think we should call the sheriff or something? Aren't you worried that your granddaughter has disappeared without even leaving a note?"

Levi sighed. "It's happened before, Rafferty."

"It has?"

"Yep, when somethin's upset her."

"And you think that's what happened this time? Something upset her and she took off?"

"Most likely."

"Well, hell, man—where does she go?"

Levi carefully measured coffee grounds into the percolator. "Don't rile yourself, she's safe enough. She probably got to stewin' over this park business and couldn't sit still. I reckon she'll be back in the mornin'."

Rafferty ran his good hand through his hair in agitation. "But I had so much to tell her, to talk to her about. I don't understand her just running away like that."

"Ain't supposed to understand women, son."

"Okay. I'll give her until morning. But if she's not back here by then, so help me, I'll go after her and drag her stubborn little butt back for her."

The anticlimax of the evening nearly killed Rafferty. He had respected LaRue's decision not to attend the meeting, and in the long run, it had only made him more anxious to get back to her. But to return to the ranch full of news and plans for the future and find her gone without a word was almost more than he could handle. Didn't she even care what had been decided? Why wasn't she more eager to start mapping out the rest of their lives?

Rafferty went to bed, but he didn't sleep. He tossed and turned, finally getting up at the break of dawn, looking tired and haggard. He sat on the front porch with a mug of coffee that grew stone cold as he held it and stared down the long lane. Where in hell was LaRue?

By noon he was worried again, pacing the floor and trying to convince Levi that they should call the sheriff.

"Son," Levi finally said, "relax. I know where LaRue is. I done some checkin' and both the old truck and her bedroll are gone. That can only mean she's run off to the hills for a spell. She always does this when she gits real mad or upset about somethin'."

"But what upset her?" Rafferty demanded. "She was fine when we left her here. What could have happened?"

"Now, don't jump to no conclusions, but I think I might know what happened."

"Tell me."

"One of the boys down at the bunkhouse said he saw 'Rue leave here t'other night. Figured she changed her mind and was goin' to the meetin'. Anyway, about forty-five minutes later, she came barrelin' back down the lane and ran into the house. In jist a bit, she came out with her campin' gear and roared off again."

"But . . . why?"

Levi scratched his head, looking less than happy. "You don't reckon she heard somethin' at the meetin' that got her dander up, do ya?"

"What could it have been?"

"Think about it, son. She couldn't have stayed for the whole thing. What if she jist heard a part of yer arguments and got the wrong idea?"

"Then she should have waited around for my explanation."

"Ain't her way, Rafferty, and you oughta know that by now."

"You're right, naturally. LaRue never does anything the simple way. If she can complicate it beyond belief, why then, of course that's what she'll do. God, I'd like to shake some sense into her."

"Best thing you can do is jist sit tight and wait till she cools off. You'll have yer chance to explain things."

"There wouldn't be any need to explain if she had one ounce of maturity," Rafferty snapped, stalking out of the house and crashing the screen door behind him.

That night he received another phone call from Terence Whitelow, the head of the Tallgrass Committee, and this time there was no reason to put the man off any longer.

"I'll be on my way back to Washington day after tomorrow," Rafferty promised.

"Sure you can't make it any sooner?" Whitelow questioned.

"No . . . there are a couple of loose ends I need to tie up here before I leave. Holly and I'll drive up to Topeka to leave our car, and then we'll be on the first plane home."

Home? The word nearly stuck in his throat. When had *home* ceased to mean the comfortable town house in Georgetown? At what point had he started equating it with an 1890s ranch house on the Kansas prairie?

When he had fallen completely under the spell of a rowdy, gun-totin' cowgirl with a big chip on her shoulder, he answered himself.

With a heavy sigh, he finished his conversation with White-low, then went to find Holly. One more day and they would be gone. He only hoped LaRue saw fit to show up before then.

She didn't.

But, Rafferty realized, it was probably just as well.

If he could have gotten his hands on her, he'd have turned her right over his knee and given her what Levi would call a proper hiding. Each hour that passed without her putting in an appearance added more fury to his already-blazing temper, like dry sticks being tossed into a raging bonfire. By the morning he was to leave, he was well aware that they had gone far beyond the point of rational discussion. And he'd come to the hurtful conclusion that maybe they didn't have all that much to say to each other, anyway.

He slammed his luggage into the trunk of the car and turned to Levi. Tate had said his goodbyes to Holly, and now looked at Rafferty, an undeniable guilt evident on his weathered face. He had steadfastly guarded the secret of LaRue's where-abouts, but Rafferty could tell he wasn't happy about it. No doubt he'd thought she would show up to iron out the problems long before this. Rafferty had thought so himself, but the morning was nearly gone, and she hadn't put in an appearance yet. He couldn't afford to wait any longer.

"Well, guess we'd better get on the road," Rafferty said. "Thanks for everything, Levi."

The older man shook the hand Rafferty offered. "Sure ya cain't stick around another day or two?"

"There's no point. Besides, Holly and I need to get these reports back to Washington. Those fellows have been about as patient as they're going to be."

Levi scuffed at the ground with the toe of his boot. "Hell, son, I'm real sorry things turned out like this. I figured you and 'Rue had somethin' good goin'."

"I figured the same way," Rafferty admitted. "Guess we were both wrong."

"Hell," Tate muttered again.

"If she ever decides to come down off her mountain," Rafferty said wryly, "tell LaRue goodbye for me, will you?"

"Damned stubborn little twit," Levi snapped. "Her...not you."

Rafferty had to chuckle. "Believe me, I knew exactly who you meant. How someone as reasonable as you could have such a spiteful, pigheaded granddaughter I'll never know."

"Well, I have to admit that she's gotten a lot worse since you came along."

"Maybe that just goes to prove we weren't really suited for each other. And who knows, maybe things turned out for the best. Goodbye, Levi—take care of yourself."

"You, too, Rafferty."

Shoulders slumped, the white-haired rancher watched until the government man's car had disappeared down the lane. Then, with sudden determination in his eye, he turned and strode off toward the barn.

LaRue leaned against an outcropping of flintrock and stared down across the valley below. Sin Creek, swollen from the recent rain, zigzagged its way across the land, glittering in the noonday sun. A herd of Hereford cattle moved along its banks, grazing in a desultory manner, as if they weren't terribly hungry but had nothing better to do.

That was pretty much the way LaRue was feeling. She had heated a can of ravioli over a small campfire, but now she didn't feel like making the effort to eat it. She set her plate aside and rocked forward, resting her chin on the heel of her hand.

She couldn't help wondering what Rafferty was thinking, what he was doing. After her initial anger had worn off, she'd half expected him to come after her. She'd envisioned them out here in the middle of nowhere, arguing and shouting at the top of their lungs. But working through their problems somehow.

She'd even been crazy enough to believe that, given the chance, Rafferty could make her understand why he had chosen to sacrifice Sin Creek—that somehow he could make everything all right again.

She heaved a bitter sigh. She'd come up here to get her jumbled thoughts straightened out, but instead all she'd done so far was wait for Rafferty to come looking for her. When was she going to face the fact that he wasn't coming? He'd made his choice... and it didn't include her.

Unexpectedly, she heard the ring of hooves on rock and sprang to her feet. Her smile of welcome died quickly when she saw her grandfather top the hill on his pony and ride toward her.

Upon closer inspection, she decided he didn't look too happy to see her, either.

She stood her ground, though her instincts were already telling her the news wasn't good.

"Rafferty's gone," Levi said with an economy of words.

"Gone?" LaRue croaked. "What do you mean?"

"I mean he left for Washington jist a while ago."

"But... he didn't even say goodbye," she half whispered, shocked at the pain she felt.

"Well now, that woulda been a little hard, wouldn't it? With him down at the ranch and you the hell and gone up here in the hills!"

"You knew where I was," she accused.

"Shore. But I figured you didn't want Rafferty to know or you'd a left him word. Shoot, sister, what was you thinkin' of to run off like that?"

"I heard Rafferty at the meeting," she replied, her chin tilting upward. "I know he decided to back the tallgrass park...."

"You don't know any such dad-blasted thing," Levi shouted. "Did it ever occur to you that you might be goin' off half cocked?" Before she could answer, he went on, "No, it never does. You jist jump from one conclusion to the next, never lettin' a man explain hisself."

"Grandpa, are you saying...?"

"I'm sayin' I don't know how yer grandma and me raised you to be such a dumb butt. You jist kicked the best man you'll ever know right in the teeth, and yer too all-fired bullheaded to admit it. Well, you jist sit up here growin' moss if you want to, and let him git away. Mebbe the next woman who gits her clutches on him won't be so damned obstinate.''

He tugged at his bushy moustache in agitation, and LaRue managed to get in a couple of questions.

''Why are you mad at me? What *did* Rafferty say at that meeting?''

''I'm mad cuz yer actin' like a snivelin' coward. Ain't no Tate ever been a coward! As fer t'other question, you shoulda had the good manners to be there when Rafferty came home. You coulda asked him yerself.''

''Then you think we had something to talk about?''

''Rafferty seemed to—he hung around waitin' on ya to show up longer than any sensible man would've.''

''Grandpa, did he decide against the park?''

''I think you owe it to Rafferty to ask him that question, sister.''

''How can I do that?''

''Well, the way I see it, ya cain't if'n ya stand there yammerin' all day.''

''You think I should . . . go after him?''

''I think yer a poor excuse fer a Tate if'n ya don't.''

''I don't even know where he's gone.''

''He's on the turnpike, headed to Topeka to drop off the car he's drivin'. Left about thirty minutes ago.''

''Maybe I can catch up with him,'' LaRue said, glancing at her watch. ''But I don't have time to gather up the tent and all.''

Levi grinned. ''I'll take care of it. You jist git on down the road.''

''Thanks, Grandpa . . . for everything.'' She threw her arms around his shoulders and kissed his leathery cheek.

''Promise you won't use that gun yer totin'?'' he asked with a twinkle in his eye.

''Sorry, I can't promise anything,'' she replied, heading for the truck. ''I'm going to bring Mr. J. B. Rafferty back one way or the other.''

''Spoken like a true Tate. Oh, 'Rue—one more thing.''

''Yeah?''

''You through with that ravioli? I'm plumb starved.''

"Help yourself, Grandpa." She laughed, climbing into the cab of the old red pickup.

Lukewarm ravioli was the last thing on her mind right now. If Rafferty had gotten a thirty-minute headstart, she was going to have to hurry like hell. There was no time to have a shower or change clothes or put on makeup. She was just going to have to go after him looking like a dusty cowboy. But after all, it wasn't anything he hadn't seen before!

Chapter Nineteen

"When all's said and done, you never live your life for
yourself. You live it for the land, for the one you love,
for your children, your friends, your neighbors. But
otherwise, life would be a pretty lonely prospect...."
                    —Rutherford Tate, Sin Creek Ranch,
                         Chase County, Kansas, 1887

Good Lord, J.B.," exclaimed Holly. "I can't believe you."

"What? That I finally got smart enough to get the hell out
of there?" Rafferty gave a slight snort of disgust and studied
the passing landscape.

"No, that you'd leave without even talking to LaRue."

"You seem to forget—she's the one who didn't want to talk
to me."

Holly pounded the heels of his hands on the steering wheel,
causing the car to swerve across the center line. "You ought to
know by now that LaRue Tate isn't very good at tackling
problems close to her heart. Remember the education thing?"

Rafferty only grunted, causing Holly's frown to deepen.

"Good gracious, man," Holly continued, "she probably thought you had thrown Sin Creek right out the window."

"Then she should have asked. And anyway, if she didn't trust me any more than that . . . well, to hell with it all."

"You're going to be sorry, mark my words."

Rafferty reached for the packet of photographs lying on the car seat between them. "Either tell me about your magazine article, Holly, or do me the favor of keeping quiet."

Hollister's aggrieved sigh plainly expressed his opinion of that idea. He pursed his lips and drove a little faster.

Rafferty shuffled through the pictures, almost sorry he'd picked them up. They brought back a disturbing array of memories.

He stared at the one taken of the wagon train just after they'd left the cottonwood grove that first morning. If he remembered correctly, he'd been feeling rather smug about then, despite a wet saddle. He'd certainly confounded LaRue by escaping the dip in the pond she'd had planned for him.

The next photo was one he'd had no idea Holly had taken. It was of him surreptitiously applying raspberry lip balm to Mert's upper lip! He almost chuckled aloud. Mert had proven to be quite a unique animal. Even this morning, when he'd slipped down to the stables to tell her goodbye, he'd have bet a month's wages there were tears in her eyes. Of course, his own eyes were so misty, it had been hard to tell for sure.

With a stern admonition to himself, he went on to the next picture: Levi, looking as if he'd walked straight out of a Louis L'Amour novel. And there were Ragweed and Gertie, posing in front of their chuckwagon.

He paused over a wonderful shot of a prairie sunset. It brought back so many things—the pungent smell of the bluestem grasses, the caress of a balmy evening breeze, the call of the bobwhite quail. He had loved the beauty of the prairie, the freedom. The camaraderie of his fellow travelers. But most of all, damn it, he'd loved—

LaRue! He sat looking at her photograph, neglecting to breathe. How in God's name could he have forgotten how beautiful she was? And in all of this mess, how had he managed to block out the memory of this moment, captured forever by Holly's camera?

The snapshot showed a laughing young woman wearing a crown of wildflowers. With skin kissed by the sun and long hair that tangled in the wind, LaRue looked like an earth goddess. That had been the moment Rafferty had first known he loved her. Now, experiencing the recreation of that moment, he knew he loved her still. Knew he always would love her.

A sling cradled Rafferty's left arm against his chest, and he realized he had spread that hand over his heart, as if to ease the ache he suddenly felt there. With a flash of honesty, he knew that the pain came not from seeing LaRue's photo but from self-reproach at his own idiocy in leaving without attempting to talk to her.

"Holly, I've been a real jackass," he muttered.

Holly's grin spread from ear to ear. "Now you're talking!"

"I've got to go back to Sin Creek as soon as possible...."

"No time like the present."

With those words, Holly slowed the car and, heading for the rutted strip of grass between the north- and south-bound lanes, executed a U-turn. As they bumped back onto the roadway, Rafferty's breath whistled out between his clenched teeth.

"Jesus, Holly, you can't turn around on the turnpike! It's against the law!"

"They'll never notice," Hollister blithely assured him. "And even if they do, all you have to do is tell them you're the secretary of the interior."

Rafferty had to laugh. But as crazy as his friend's actions had been, at least they were headed back to Sin Creek.

LaRue tugged her battered cowboy hat down tighter. With the wind streaming in the open windows, it was hard to keep it from blowing off, and she needed it to hold her hair out of her eyes. Driving the old pickup as fast as she was, she didn't need any distractions.

She scanned the turnpike up ahead, but saw nothing that looked even remotely like the green government sedan. With a sinking heart, she realized she had probably missed Rafferty. He could be at the airport right now, boarding a plane back to Washington.

And Louise, she reminded herself. Her foot jerked involuntarily and the pickup surged forward.

Fine time to decide to get jealous, she thought with a half smile. She should have thought of the consequences two nights ago when she had walked out on Rafferty so high-handedly.

Just catch up with him, she advised herself. *You can worry about groveling and begging his forgiveness later. Right now you'd better concentrate on keeping this old junk heap between the ditches.*

Suddenly, a car coming from the opposite direction seized her attention. If she didn't know better, she'd almost think it could be the government car....

Her eyes followed it past, and as she ascertained it had indeed been Hollister Ames driving, she heard the ear-splitting screech of tires grabbing the pavement. She hit her own brakes, skidding around. As the pickup careened over both lanes of the highway, she could see that the car on the opposite side was making a hasty U-turn. That could only mean one thing: Rafferty was in it!

LaRue didn't hesitate to pull onto the median. The green car came to an abrupt halt, front bumper against the front bumper of the pickup. Holly sat behind the wheel, grinning broadly. Rafferty, on the other hand, had jumped out of the car and definitely was *not* smiling. LaRue swallowed deeply and opened her own door.

"What are you trying to do?" he demanded. "Get yourself killed driving like that?"

"I didn't notice you and Holly driving any more safely."

"That's beside the point. Where were you going?"

"After you."

He looked as if he didn't believe her. "What for?"

"To let you know you weren't going to get away with running out on me."

Rafferty's mouth fell open. "Who ran out on who?"

"Shouldn't that be *whom*?" she asked calmly.

"Don't get smart with me, LaRue. Just answer the damned question."

"All right, it may have looked like I ran out on you," she conceded. "But I didn't."

"What do you call it, then?"

"I call it needing a little time to make certain adjustments in my thinking."

"Adjustments to what?"

"Adjustments to the fact that you were going to advocate the prairie park . . . that my home and my whole way of life was going to be destroyed."

"I didn't advocate the park," he argued.

"So I've gathered . . . but, I didn't know that then."

"And you didn't hang around to find out, either."

"Well, at least I didn't try to leave the state."

"I wasn't leaving because I wanted to. Some of us have responsibilities, you know. Jobs and bosses . . . things like that."

"What about your responsibility to me?" she queried. "Did you just think you could run out on me with no word?"

"I didn't think I owed you anything. Not after the way you acted."

LaRue rested her hands on her hips. "What about your legal obligations?"

"What legal obligations?"

"Have you forgotten a certain marriage ceremony we went through?"

"Of course not. But it was as bogus as the rest of our relationship."

"No need to get insulting," she said, smiling demurely. "And for your information, that ceremony wasn't so phony, after all."

Rafferty took another step toward her. "What do you mean?"

"It just so happens that in the state of Kansas, when two people represent themselves as a married couple, it constitutes a common-law marriage."

"Bullsh—"

"Ah-ah, Rafferty. Don't profane our enlightened legal system."

"We're no more married than . . . than . . ."

"Don't be so sure. I'm positive that I could have sent the law after you if I'd wanted to."

"What for?"

"To charge you with desertion."

"You're crazier than I thought."

"If you don't like desertion, how about breach of promise?"

"Another Kansas mantrap, I take it?"

"You've got it."

Rafferty shifted his stance and rubbed his wrist where it protruded from the cast. His arm had begun to ache intolerably.

"Good Lord, what are we doing standing out here stopping traffic?"

He indicated the several cars going by, most of them moving at a snail's pace, trying to figure out what was happening on the median strip.

"I guess we're having the talk we should have had two days ago," she answered.

"It wasn't my fault we didn't have it."

"Maybe not," she agreed, "but you're dragging your feet now."

"Well, excuse me," he drawled sarcastically. "It's just that I'm not used to having meaningful discussions in the middle of a turnpike."

"Neither am I, but this is as good a place as any. Tell me what you said at the meeting, Rafferty."

"If you were so interested, why didn't you bother to go to it?"

"I did bother," she snapped. "And I didn't like what I heard."

"Which was?"

"You telling the townspeople how government intervention was the only way to prevent big business from moving into the Flint Hills."

"You heard me saying it is ordinarily the only way. What you didn't hear was the plan I proposed for the public to do something about the situation."

"What plan?"

"I asked their opinion on forming an association of landowners whose purpose would be to protect the area from industrial development. If the owners band together and create a legal association, they could collect dues, hire legal counsel...you get the idea, don't you?"

"I'm not sure. How would that keep industry out?"

"If someone wants or needs to sell their land, the members of the association could buy it, or at least, oversee the sale, keeping out big businesses. We aren't clear on the legalities just yet, but the county attorney is checking into it."

"Then...the townspeople were in favor of your plan?"

"It would seem so."

"Why would they trust you?" she asked. "You're an outsider."

"Funny how you keep finding ways to remind me of that."

"Don't get smart with me, Rafferty. Just answer the question. Why would they trust an outsider?"

He glared at her, then deliberately tore his gaze away to stare over the tops of passing cars, to the hills beyond. "Because this outsider was stupid enough to tell them all how I was going to marry one of their hometown girls and settle down. My God, I even mentioned something about wanting to raise my own family in Chase County."

LaRue bit her lower lip. "You—you told them that?"

"Hilarious, isn't it?"

"Not to me." She shook her head in puzzlement. "But, Rafferty, what about the park? I heard you saying that it was necessary to preserve the tallgrass prairie."

"And it is. Had you given me a little credit and stayed around, you'd have heard me say I thought the people of the Flint Hills were doing a fine job of protecting the land. I went on to say I was going to recommend to the committee that the government involve itself in areas farther north, say in the vicinity of Chicago or Minneapolis, even the Dakotas, Iowa and

Nebraska—where the prairies are smaller and individual citizens have less chance of keeping large bands of tallgrass intact. These parks would be of lesser size, perhaps, but they'd preserve land more immediately endangered. And then I—'' He broke off abruptly, swinging his gaze back to her.

"And then you what?" she prompted.

"Like a damned fool, I volunteered my services to help out on the local front."

"In what capacity?"

"You'll get a kick out of this," he promised grimly. "I was going to head up a committee to organize and educate the Flint Hills farmers and ranchers about their individual duties and responsibilities as landowners. I thought an involvement like that could do as much good or more than government interference. After all, folks here already have the right idea. Think what presenting a united front could mean!"

Despite everything, Rafferty felt a stirring of the excitement he'd experienced at the town meeting. It had been important to him that he establish himself as a constructive influence in the community.

"Rafferty," LaRue said slowly, "are you saying that instead of advising the government to take over our land, you were willing to stay on yourself and help out? Live here, I mean, and—and everything?"

"Yes. That's what I wanted, if you'd given me the chance."

"Why didn't you just tell me?" she asked. "Why did you make me wait until the meeting? Was it asking so much for you to confide in me?"

"Oh, now wait one minute! If memory serves me correctly, I did try to tell you beforehand. On more than one occasion."

"Oh, that...."

"Yeah, that."

"Well, I didn't want to influence your final decision."

"Did you think I was so wishy-washy?"

"You're too obstinate to be wishy-washy," she exclaimed.

A new, deeper voice sounded. "All right, buddy, what the hell is going on here?"

Rafferty and LaRue turned to see a huge man in a state trooper's uniform. Their startled reflections looked back at them from the lenses of his mirrored sunglasses.

"Excuse me, officer," Rafferty said politely. "I was just about to strangle this woman."

"Oh, yeah?" challenged LaRue.

"What's the trouble?" the patrolman asked. "This man threatening you, ma'am?"

"He thinks he is," she retorted, "but God only knows, I'm not worried by him. In fact, I'd bet he's more afraid of me than I am him."

"But—"

"Why wouldn't I be?" Rafferty interjected. "A lunatic with a gun!"

"You're armed?" gasped the trooper, obviously shocked at his own failure to determine such a thing immediately. He half turned to address a second officer. "Dwight, you'd better radio for that backup again."

"Sure thing, Marvin." The other man turned and started back to the patrol car.

"Oh, hell," scoffed LaRue with a withering glance at Rafferty. "This gun isn't even loaded." She snatched the Smith & Wesson from its holster and aimed it to one side, ostensibly pulling the trigger.

The roar was deafening, followed by a stunned silence. The *phfffft* of air escaping from the front tire of the patrol car was clearly audible.

"Son-of-a-bitch!" shrieked Dwight, diving for the ditch as he drew his own gun. "She fired on me!"

LaRue's face was chalky white as she gazed at the gun in her hand, then dropped it into the mud at her feet.

"It was unloaded, I'd swear it," she murmured.

The big trooper, his own gun in hand, towered over her. "That was a hare-brained thing to do, miss."

"God, I know it," she gulped. "I've been handling guns since I was nine years old—and I've never done anything like that before. Grandpa will kill me!"

"Your grandfather wants to kill you, too?" The trooper was more than a trifle confused.

"You can see what a menace she is," Rafferty pointed out.

"Stay out of this," LaRue yelled. "It was all your fault, anyway!"

"Why is everything always my fault? It's about time you grew up and started taking responsibility for your own actions." Rafferty turned to the officer, "Look, you seem like a reasonable man...."

Holly, greatly delighted by the scene he'd been witnessing, chose that moment to get out of the car. "Is everything okay, Mr. Secretary?" He cast a curious glance at the trooper named Marvin. "I don't suppose you realize that you're addressing the secretary of the interior."

"Secretary of the what?"

"Oh, Holly," snorted LaRue, "you're as full of it as Rafferty."

"Who are you?" Marvin demanded suspiciously. "Let's see some ID here, folks. But just watch what you do with your hands."

"I'm wearing a goddamned sling," Rafferty remarked. "I'm not exactly a threat."

"Dwight, get over here. Keep these nut cases covered while I look at their identification."

Dwight did as he was told, though he chose to move cautiously. He couldn't seem to keep his eyes off the gun lying at LaRue's feet.

"I didn't bring a purse," she was explaining, "so I'm afraid I don't have my driver's license with me."

"How very interesting," observed Marvin, taking the wallets Rafferty and Holly were extending.

"Why don't the three of you get up against the hood of the car?" suggested Dwight. "We can keep a closer eye on you that way. You there," he said, nudging Rafferty, "spread those legs . . . no funny business now."

"If you want to call him by name," LaRue said nastily, "it's *Julian Beauregard*."

"Julian Beauregard?" Holly repeated incredulously. "Julian Beauregard?"

"You little snitch," Rafferty said.

"You deserved it," LaRue declared. "And you know it."

"God, I can't believe this," Rafferty moaned. "And to think, if we hadn't stopped to talk to *you*, we'd be on a plane back to Washington by now." He favored LaRue with a black look, but she only tossed her head and turned her back on him.

"Washington, huh?" the trooper queried, studying Rafferty's ID. "Says here you are a government man...though not, as your accomplice alleges, the secretary of the interior."

"Just a little joke, officer," Holly said cheerfully.

"Not a very funny one." Marvin gave Holly a toothy smile. "Not nearly as funny as the fact you're driving with an expired license."

Holly's face registered his disbelief. "What! You've got to be kidding!"

"Did you or did you not have a birthday last month?"

"I did, but...oh, shoot! We were on the road. Guess I just didn't think about renewing my darned license. Wait a minute, what about...?"

"Don't bother to try that diplomatic immunity crap with me, son. We've had government people through here before this." Marvin's grin grew broader. "Looks to me like we'd better take the lot of 'em in, Dwight. We've got a couple of illegal drivers, illegal use of a firearm, destruction of police property..."

"But you don't understand," LaRue cried.

"Obstructing a public highway, illegal parking..."

"Wait just a minute," insisted Rafferty.

"Impersonation of a government official. And, if we're lucky," emphasized Marvin, "we might come up with resisting arrest. Read 'em their rights, Dwight."

"This is your fault, LaRue Tate," Rafferty fumed. "Couldn't you do something normal, for once in your life?"

"My fault? Why, you—you arrogant lowlife...tinhorn!"

"You have the right to remain silent..." began Dwight.

"Lady, that had better be the last time you ever call me a tinhorn," Rafferty warned. "If I haven't proven myself by now—"

"You have the right to remain silent," the trooper said in a tired voice, "and I wish to God you'd exercise it."

Two backup cars arrived simultaneously, sirens screaming and red lights flashing. A bevy of state troopers, armed to the teeth, rushed forward to surround the desperadoes.

LaRue watched as one of them clamped a handcuff around Rafferty's good wrist, looking perplexed as he studied the cast on the other arm.

"Rodeo injury," Rafferty said proudly.

The trooper swept an unbelieving gaze over Rafferty's business suit. "Sure, mister."

"He's telling the truth," LaRue said hotly. "He tangled with one of the meanest broncs east of the Arkansas River."

LaRue intercepted Rafferty's stunned look. "Well, I figured maybe it *was* time to upgrade your greenhorn status a little," she muttered as they were led away.

Four hours and several long-distance phone calls later, the three offenders looked through the bars of the holding cell to see Levi Tate, accompanied by the sheriff.

"Grandpa, at last you're here," LaRue exclaimed. "I thought you weren't coming."

"Well, I considered it—but then I took pity on Hollister and decided to put up bail."

"Thanks, Levi. I appreciate it," Rafferty said, pointedly ignoring LaRue.

The sheriff unlocked the door to the jail cell and motioned for Holly to step out. Then, to their mutual surprise, Rafferty and LaRue found the door relocked, with them still on the wrong side.

"What's going on?" asked LaRue indignantly. "I thought you'd posted bail."

"I did...for Holly. But, sister, all us folks are gittin' real tired of you and Rafferty actin' like a couple of spoiled kids. Once you git yer differences solved, I'll hand over the bail and the sheriff'll let you outa here. But not before then.''

"That's blackmail," shouted Rafferty at their retreating backs. "You'll hear from my lawyer about this!"

"Grandpa!" yelled LaRue. "Come back here, you stubborn old fart!"

"Watch yer mouth, girl," Levi cautioned as the outer door closed with a well-defined bang. Thirty seconds later, the two prisoners reluctantly faced each other.

"Well," said Rafferty, "what do we do now?"

LaRue studied her fingernails with intensity. "I guess we could...try to patch up our differences, like Grandpa suggested."

"Funny thing," Rafferty mused. "This time last week, we didn't have any trouble getting along."

"I know."

"What do you suppose happened?"

"Right now I'm too tired to remember," she confessed.

"I'll bet you're hungry, too. I know I am."

"Yeah. Guess they don't feed you in this jail."

"Levi would probably insist on bread and water, even if they did."

LaRue looked up, chuckling slightly. "We sure owe him one, don't we?"

"Let's worry about that later. Right now we should concentrate on getting out of here. Then we can go to a café somewhere and order everything on the menu."

"Mmm, sounds good."

Rafferty moved closer to her. "You know, I'd like to forget today ever happened. It's been the worst fiasco of my life."

"Mine, too."

"Why don't we make a pact to back up and start over again, from say...the night of the rodeo?"

She smiled shyly. "Yes, that was a nice night."

He put a forefinger beneath her chin and tilted her head upward. "The crazy part of all this is that we could be having nights like that for the rest of our lives. If only we could resolve our problems and get on with it, that is."

"Do you think we can?"

He smiled down into her earnest gold-flecked eyes. "We did it before, if you'll remember. The pushy government man and the dusty little cowgirl forgot their differences long enough to fall in love, didn't they?"

She nodded. "Yes, they did." She took a deep breath. "Rafferty, this has all been my fault."

"No, we're both to blame."

"But I see now that I wanted everything my way," she admitted in the low, husky voice he found so appealing. "I wanted the ranch, but I wanted you, too. I think I expected you to make all the sacrifices."

"You didn't ask me for any favors, sugar."

"Maybe not, but somehow, deep down inside, I must have thought you would find a way around the problems. I just assumed everything could be smoothed out to my satisfaction." She smiled. "Would you believe that I've finally grown up enough to realize that love doesn't work that way? It isn't right to expect you to bend all the time. Rafferty, I want you to know that . . . well, if you'll give me another chance, I'll try as hard as I can to meet you halfway. More than halfway, if necessary."

He slipped his good arm around her waist and drew her tight against him. His mouth settled over hers with an ardency that put an end to her apology. "Just love me—that's all I ask."

"I do." Her warm, willing response expressed all the things she had been unable to say with mere words, and just that easily, the rift was healed.

"We've got to remember," she whispered into his ear, "that, next time we feel like yelling at each other, we need to try kissing instead. It works so much better."

"Mmm, and it's so much more fun."

After a few minutes, Rafferty raised his head long enough to call for the sheriff. The man came in, Levi following closely.

"Is there a justice of the peace handy?" Rafferty asked, ignoring Levi's delighted chortle. "We thought this might be a very romantic place for a wedding."

"Romantic?" echoed the sheriff.

"Don't argue," warned Levi. "Jist git the damned justice of the peace, will ya?"

Epilogue

LaRue looked up from her book as the door opened and Rafferty stepped into the bedroom. She knew he had just come in from outdoors for, although he'd shed his coat and boots before coming upstairs, there was a powdering of snow in his black hair.

"Whew, it's wicked out tonight," he announced, striding across the room to settle his rangy body on the edge of the bed. "The kind of night when a man needs a wife to warm him up...."

She uttered a small scream as he thrust the bedcovers aside and hauled her onto his lap, kissing her with enthusiasm.

"How did your meeting go?" she asked, snuggling closer to share her body heat.

"Great. The association outbid the factory owners on that property. They think they can rent it out for pasture to make their initial investment back."

"That's wonderful, Rafferty. I'm so proud of all you've done in the past six months."

"Everything has turned out pretty well, hasn't it?"

"Only because you've worked so hard," she stated, rubbing her cheek against the red-and-black wool shirt he wore. Finding it somewhat scratchy, she unbuttoned it and stroked the softly furred chest beneath.

"Quincy tells me he expects the second shipment of buffalo to arrive within the week," Rafferty said in a distracted voice. "As soon as we get them vaccinated, we can turn them in with the others."

"And next summer when we make the overland trip, there'll be buffalo in the pastures again."

"Yeah, just like the old days."

"Grandpa thinks it's a wonderful idea," LaRue told him. "In fact, he thinks everything you've done at Sin Creek is wonderful."

"He's registered a complaint or two in one department, however," Rafferty chuckled.

"Oh?"

"He doesn't seem to think much of the fact we're not producing great-grandchildren yet."

"He actually told you that? Why, the old reprobate!"

"I politely explained we had decided to wait until after you've graduated from college. He took it fairly well, I think."

She sniffed. "You don't know my granddad. He'll try some other approach, I guarantee it."

"I'll be glad when Holly gets here for Christmas. Maybe he'll prove to be a diversion."

"Unless, of course," LaRue pointed out, "the two of them join forces against us."

"You're right. By the way, did I mention how pleased I was to hear Holly had sold his wagon-trip article?"

She smiled indulgently. "Only two or three dozen times."

"Well, it'll be fun reading about ourselves." He nodded toward the bedside table and a framed photo of LaRue wearing the wreath of flowers. "And it's not every day my wife gets her picture on the cover of a national magazine, either."

"I'm still not certain how I feel about that kind of publicity," she murmured.

"It'll be a piece of cake," Rafferty assured her. "No worse than having our wedding covered by that Kansas City newspaper."

They both smiled at the memory of the elaborate, old-fashioned wedding they'd had two weeks after the simple civil ceremony performed in the county jail. The event had taken place in the historic courthouse in Cottonwood Falls, with virtually the entire population of the town and surrounding countryside in attendance.

"You know, I've been thinking," mused LaRue.

"Oh-oh."

"Now listen, you might like this idea." She patted his cheek fondly. "We got a letter from your mother today, and she says she is furious that you didn't wait until she could be here for the wedding. But since she and her husband are coming for a visit in February, I was wondering . . . why don't we have another wedding while they're here?"

"On Valentine's Day?" questioned Rafferty, clearly interested.

"That's a wonderful idea! And since it will be a small wedding—mainly family—we could have it in the old Sin Creek schoolhouse. Would you mind?"

"Why should I mind? As long as weddings are followed by wedding nights, how can I complain?"

She brushed a kiss over his mouth. "I love you, Rafferty."

"Can you imagine? By my count, we've been married three times so far, and I still love you, too."

"I should hope so," she remarked, kissing his ear.

"Of course, loving a cowgirl isn't as easy it sounds," he stated solemnly.

"Don't start with me, Rafferty . . . at least, don't start *that*."

"But you do want me to start something . . . ?"

"That's the general idea."

"All right—did you miss me tonight?"

"Of course."

"Bet you didn't," he teased. "You had your nose buried so deep in that school book, I'll bet you didn't even know I was gone."

"That's one bet you'd lose, mister." LaRue lifted her arms to encircle his shoulders and then began kissing him beneath the chin. She let her lips trail softly up and over his jaw, seeking and eventually finding his mouth. She traced the outline of his smile with her tongue, and small sounds of pleasure issued from his lips.

"What about your homework? You finished with it yet?"

"I was studying anatomy," she whispered.

"Oh. Well..." he said, shrugging out of his shirt. "That's something we college boys know a lot about."

"I thought so." LaRue scrambled off his lap and back under the covers. As soon as he had shed the rest of his clothing, he joined her, pulling her into his arms.

"Damn, these sheets are cold," he complained, letting his hands investigate the sheer laciness of her nightgown.

"They'll warm up quickly," she promised. "Turn out the light, Rafferty."

"Yes, ma'am."

The darkness was filled with low murmurs and pleasant sighs. After a time, LaRue posed a question.

"Rafferty, someday when we do have children—if we have a son, what do you think of the name Julian Beau—"

"You know damned good and well what I think of that name," he growled. "And if you keep bringing it up, I'll just have to think of some creative way to silence you."

And there, in the intimate darkness of their bedroom, he did, indeed, become most inventive.

* * * * *

COMING NEXT MONTH

#607 BEST MAN—Jo Ann Algermissen
Sylas Kincaid detected the pain masked by Alana Benton's brittle poise, and he sensed that masculine cruelty had put it there. But surely the love of a better man would bring her heart out of hiding...

#608 A WOMAN'S WORK—Laura Leone
Hardworking Marla Foster stunned her firm by capturing Brent Ventura's account. But Brent's dangerously unprofessional mix of irreverence and relentless sex appeal soon proved Marla's job had only just begun!

#609 THE OTHER MOTHER—Pamela Jerrold
Her suddenly widowed sister left pregnant surrogate mother Caitlin O'Shea high and dry. But prodigal brother-in-law Sam Ellison seemed oddly eager to keep Caitlin's bundle of joy all in the family.

#610 MY FIRST LOVE, MY LAST—Pat Warren
Rafe Sloan's motives for helping Nora Maddox find her missing son weren't entirely altruistic. The abrupt ending to their old affair had left burning questions, and Rafe was prepared to probe deeply for the answers....

#611 WITH NO REGRETS—Lisa Jackson
Jaded attorney Jake McGowan rationalized that he was helping beautiful, desperate Kimberly Bennett with her child-custody suit merely to win *him* sweet revenge on Kimberly's shady ex-husband. So why was his trademark cynicism beginning to feel like caring?

#612 WALK UPON THE WIND—Christine Flynn
A hurricane blew sheltered Nicole Stewart into Aaron Wilde's untamed world. Their island idyll couldn't last, but could she return to privileged society once she'd tasted primitive passion, once she'd walked upon the wind?

AVAILABLE THIS MONTH:

Silhouette Romance®

CIMARRON STORIES

A TRILOGY BY PEPPER ADAMS

Pepper Adams is back and spicier than ever with three tender, heartwarming tales, set on the plains of Oklahoma.

CIMARRON KNIGHT ... available in June
Rugged rancher and dyed-in-the-wool bachelor Brody Sawyer meets his match in determined Noelle Chandler and her adorable twin boys!

CIMARRON GLORY ... available in August
With a stubborn streak as strong as her foster brother Brody's, Glory Roberts has her heart set on lassoing handsome loner Ross Forbes ... and uncovering his mysterious past....

CIMARRON REBEL ... available in October
Brody's brother Riley is a handsome rebel with a cause! And he doesn't mind getting roped into marrying Darcy Durant—in name only—to gain custody of two heartbroken kids.

**Don't miss CIMARRON KNIGHT, CIMARRON GLORY and
CIMARRON REBEL—three special stories that'll win your
heart ... available only from Silhouette Romance!**

Take 4 bestselling love stories FREE

Plus get a FREE surprise gift!

Silhouette Intimate Moments®

**Beginning this month, Intimate Moments brings
you the first of two gripping stories by Emilie Richards**

Coming in June

Runaway
by EMILIE RICHARDS
Intimate Moments #337

Coming in July

The Way Back Home
by EMILIE RICHARDS
Intimate Moments #341

Krista and Rosie Jensen were two sisters who had it all—until a
painful secret tore them apart.

They were two special women who met two very special men who
made life a little easier—and love a whole lot better—until the day
when Krista and Rosie could be sisters once again.

You'll laugh, you'll cry and you'll never, ever forget. RUNAWAY is
available now at your favorite retail outlet, or order your copy by
sending your name, address, zip or postal code along with a check
or money order for $2.95, plus 75¢ postage and handling, payable
to Silhouette Reader Service to:

Silhouette Books ®

RUN-1A

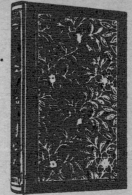